LOVE'S SWEET RAPTURE

Rome's eyes went to the front of Adrian's camisole. Looking down, she could see that the fabric was all but transparent when wet. She heard Rome's indrawn breath.

Then his eyes drifted up to her face and their gazes met. She could see the desire turn his eyes a deep turquoise. Her heart slammed to a halt, then raced so fast she could feel it pounding against her ribs.

His head came down. His eyes continued to watch her. His lips reached for hers. For the first time Adrian didn't think before acting. She wanted Rome's kiss, longed for it. She'd waited, hoping the attraction she felt would eventually subside. But it had grown, taking on a life of its own. And now, she wanted a small measure of what she knew she could never wholly have.

His lips were warm and firm, his hands strong against her back and legs. His heart beat faster and she could hear its rapid staccato as he gathered her close.

She forgot everything in his embrace. There was no room for doubts or worries. There was only pleasure, real and intense.

Other *Leisure* and *Love Spell* Books by
Marti Jones:
A LOVE THROUGH TIME
DREAMWEAVER
TIME'S HEALING HEART

STARDUST TIME

MARTI JONES

LOVE SPELL ◆ **NEW YORK CITY**

LOVE SPELL®

June 1995

Published by

Dorchester Publishing Co., Inc.
276 Fifth Avenue
New York, NY 10001

Printed in the United States of America.

This book is dedicated to Andy Gurene for not letting me down even when my computer did.

STARDUST TIME

Prologue

Southern Alabama
March, 1895

Rome Walker stared up at the night sky, a heaviness weighing down his broad shoulders. Behind him, the small cabin was dark. He sipped whiskey from a bottle, hoping his mind would shut down long enough for him to get some much-needed sleep.

But he knew sleep wouldn't come. It had deserted him nearly a year ago and visited rarely, if at all, now. The months since Lorraine's death had taken their toll. He'd lost weight. The face that looked back at him from his shaving mirror was barely recognizable with its lines of fatigue and bitterness.

The bottle traveled to his lips once more and he drank deeply. He shouldn't, he knew. The children might awaken, needing him, asking for their mother as they still did with torturous frequency.

Again his responsibilities smothered him until he felt the breath in his lungs being cut off. Not that he didn't love his children, he thought hastily, superstitiously trying to ward off the fates. No, he loved the babies. Always had, even though it had been Lorraine's idea to have so many so soon.

He would have been content to wait before starting a family. He'd wanted to get the farm on solid ground before adding additional expenses and duties. But Lorraine wouldn't wait, despite the lambskin sheaths the doctor had given him before their wedding.

She refused to allow him to use the devices, claiming it was God's choice when and if children were conceived. He couldn't argue with her, though he always remembered the phrase *God helps those who help themselves.*

Now Lorraine had her children. Three of them. But Lorraine was gone, taken away from them by what had seemed like a minor infection. And Rome was left to raise the children alone.

Three small children, and him with planting time upon him and no help. What was he supposed to do? How could he manage it all on his own?

The bottle found its way to his mouth once more, despite his resolve. He hated the impotent way he felt lately, the weakness that threatened to beat him down. But he had to admit he was afraid for the first time in his life.

At first, the pain of losing Lorraine had blocked all other thoughts from his mind. But, too soon, he realized he couldn't go on without someone's assistance.

With regret, he remembered some of his earlier ideas. He'd been so overwhelmed by grief he hadn't been thinking clearly. Desperate, he'd even penned a bold invitation to his sister-in-law, a woman he hadn't seen in nine years. He was thankful at least that she'd never replied and he hadn't been faced with following through on that ill-thought plan.

Despite the anguish in his heart, he'd eventually done the unthinkable. He'd advertised for a wife. It was common practice, but having married for love, Rome always thought it cold and calculating. Now he understood the desperation that drove men to such extremes.

The problem was, there were very few unattached women around these parts and none, it seemed, who wanted a man with three small children.

There were enough single men, however, for those same women to pick and choose from without walking into a ready-made family. Besides, most women wanted their own children and he knew adding to the ones he already had would be a huge responsibility.

He'd placed the ad two months ago, but not one woman had responded. Now he didn't know how he was going to get the planting done while caring for the babies.

The pain of his own loss had dulled over the months, but Rome always shed a tear when he thought of his motherless children. Again, his gaze went to the heavens.

"Lorraine, Lorraine, what am I going to do? If I stay with the babies, the farm will go to pot and they'll go hungry. If I leave them to go to the fields, there's no telling what'll happen to them. Can you hear me, Lorraine? God, can anyone hear me?"

Rome hadn't prayed since the night Lorraine took sick, but he fell to his knees now. The bottle rolled away, spilling its contents onto the hard-packed ground. The denim coveralls chafed his knees as he knelt down.

"God, help me. I need help, and I don't have anywhere else to turn."

Though he'd consumed a good bit of the whiskey, Rome was far from drunk. Liquor couldn't dull his fear, his pain. He turned his face to the sky, searching the darkness for an answer which had heretofore eluded him.

A fiery flash shot across the sky, its head a ball of white flame, its tail a streak of blue against the clear moonlit night. He gasped, scrambling backward in haste.

12

"Great God almighty," he shouted, falling on his butt. His eyes shot wide as the orb split the darkness, raining bright teardrops of color down on the hot Southern soil.

Thank the Lord his fields weren't planted yet. No telling what the devil the strange fragments would do to them.

His fear of the unknown almost got the better of him and he considered running for the cabin. But he stayed where he was, watching the spectacle for a long minute. Suddenly it faded away, leaving a blue haze across the ebony horizon.

Rome knew he'd seen a miracle. Filled with wonderment, he scrambled to his feet, kicking the bottle away in his haste. He paid it no mind, certain of a sudden that he wouldn't need the liquor anymore. No, everything was going to be all right. He had his answer.

He'd prayed and the heavens had sent him a reply he wasn't likely to miss.

Still, he didn't move for a long time. In what way would his answer come? Would it be soon enough to save them? Finally he shook off his worries and allowed a surreal confidence to overtake him. Who was he to question a miracle?

With a certainty he didn't dare challenge, Rome strode toward the cabin. Glancing back over his shoulder, he nodded. Help was surely on the way.

Chapter One

Southern Alabama
March, 1995

Adjusting the focus on the binoculars she held before her face, Adrian Sheppard wondered why there wasn't a crowd here to watch such a spectacle. She had the old helicopter field to herself.

Climbing onto the hood of her sunshine-yellow car, she settled her back against the windshield. Maybe, in her excitement, she was just early.

The full moon hung low overhead, veiled by the white, puffy clouds dotting the sky like tufts of cotton stuck to black velvet. Adrian hoped it wouldn't be too cloudy to see when the time came.

Thinking she heard the engine of a car, she again scanned the paved side road leading to the airstrip. Fog blanketed the ground of the low-lying field, giving it a ghostly glow and causing a shiver to run along her spine.

She would have thought droves of sightseers would have come out to catch a glimpse of the famous Fable Comet. After all, it wouldn't appear again for another hundred years.

The thought struck her then that a hundred years ago people had gazed upon the same sight she was about to see. It awed her to think of something so untouched by time. The comet would come, again and again, while life as they knew it would pass away. Generation after generation would grow old and die, but the Fable Comet would continue to orbit the atmosphere every 100 years.

The knowledge was overwhelming and again Adrian wondered where the spectators were. Maybe, in an age when space travel was as common as commercial airline flights, folks just weren't interested in things like comets anymore.

Adrian couldn't understand that, though. She'd been antsy all day waiting for the moment when the display would begin. Of course, she reminded herself, she had ulterior motives.

Clutching her camera with the expensive

night lens attached, she pointed it up in an effort to assure herself it would work. She needed these photos to turn out well in order to impress the professor at the local college tomorrow when she went for her job interview.

She'd never worked at a planetarium before, but she felt sure it would be just the thing she'd been looking for. Of course, didn't she always feel that way before starting a new job?

She experienced a moment's dismay as she remembered the disaster at the pool a week ago. Another occupation down the tubes. And this time, she knew her failure could have tragic consequences.

Another example of her irresponsibility, Alex would say. If he were speaking to her, she thought with sadness. Her brother had long since given up on her, tired of her feckless lifestyle and bitter over a decision her parents had made before their deaths. He would tell her she was running again, quitting when things got tough.

That's why she'd decided to be patient this time and find just the right position. No more jumping in without thinking. No more going in half-prepared.

And then she'd seen the advertisement for a lab assistant at the planetarium. She hadn't thought much about stars and planets before that, but she really wanted the job now. It felt right.

Of course, she'd said that before, she reminded herself.

But this time would be different. This time she'd go in prepared. She'd talk about the Fable Comet and show the professor the pictures she'd taken. He'd have to be impressed with her enthusiasm. And she was bright, eager, ready to learn.

Besides, it wasn't like she could hurt anyone as a lab assistant. It seemed safe enough.

After adjusting the focus on the camera, she set it aside and picked up the binoculars again. No more blunders. No more scrimping to get through nursing school only to faint at her first emergency. No more training to be a lifeguard only to get a cramp the first time she had to haul a man to safety. Never mind that he weighed 300 pounds and she only 115. Every time she thought of that near-calamity her legs trembled with terror.

But this time would be different, she assured herself again. This time she'd stick with it and succeed.

Time dragged on, but Adrian's enthusiasm didn't dim. She would wait all night if she had to. She meant to take the best pictures of the Fable Comet that Prof. Richard Kenyon had ever seen. She'd remember every detail of tonight's experience so they could share it time and time again. They'd have something in common right from the beginning.

For the first time she wondered what the professor looked like. She'd only spoken to him once on the phone, but he sounded nice. He had a smooth, pleasant voice. The kind that inspired confidence and trust. What if he turned out to be young and handsome? She certainly wouldn't mind working for a man like that. Lord knew, her social life wasn't going any better than her professional life right now. And hadn't for a while, she had to admit, as long as she was being honest.

With her luck, though, he was probably in his sixties with a wife and several children almost as old as she. She told herself it wouldn't matter. As long as she got the job. As long as she didn't screw up this time. She wouldn't care if she never got another date.

Carefully laying the binoculars on the hood beside her, she stared up at the diamond-studded sky. The stars twinkled and flashed, and for the first time in months she let her feelings go. She'd been lying to herself. She wanted someone in her life. Everybody had somebody, it seemed. Except her.

Because her parents had liked to travel, and took pleasure in their time alone more than they enjoyed being saddled with two children, Alex had always been her closest family member. And now even they were estranged, leaving Adrian on her own.

She'd like to mend the rift between them, but

Alex didn't share her concerns. He had a wife, twin boys. A job he loathed, but was forced to work at. And the only home either of them had ever known. He resented her carefree attitude, her wandering spirit.

But hopefully that was all about to change, she thought, grasping her camera. She was determined to make a go of this job. She'd get her career in order, and then she'd work on her relationship with Alex.

With her resolve firmly in place, she knew she'd find the perfect job one day. As the sky lit up above her, she thought perhaps she had.

The Fable Comet came unexpectedly from the left side of the sky, arcing across the black expanse like a streak of lightning. The air sizzled with the electric tide it left in its wake. Even the fog seemed to dissipate a bit.

Adrian was so surprised, she fumbled for a split second before remembering to grab the camera. Her jeaned bottom slid on the wax-slick hood and she grappled for a hold. Scrambling to her knees, she aimed the camera straight up.

God, what a thrill! She watched the heavenly body soar above her as though in slow motion. She poised the camera, but couldn't bring herself to take her eyes off the spectacle long enough to look through the square of the camera's viewfinder.

Suddenly a burst of tiny diamonds flew from

the comet's tail as though something had exploded, and hundreds of sparkles began to rain down to earth. Knowing she was about to miss the chance of a lifetime, Adrian forced herself to aim the camera. She snapped off several pictures of nature's amazing fireworks.

Scooting up the windshield to the top of the small compact car, she stood to get a better shot. Any second now she knew the comet would disappear for a hundred years. This was her only chance to see and photograph it.

She followed it across the sky, awed by the trail of stardust racing behind it, and snapped pictures as fast as the camera could automatically wind to the next frame.

A thrill of excitement shot through Adrian's chest and she felt herself tingle all over. She was watching history. Where was everyone? Didn't they know what they were missing? It was an experience she desperately wanted to share with someone.

Just then, a bright light caught her attention. She lowered the camera and saw a falling star. For a moment she couldn't breathe, it was such a brilliant sight. Then she frowned. Was it her imagination or was it falling directly toward her?

She began to snap pictures again. Vaguely an old rhyme played across her mind. *Wish upon a falling star.*

She could see where the old wives' tale had

come from. There was something almost magical about seeing the bright light coming toward her. Knowing that what one was seeing had happened so far in the past, time had no meaning.

Funny, but she found it difficult to think of the planets and stars as being light years away. Especially with the falling light growing closer by the second.

Adrian lowered the camera. Off to the right she saw the comet disappear as quickly as it had appeared. She felt momentarily bereft, knowing it was lost to her forever.

Quickly she looked back at the sparkle growing brighter as it descended. It looked so close. Almost as if it were heading straight for her.

With a shock of fear, she realized that was exactly what was happening. One of the blazing particles that had burst from the tail of the comet was falling to earth, right above the helicopter field.

Adrian cried out with giddiness. Oh, this was too good to be true. She couldn't believe her luck. What a coup! The professor at the college couldn't help being impressed when she showed him a piece of the Fable Comet.

Bless the mystical comet, she thought. Maybe it did have magical powers the way people used to think it did. It would certainly make an uncanny difference in her life if she could get a piece of it!

As the light drew brighter, descending through the inky sky toward the field, her excitement soared. She scrambled down from the roof of the car so fast her legs went out from under her. She lost her grip on the camera and it skidded across the hood toward the front fender.

"Oh, no!" Adrian cried, grasping frantically for the strap. She rolled onto her side, her nails scraping the bright yellow paint of her hood. The camera disappeared over the side just as Adrian realized the enormous amount of light illuminating the area. She spun around and stared up in shock and horror.

It was coming right at her!

She lunged across the hood and propelled herself over the edge of the car headfirst. Her hands hit the ground, her palms scraping the gravel as she tumbled end over end. She heard the sound of glass breaking as the expensive camera hit the ground. She landed hard on top of it.

But she couldn't think about the monetary loss at that moment. All she could do was look back at the falling star as the white-hot light flashed before her eyes, temporarily blinding her.

A crash resounded in her ears even as she clasped her arms around her head in an effort to shield herself from the falling debris. A fiery pain exploded in her body and she cried out, the sound sucked up in the deafening roar of heaven and earth colliding.

Chapter Two

Adrian rolled over and faced the black sky. The stars twinkled and the moon glowed, illuminating the area. But all she could see were spots. White dots danced crazily across her vision, as if a thousand-watt bulb had gone off in her face.

Her head ached and her palms burned, but otherwise she seemed fine. She slowly crawled to her knees and, reaching blindly for the bumper of her car, started to pull herself to her feet.

"Aargh," she cried, her hand meeting only air and her move sending her back down into the dirt face-first.

Blinking rapidly, she tried to bring the area into focus. It was no good. Skyrockets of color did a dance in her head and she couldn't seem to chase them away. Feeling more than a little foolish, she began to search the ground with her hands.

After several minutes her head cleared slightly, but her irritation only grew. Where the devil was her car? Had she fallen that far away? She rolled to sit on her bottom, rubbing her burning eyelids as she tried to see through the darkness.

For a brief second her vision cleared and she quickly looked around. Nothing. All she could see were dark shadows. Her head was pounding.

If she could get to her car, she could turn on the lights. Or better yet, she could get a ginger ale from the small cooler she'd brought along and take some aspirin.

Just then she remembered the camera, and the sound of it as it landed on the hard ground, and she cringed. Shoving her long red curls back out of her face, she shook her aching head.

She'd charged that camera, along with the lens, certain they'd help her get the job with the planetarium. Now she had nothing to show for her efforts except a headache and a credit card bill she wouldn't be able to pay without dipping into her inheritance, something she refused to do.

Finally her eyes cleared enough for her to stumble to her feet. But the moon only afforded a meager amount of light, not enough for her to see more than a few feet around her.

Adrian took a step forward and frowned. Her Keds disappeared into the grass up to her shins.

"What the heck . . . ?"

The helicopter field was a popular exercise area during the day: people walked and jogged around it regularly. There had never been a time when the grass wasn't beaten down to short nubs. Except in the very middle.

"Good grief, how did I get out here?"

Knowing the field was huge, and the middle would have been a good hundred yards from where she'd parked, Adrian rubbed her temple in confusion.

Was she thrown away from the car? Had she wandered away without remembering it? If so, how far had she gone? Was she still in the field at all?

A shiver of fear feathered up her spine. The helicopter field was in the middle of nowhere, a deserted clearing at least four miles from the edge of town. And she was out here alone, without even a flashlight, unable to locate the safety of her car.

"Settle down, Adrian," she told herself, fighting the sudden disquiet threatening her composure. "You're alone. There isn't anyone close by and no one will know you're here if you just keep quiet." And stop talking out loud to yourself, she thought, glancing around frantically.

She brushed herself off, more for something

27

to do than because she cared what she looked like. As her hands brushed over the flowing white ruffled shirt, she paused. Pulling the fabric away from her body, she stuck her finger through a hole just above her navel. As she checked the shirt out more closely, she gasped. It looked like Swiss cheese!

Small burn holes dotted the silk everywhere she touched. The ashes—or debris, or whatever—from the comet had actually fallen on her. It had burned dozens of little holes in her blouse. She lifted the silk and touched her flat midriff. Nothing. Thank goodness, it hadn't been hot enough to sear her skin.

She had to get out of here. She had to get home. Then she could sit down and rationally think about what had happened. Tomorrow she'd come back out here, in broad daylight, and search the area. Surely if the debris had fallen so close to her there would be pieces of it lying around. Her plan could still work, even without the pictures.

But first she had to find her car. No easy task in the dark, even with the moon for light. She decided the best thing to do would be to take precise steps in each direction. Then, if she didn't see anything, turn around and retrace her steps so she wouldn't get lost.

Carefully putting one foot directly in front of the other, she paced off 20 yards through the layer of fog. Straining, she looked around.

Nothing. Spinning on her heel, she turned and retraced her steps.

After an hour, Adrian was cursing and stomping. This was ridiculous. She'd walked in every direction but hadn't found anything except more tall grass and weeds.

Would she have to wait until morning to find her car? That could be hours from now. Unless she'd been knocked out. Why hadn't that occurred to her before? It had seemed as though she'd been conscious the whole time, but had she? She'd gotten into the middle of the field somehow and she didn't remember walking there.

Good grief, she might have a concussion or something. Could a person be knocked unconscious and not remember it? She supposed it was possible.

A sudden weakness stole into her limbs and she sank to the damp grass. Maybe she should just wait until daylight. She could rest a while in case she was injured and didn't realize it.

She lay back on the cool ground and closed her eyes. Almost immediately, she reopened them. Whenever she shut her lids the wild colors danced again. Resigned, she stared up at the sky, trying to relax and calm herself.

She must have dozed because when she opened her eyes again the sun was just peeking over the horizon. Energized, she jumped to her feet, determined to get to her car and leave as soon as possible.

Which might be a problem, she thought, scanning the area. Her legs trembled beneath her and she sank her hands in the front pockets of her jeans. Where the hell was she? This was not the helicopter field. She was in the middle of nowhere!

Stay calm, Adrian, she told herself. It's daytime now, you don't need to be afraid. Obviously you wandered away from the field and your car. But you couldn't have gone far. They have to be around here somewhere.

But where? She could see now in every direction and what she saw was nothing. No power lines, no road, no houses. God, wherever she was, she knew she'd never been here before.

"If I miss my interview I'll never get that job. And without a job soon I'll have to use the money Mom and Dad left," she said, tightening her jaw. "No, absolutely not. I won't touch that money even if I have to work at a fast-food restaurant until I get a better position."

She'd just have to walk. That was all there was to it. She'd walk until she came to the road, or a store with a phone. She could orient herself, get her bearings.

"Well, quit dawdling and get going," she chastised herself. "Or you'll be flipping burgers for sure."

The problem was, she didn't know which way

to go. If she'd wandered away from her car without even realizing it, how was she supposed to know in which direction she'd come?

The grass.

No one ever said she wasn't smart, she thought. Glancing around, she searched the area for tracks. In grass this thick she was bound to have left a trail. Turning in a circle, she frowned. All around her the grass grew tall and straight. She could see where she'd paced off her steps the night before in an effort to find her car. But at the end of each path the trail abruptly ended. There wasn't a single broken stalk. Nothing.

She felt as if she were caught in one of those weird circles that appeared in farmers' fields and were supposed to be caused by UFOs. How could someone get into the middle of a field without trampling the grass?

The whole episode was beginning to bring back her headache and she finally decided to stop thinking and just start walking. Sooner or later she'd have to come across something.

"Wouldn't you know it would be later," she told herself irritably. She'd been walking at least an hour and she still hadn't come to the road. She'd found a dirt path, however, and she figured it must lead somewhere. But so far she hadn't seen anything except a few trees and more empty fields.

The sun was reaching higher into the sky, and Adrian shaded her eyes as she glanced around. Suddenly her heart gave a leap of joy. A giggle of relief burst from her lips.

She'd been walking up someone's driveway. Gazing happily at the small cabin, she had to admit it didn't look like much. But surely they'd have a phone. And they could tell her exactly where she was.

She hurried toward the house, admitting that was a charitable term for the rough-hewn shack. Planks were chinked together with red clay to make up the four walls, and a fireplace of flat, slate rocks leaned against one side. The house was up off the ground and she could see a small rabbit grazing on the tall grass growing underneath.

"Hello," she called, not wanting to sneak up on anyone first thing in the morning. Especially out here in the middle of nowhere where they probably didn't get many unexpected visitors.

"Is anyone home?" Another shiver of apprehension slid over her. What if no one was here? The way the place looked it could be a deserted shack from another era.

But then she glanced around and saw the cleared field nearby, and a few outbuildings scattered around. The yard had no grass, but strange circular patterns had been drawn in the orange dirt. Curiouser and curiouser, Alice.

The door creaked open and Adrian jumped.

"Hello? I was wondering if you could help me. I'm lost and I'm late for a job interview."

She couldn't see the person who'd opened the door, and she was just about to conclude it had moved on its own when a man came from around the back of the cabin, fastening the hook on a pair of baggy, faded overalls.

The other hook was missing and, as he stopped and stared, Adrian saw the strap swinging across his back. The bibbed front drooped, revealing the soiled neckline of what looked like the top of a pair of long johns. The sleeves had been pushed up to his elbows.

Tall and lean, with a face made exclusively of hollows and planes, the man stared at her. His eyes squinted against the rising sun, and the tiny lines fanning out from the corners were white, acknowledging that he squinted often. Deeper lines bracketed his mouth, lines she suspected were not caused by laughter. His eyes continued to watch her, no sign of welcome in their blue-green depths.

Neither of them moved for a long moment; then Adrian shook off her shock and took a step forward. She forced a smile as she brushed the springy red curls away from her face.

"God, am I glad to see you," she said without thinking. "I've been wandering around for more than an hour. I'm lost and I was wondering if you could help me." He didn't answer for a minute and she went on, trying to convey her urgency. "You see, I'm going to be late for a job interview."

A light came into the man's eyes and she thought she saw the ghost of a smile. Then confusion skidded across his harsh features. "A job interview? Well, I wouldn't call it that exactly." His expression cleared once more. "Course, I guess you might look at it that way. No matter, we're sure glad you're here."

"You are?" Adrian asked, looking around in confusion. Did he think she was someone else? If so, who?

"Yep. Right glad. And a little surprised, too. I didn't expect you first thing this morning. Course, the sooner the better," he added with a grin.

The smile transformed his face and Adrian caught her breath. He couldn't be called handsome: his appearance made her think he'd had a hard life. But the smile lit his eyes and touched something in her. Slowly, she relaxed.

"I'm sorry, Mr. . . . "

"Walker, just like the ad said. But you can call me Rome. In fact, under the circumstances formality seems kinda out of place."

"It does?" Adrian's face fell. What was going on? Obviously there'd been a mistake.

"Just call me Rome," he said stepping toward her. The heavy work boots he wore stirred the orange dust around his feet and she could see the particles settle on the tough black leather. "And your name is?"

Adrian stepped back. Better to get this settled as soon as possible. "I'm sorry, Mr. Walker—"

"Rome," he stressed.

"I'm sorry, but I think there's been some mistake. I'm lost. I just came here to ask directions. I need to get to a telephone and call someone to come and pick me up."

"There's no mistake. I'm the one who placed the ad. If you're looking for a job, you're not lost. And Newhope hasn't got a telephone. It's nothing but a wide spot in the road. Not what you'd call a town exactly."

Adrian frowned. How could he refer to Newhope as a wide spot in the road? They weren't a big city by any stretch of the imagination, but they'd grown to over 50,000 residents and the town itself covered at least a 20-mile radius.

Adrian held her hands up and waved. "There's been a mistake. Obviously you're expecting someone, but not me. I drove out here from Newhope last night."

"You drove by yourself?" His mouth dropped open in surprise. "Where's your cart?"

"My what?"

"Your cart. Or did you rent one of them carriages from Sam at the livery?"

"I didn't rent anything. I drove my car. Only I somehow got lost and now I can't find it."

She stopped talking, noting the way his mouth still hung open. He didn't seem aware of the fact that he looked like a widemouthed bass.

She nervously tucked her hands into her jeans pockets.

His eyes followed her movements and his mouth snapped shut with a click. Frowning, he studied her.

"What happened to your clothes?" he finally blurted.

Adrian remembered the ruined blouse and crossed her arms in front of her breasts. "You wouldn't believe it," she told him.

He just shook his head. "No matter," he said. "It isn't like I mean to be picky, or anything. Nope, I'm just glad you're finally here."

He seemed to remember his manners then, and he brushed his palms on the denim covering his narrow hips. "Won't you come inside, Miss . . ."

"Sheppard. Adrian Sheppard." She looked at the hand he pointed toward the little cabin. "Maybe I should just walk back. If you could tell me which way the helicopter field is from here, I'm sure I can find it."

"The what?" Before she could answer, his features hardened, and she saw the desperation in his beautiful teal eyes. "You don't mean to stay, then?"

"Stay?"

"I know the place looks kinda rough right now, but I've been without help for almost a year. It won't take much for you to get it looking tidy again."

"Me?" Adrian felt like an idiot. She didn't understand a word this man was saying to her and she couldn't seem to make him understand that she wasn't who he thought she was. Whoever that was.

"If you want the position."

Adrian was shaking her head. Then his words registered and her ears perked up. Was he offering her a job? Something more challenging—and prosperous—than asking, "Would you like fries with that?"

She'd done too much scouting to pass up a golden opportunity like this. It wouldn't hurt just to inquire about the position.

Besides, even if she left now there was no way she'd make the interview at the planetarium. The least she could do was hear the man out.

After all, beggars couldn't be choosers, she thought, remembering the lost camera and the credit card bill she would have to pay.

"What kind of position are you talking about, Mr. Walker?"

His brow furrowed, and she thought she saw a flush of red creep over his neck. "The advertisement spelled it out," he said, eyeing her with what might have been distrust.

"I'm sorry, I don't have a copy of it. Could you tell me again?"

"What did you say your name was?" he asked suddenly, suspicion blossoming on his face.

Adrian heard a squeak and glanced over to

see the door move once more. She thought she saw a small face peer around the edge; then it disappeared before she could be sure.

"Adrian Sheppard."

"Miss Sheppard, there's nothing around here for miles but my place. What did you come out here for if you're not interested in the advertisement?" His patience evaporated and a look of resigned displeasure covered the hard lines of his face.

Adrian hurried to reassure him, seeing another opportunity slipping through her fingers. "I'm interested, I am," she said. Stepping forward, she pasted on her best smile and decided to be blunt. "In fact, I'm just about desperate for a job right now. But would you mind telling me what exactly you're looking for?"

He narrowed his eyes and studied her face for a long moment. Then he seemed to make a decision and he nodded. It seemed he needed help as badly as she needed a job.

"I advertised for a wife, Miss Sheppard. A wife," he said as Adrian heard the door of the cabin creak all the way open. "And a mother."

With a gasp Adrian turned to look at the porch of the shack. Three ragtag children stood there, lined in a row across the uneven planks.

"These are my children, Emily, Tobias, and Eli."

They stared at her for what seemed like an

eternity and then the littlest one toddled forward, his thumb stuck in his mouth. As he reached the steps he held out his arms.

"Mama," he cooed.

Chapter Three

"Oh, no. No!" Adrian shouted, taking a hasty step back. "There's definitely been a mistake here," she babbled. Her eyes darted between the man and the kids. "I don't know who you were expecting, but it wasn't me. I just came out here to watch the sky last night. I didn't come out here to get—well, for any other reason."

The harsh lines were back on the man's face. He glanced at his children and then back at Adrian, bitterness pulling down the corners of his mouth.

"If you've changed your mind, that's fine," he said, obviously disappointed in her reaction. "But I didn't try to misrepresent myself or my circumstances. I made it clear I had three children."

"Honestly, Mr. Walker, I didn't come here because of your ad," she rushed to assure him. "I'm sorry about the misunderstanding, but I really am just lost. I wandered here by mistake."

"Mistake? That's a far piece to wander accidentally. And why did you ask about the position? Why did you make me think you'd come in answer to my pr—my advertisement?" he said shortly.

"It's a long story, really." She turned to look at the children. The toddler had replaced his thumb in his mouth and was standing close to the edge of the porch. She thought she should warn him to step back, but realized it wasn't her place. The other two children caught her attention and she took a moment to scrutinize them.

Another boy and a little girl. The boy looked hopeful, almost eager, and she turned away from his little face quickly. An unattractive pout pushed out the little girl's bottom lip and her blue eyes stared hard at Adrian. Stung by the undeserved anger, she turned back to the man.

"I'm sorry," she repeated, not certain why she felt she owed them an apology. "But I really can't accept your offer." God, her ex-husband would bust a gut laughing if he could see her now.

Adrian wasn't amused. This man must be crazy. No one just advertised for a wife and mother. Or maybe someone did. She'd never read a singles magazine but she'd heard about

42

them. SWM seeks SWF for a good time, must like Jell-O and contact sports.

She shuddered and took another step back.

The man looked at the three small faces staring up at him and he sighed deeply. His features softened then. "It's all right," he said. "I guess we would kind of overwhelm a person."

He faced Adrian and she could see the sadness in his expressive eyes. This man was in desperate straits, she realized. He'd have to be to advertise for a wife in these times.

She wished she could help him, but there was no point in getting their hopes up for nothing. She would never, ever agree to such an outrageous offer. Just the thought of marriage and children left a bad taste in her mouth after the disaster with Tate.

"Would you like something to eat? We were just about to sit down to breakfast."

Although startled by the unexpected offer, Adrian felt her stomach rumble and she remembered she hadn't eaten dinner the night before. She'd been too excited about the comet and the interview at the planetarium. But she couldn't—wouldn't—accept anything from this poor family. No doubt they needed whatever they had.

"No, thank you," she said, forcing a brittle smile. "But I could use a ride back to town after you're through."

The man waved the children back into the

house and they went slowly, shuffling their feet dejectedly. Adrian wished she could do something for them. What a terrible life for such little kids.

"I'm sorry, miss. But I've only got the one horse and, help or no help, I've got to get him behind the plow this week. I'm already behind and I can't afford to lose a full day and night going to town. I know it's a lot to ask but if you could stay, just for the month, I'd be happy to take you to town when I go in for supplies."

"A month! What are you talking about? Can't you just drive me in your car?"

"My what?"

Oh, God, Adrian thought. This is a nightmare. No matter how poor the man was he had to have a car. Then she realized how foolish that sounded.

"I'll walk back," she said. "Thank you anyway, but I can't stay here for a month."

"Begging your pardon, ma'am, but you can't walk to town either."

"I can't? Why not?"

He raked the light hair off his forehead and scratched his jaw. "It's nearly thirty miles. You'd never make it. Besides, there are panthers out there at night."

Adrian stared, stunned. She didn't know which to react to first, his mileage to town or his reference to panthers. She shook her head. "What are you talking about? The edge of town can't be more than four or five miles. And there haven't been panthers in these parts for decades."

Again, Walker stared at her closely. His gaze swept over her wild hair, flushed face, and ruined shirt.

"Ma'am, maybe you ought to come on inside and have a bite. I think you're a bit confused."

Adrian couldn't disagree with that. She'd been confused ever since the falling star fell on her. Could she have possibly wandered so far? She looked at Rome Walker and saw only the sadness and concern that seemed to haunt his eyes. He didn't look dangerous. And she didn't think there was anything to fear as long as they were surrounded by his children. The love he felt for them had been plain to see when he looked at them.

"I could use a cup of coffee," she admitted. "I'm beginning to think I might be even more lost than I thought."

Again he waved his hand toward the cabin. After a moment of nervous consideration, Adrian stepped toward the porch. She eased her foot carefully onto the first step and then looked back at Rome Walker.

He stood behind her, his eyes now level with hers. He really did have beautiful eyes, she thought. If only they didn't look so sad all the time. She could see the deep brown of his skin, and she knew he spent a lot of time in the sun.

His arms were muscled, his stomach flat, his hips lean. *Rangy* was the word that came to mind. Almost as though he'd lost a lot of weight in a short time. There was a hunger in his gaze. Not a sexual desire, but as though he needed something desperately and had no hope of getting it. She wished there were more she could do for him and his children, but she knew there was nothing.

She turned and stepped across the porch to the door, pushing it aside. Her eyes quickly adjusted to the dim interior and she gasped. It was even worse than she thought. The cabin looked like something out of "Little House on the Prarie." She could see only one room, a combination living/dining/bedroom. A door led off the left side, but she couldn't see inside it. The main room had only two windows, one facing the front of the property and the other facing the rear. Out the back she could see a porch and several smaller buildings farther away.

Adrian jumped and whirled to face Rome Walker. For the first time she scrutinized everything around her closely. His overalls looked normal, his boots old but not strange. The children had been dressed in cheap clothing, the little girl's dress reaching almost to her ankles, but that was understandable since it was most probably a castoff if they were as poor as it seemed.

But nothing could have prepared her for the

sight of the run-down shack. Dust covered the uneven planks of the floor and Adrian could see daylight between the boards on the walls. The furniture consisted of a long picnic-type table with two benches, and two small cots, one on either side of the fireplace.

She smelled bacon, and turned to find the little girl dishing the strips onto a plate from an iron skillet on the hearth.

Without thinking, Adrian rushed forward. She grabbed the girl by her shoulders and pulled her back. "Good Lord, you shouldn't be that close to a fire." She could feel the heat of the flames on her cheeks and she shot Walker a harsh look.

"I always dish the food," the little girl said angrily. She plunked the plates down on the table with a thud and turned back to the fire, taking a minute to narrow her eyes at the intruder.

"Mimi, there's no cause to be rude."

The girl wore a small apron over her dress and she used it to reach for a metal coffeepot hanging close to the fire.

Adrian gasped and stepped forward, but the girl's glare stopped her in her tracks. She set the pot down next to the plate and looked up at her father. He nodded sharply.

"Apologize."

"I'm sorry," she mumbled, not sounding the least bit repentant.

Adrian took another long look at the occupants of the room. She had never seen such poverty in her life. Did people actually live like this? She felt a wave of shame wash over her. Of course they did. She hadn't been living on the moon for the last 29 years. She knew all about the destitute, the homeless. She'd even helped serve Christmas dinner at the soup kitchen last year and seen the hopeless faces of the poor up close. But she'd never come face-to-face with the reality of their lives.

But wouldn't social services do something about children living in this environment? Wouldn't they help them in some way?

"Miss Sheppard?"

Adrian snapped out of her musings and saw the little girl scooping eggs onto another plate. She might not agree to be their mother, but she could at least help out until she got back to town and notified the proper authorities.

"Here," she said, stepping forward and kneeling before the fire. "Let me do that."

She finished off the eggs and set the plate on the table. The girl had added several slices of bread and a ceramic pitcher of milk.

She took more plates from a shelf over the fireplace and set the table. As she laid down the last plate, all eyes turned to Adrian.

An expectant silence filled the little room and she shuffled nervously, feeling somehow responsible. She saw the older boy, a child of maybe three or four, stare up at her with tears in his eyes.

"Did I do something? What . . . ?"

"I'm sorry, Miss Sheppard. It's been a long time since we had a lady sit with us at this table. I guess we've missed it, is all."

Adrian's heart swelled. She saw Rome Walker scan the cabin critically as he pulled out the bench for her to sit down.

"I hadn't realized how we'd let the place go," he said, his tone apologetic. "I guess it must look pretty bad to you."

"We've still got some of Mama's pretty things, like the plates," Mimi added, the pain in her blue eyes matching her father's. "We have a real stove, too, out back in the kitchen. But Daddy does better with the fireplace."

Adrian longed to tell Rome Walker no one should be cooking over an open fireplace. Especially with children in the house. But with herculean effort she managed to hold her tongue.

"I'd started adding another room before Lorraine died, but I haven't had a chance to finish it."

Adrian felt an embarrassed flush creep over her cheeks. Why did he feel the need to explain things to her? Had he read her thoughts? Was he afraid she would sic the Social Services people on him and they'd take his children away? Obviously he was doing the best he could.·

Still, she couldn't just forget what she'd seen. Once she returned to Newhope, she would have to see that something was done about these children. No matter if Rome Walker did seem like a nice man.

Without a car, he couldn't offer her a ride back to town. As Adrian ate the simple but tasty meal he'd prepared, she considered what she would do. After breakfast, she would start walking back. It would take her most of the day if she truly had wandered 30 miles from town. But once she found a telephone she'd call someone to come and get her. The idea wasn't pleasant, but she knew she'd be home by nightfall at least.

Meanwhile, she would try to think of a way to help these poor children without causing Rome Walker any more trouble.

They polished off the food and she helped the little girl clear the table. On the cabin's back porch was a huge sink with an old-fashioned pump attached. The girl cranked the handle and ran water over the dirty dishes, then took a bar of soap and started scrubbing them.

Adrian had seen enough. No matter how much Rome Walker loved his children, this was ridiculous! They didn't even have running water. It was absolutely primitive. Children couldn't live like this.

She stormed back into the house, determined to get to town as soon as possible. Her own problems were all but forgotten in her anger at Rome Walker. The man was a barbarian to keep children in this place.

When she reentered the house, she didn't see him. Glancing around, she realized all the males had disappeared. Now what? she thought. Where had they gone? When would they be back?

The door swung open and she jumped. Walker strode in, a small trunk in his hands.

"This was Lorraine's. I figured you'd need some proper clothes if you were going back into town. You're welcome to use whatever you need."

The despair in his voice spoke volumes. He'd seen her horror when she looked at his cabin. He'd read the dismay on her face when she'd watched Mimi bending over the fireplace. He was as eager to be rid of her as she was to go. He set the trunk on the floor in front of her.

Rome turned and walked back out the door, letting it swing shut behind him. Again she wondered where the little boys had gone. She heard Mimi on the porch and decided she'd help the girl before she left.

Walking out the back door, she saw Mimi toweling off the plates. She stepped up beside her and took the towel, offering the girl a smile. Without responding, Mimi went back to washing.

Together they washed and dried in silence. Adrian had a small shock when she actually held the first plate in her hand. It was china, very fragile, and hand-painted unless she

51

Marti Jones

missed her guess. What were such expensive dishes doing in this den of poverty? she wondered.

Mimi handled each dish reverently. After they had all been scrubbed spotless, she took the stack Adrian had made and carried them back into the house, carefully replacing them on the shelf. Her eyes fell on the trunk and she shot Adrian a hard glare.

"I need to borrow a shirt," Adrian mumbled, wondering why the girl's dislike could so unsettle her. "Your father said it would be all right. I promise I'll return it."

Mimi snatched up a broom from the corner behind the door and left the cabin without a word. Adrian went to the door and watched her sweep the porch. When she had finished that, she went to the yard and began to sweep the dirt into intricate swirls.

"What on earth?" Adrian had never seen anyone sweep dirt before. Was Mimi just doing it to avoid being in the cabin with Adrian? That must be it, she thought.

Kneeling in front of the trunk, Adrian knew she couldn't get back to town soon enough. This whole experience was a nightmare. First the falling star, then getting lost and wandering so far away from her car she couldn't find her way back. Now she felt just awful thinking about Mimi and the two little boys living here.

With a sigh, she lifted the cover of the trunk.

A musty smell crept toward her nose and she sneezed. Maybe she'd be better off wearing the holey shirt she had on.

A Bible had been placed on top of the clothes in the trunk and it caught Adrian's attention. Reaching for it, she saw that it was covered in a hand-stitched, needlepoint jacket. She fingered the tiny, straight stitches. Someone had put a lot of time and love into the pattern.

She opened the Bible to the first page and read the name scrawled across the top. *Lorraine Norton Walker*.

Her first thought was to close the book and forget she'd seen it. But her curiosity won out. What kind of woman would live in a place like this? Bring children into the world with nothing but a shack over their heads and a couple of cots on the floor?

She flipped the page. *Marriages.* Only the first two lines had been filled in. The first one read *Lorraine Norton married Rome Christopher Walker.* The second line was the date. Adrian felt a small shock course through her and then she laughed softly.

Fingering the small letters, she assumed the writing had been blurred. For a second, she thought it said February 12, 1886. Obviously it should read 1986.

She flipped another page and the shock blossomed into horror. A sketch of a tree had been drawn on the page before her. At the bottom, in a small block, was written *Rome and Lorraine Walker*. Above that, three lines stretched out like branches. At the end of each branch was another square. In each square, a name and a date.

This time there was no mistake. The writing had been done by a careful hand. The print was clear and precise. Adrian's eyes widened as she read the words:

Emily Lorraine Walker, born November 28, 1886.
Tobias Joseph Walker, born June 17, 1891.
Eli Christopher Walker, born May 10, 1893.

A chill crept up her neck, raising the hair on her nape. She clutched the hard edges of the Bible until they cut into her scraped palms. Frantically, she turned the page, her breath coming in short, shallow gasps.

The next page was headed *Deaths*. She squeezed her eyes shut, trying to block out the sight. Whatever it said, she didn't want to know. All she wanted to do was put the Bible back where she'd found it and get the hell out of this nuthouse as soon as possible. Suddenly fear overtook her. All the things she'd seen were starting to fall into place and the facts threatened to drive her out of what was left of her mind.

Slowly she opened her eyelids and focused on the words. Immediately she closed them tight again. The handwriting was different. Whoever had filled in the top line of this page was not the same person who had filled in the previous ones.

Desperate for answers, and knowing with a sickening certainty she wouldn't like the ones she found, Adrian looked at the page in the Bible once more.

Her hands were trembling. Her legs felt like jelly, and she was glad she was sitting down, otherwise she'd have fallen.

Lorraine Norton Walker, died May 1, 1894.

Adrian slammed the book shut and shoved it back into the trunk. Her heart pounded so hard she could feel it beating against her breastbone. Short, rapid breaths hissed past her dry lips. It wasn't possible. She wouldn't even consider such a ridiculous notion.

But as Adrian's darting gaze flitted frantically around the sparse cabin, she knew she had to think. No matter how crazy it seemed, she'd known from the moment she arrived here that something was wrong. People didn't live like this anymore.

"Stop it," she whispered, scrambling to her feet. "You're acting stupid. That Bible can't be right; it's some sort of mistake." That had to be the answer. Anything else was incomprehensible. Because if the Bible was correct, and she

told herself again it could not be, then that
would mean one of two things.

Either she had just shared breakfast with four
ghosts, or else . . .

Chapter Four

"Miss Sheppard?"

Adrian cried out and scrambled back, the Bible clutched in her trembling hands. She pressed the heavy weight against her chest and stared up at Rome Walker.

"Miss Sheppard, are you all right?" He took another step toward her and Adrian shot to her feet, hastily backing up.

"What's the matter?"

His voice was reserved, but concerned. Adrian shoved the Bible away from her chest, holding it out where he could see it. "Explain this," she demanded, not even realizing how absurd her command sounded.

"It's a Bible," he told her, the lines across his forehead deepening. The sadness usually present in his eyes was momentarily replaced with confusion.

"I know it's a Bible," she snapped. "Explain the inscriptions. The names, the dates," she babbled.

When he said nothing, just continued to watch her, she flipped to the first page. Her fingers tapped the words she knew were written there, but her eyes never left his face.

"Here it says Rome and Lorraine Walker were married February 12, 1886. Are those family names?"

"Family names?"

"Yes, you know. Names that have been in your family for generations," she said, clutching desperately at straws.

"Not that I know of."

"What about this?" She flipped the page and rapidly tapped the rough-drawn family tree. "The names of these children, they just happen to be the same as yours?"

"No, they don't just happen to be. They are. Lorraine filled in the names and dates when the babies were born. Miss Sheppard . . ."

Adrian slammed the book shut, unwilling to look at the crazy scrawl any longer. It couldn't be true. For some reason Rome Walker, or whoever he was, was lying to her. It didn't make sense, especially since he'd indicated he wanted her to stay and work for him. No, not work, she corrected, fighting the rising panic sweeping over her. Marry him. This man wanted someone he'd never met before to marry him.

That proved he was crazy, didn't it?

She crossed her arms over her chest, forgetting the Bible now buried in her bosom. "So you're telling me you were born in . . . what year?"

He quirked an eyebrow in question, then seemed to understand. "I was born in 1860, Miss Sheppard. I realize that means I'm a great deal older than you are, but I'm not that old."

Adrian gasped and stumbled backward. She reached for the chair to steady herself, and the Bible fell to the floor, falling open to the page of Lorraine's death notice as though mocking her shock and horror. Yes, you are, she wanted to scream at Rome Walker. You are very, very old. In fact, you are dead!

"Are you all right?" he asked, stepping toward her. She tried to back up again, but the chair was behind her, and as her knees hit the wooden edge she crumpled into the seat.

"You're telling me this is your Bible? Yours and Lorraine's? That those are the correct dates of your marriage and the children's birthdays?"

His frown deepened. "Yes, of course it is. What else would it be?"

He reached down and picked up the Bible and she saw him caress the cover lovingly as he closed it. Gripping it in his hands, he stared down at her.

A wave of terror threatened to drown her, but Adrian fought off the alarm clamping down on her chest. She struggled for air to clear her thoughts. His earlier remarks came rushing at her like stones from a slingshot, hurling into her with the impact of missiles. *You drove a cart, or a carriage. Newhope is nothing but a wide spot in the road. I only have one horse and I need him to pull the plow.*

The comments had seemed curious but not threatening—until now. Not until she remembered the comet, the debris, the missing car and field. How she'd watched the spectacle and thought of the people, 100 years ago, who'd last seen it. March nineteenth, 1885.

"That would make today March the twentieth, 1895," she whispered to herself.

"That's right," Rome said, startling her. "Is something wrong?"

Her head snapped up and she met his eyes. The teal orbs held her gaze for a long minute; then she threw her hands over her face and shook her head. "Yes, oh, yes, something is definitely wrong."

Rome came to the table. He pulled out a chair and sat down across from her.

"I can see you're having some difficulties with this situation. And I can't blame you, I guess. But the truth is, Miss Sheppard, we really need your help."

Adrian's head came up slowly. Her fingers

slid down her cheeks and she watched the grief and despair cross his features. If this were really happening, if everything he said was true, he was 35 years old. He looked older. The hardships he spoke of had certainly taken a toll on him.

"I have to get the seed in the ground, and time's wasting. But I can't leave the younguns alone all day while I tend to the plowing and planting. Emily—Mimi—she's a good girl. But she's not much more than a babe herself. How can I leave her with two spirited boys for hours at a time?"

"You don't understand," she said, terror making her voice barely audible. "I don't belong here. There's been a terrible mistake."

She shook her head. That was like saying the Red Sea was a little wet. How could she make Rome Walker understand something she knew to be impossible? Something she refused to believe herself?

"I don't think so, Miss Sheppard."

Adrian glanced up and saw the hope flare in his eyes before he doused it. "I think you were sent to help us. Why else would you be out here in the middle of nowhere, so far from town and all alone? You said you were lost, but you didn't say where you were from. What brought you here in the first place?"

"I needed a job," she began, then cut off her words, knowing how they would sound. His eyebrow jumped toward his hairline. "Not the job you were advertising for," she hastily added.

"No matter. No one else has applied for the position. Are you telling me you don't need a job now?"

"I still need a job," she admitted. "But—"

"But nothing. In Newhope you might get work in the little restaurant Bob Quinn opened, but he won't be paying much. You'll have to find a place to live and we don't have a hotel yet. Besides that, there isn't much honest work for a young woman around these parts."

She watched the words form on his lips, her mind wandering as he spoke. What was she doing? How could she just continue to sit here, listening to him sell her on the position he'd advertised for?

Shock.

That must be the answer. She was in shock. Her legs wouldn't work. The urge to run screaming from the cabin had seized her, but her body was too numb to move.

"Did you see the comet?" she finally managed to say. Her tone was flat, as though she'd removed herself from the useless shell that was her body. The words seemed to drift slowly to her ears as though echoing down a long tunnel.

She saw Rome Walker nod his head. His eyes narrowed as he watched her closely.

"It was a miracle," he said. "The answer to my prayers."

Her head came up and she perused him closely, trying to see any signs of a deranged mind behind the constantly despondent eyes.

"Yes, it was like a miracle. The way the shards of light exploded from the tail and rained to earth," she said.

He smiled slightly, and again she thought how the expression transformed him. She tried to imagine Rome Walker as a younger man, happily married and starting a life with his bride. Before the grief and burdens dug lines of bitterness and despair on his face.

"I have to admit, it scared the wits out of me at first," he said, his admission sounding almost childlike. "I thought it must be the end of the world."

Adrian frowned, puzzled. Then her face fell. Of course, if Rome Walker was from the last century he wouldn't know about comets and such. She remembered the stories of how the nineteenth-century preachers had lectured about the comet being a sign from God. A prelude, even, to the second coming. Anyone who didn't know about the comet would be stunned by the brilliant sight. She could even understand his thinking it was a sign. But a sign of what?

She voiced her question before she could stop herself. Rome eyed her closely and rose to his feet. He went to the fireplace and carefully laid the Bible on the mantel. Propping his booted foot on the hearth, he breathed a ragged sigh.

"I was drinking heavy, Miss Sheppard. I'd about come to the end of my tether, and I didn't know what to do. I was desperate for help, for answers. I felt abandoned by Lorraine, and by God." He turned to face her, gauging her reaction, she thought. "I'm beyond pride, Miss Sheppard. I'm beside myself with despair. I'd be willing to beg, if it would mean you'd stay."

She could see what the words cost him. Such a large man. So able, so strong. It hurt her to see his pride stripped away.

"I can understand how I might have frightened you, announcing my desire for a wife like I did. I want you to know up front that I only did that so things would be proper. But I'm even beyond worrying about propriety. If you don't see yourself married to a man like me, I understand. But don't let it keep you from helping me. I can't pay much, but I can offer you a roof over your head, plenty of food, and a small salary that'll at least give you the means to get home if you should decide not to stay."

"Home?" Adrian's mind was whirling. Where was her home? Where was she? What had happened? She still couldn't accept all she'd seen and heard in the last hours. She still expected to look out the door and see telephone poles and electric wires running the length of a blacktop road.

"Don't get me wrong; I don't want you to

leave," he quickly assured her. "If I put off the planting for another week or so I can finish the other bedroom. Together we could get the place looking like a real home again, with rugs and chairs and whatever. I could even close off the back porch and you'd have a room indoors for washing and bathing."

She listened to his hurried diatribe, hearing the eagerness and anxiety he couldn't hide. She wanted to tell him that his home wasn't the problem. His children weren't what had her upset. She started to shake her head and he went on, talking faster.

"The kitchen out back can be put to rights in no time. I know it doesn't seem like much now, but with a little work . . ."

Adrian's head was shaking frantically now. She had to make him stop. She didn't want to hear another word. This was impossible. It couldn't be real. She'd never stay here, not in a million years.

"No," she cried, jumping to her feet. The realization of her situation overcame the shock. She had to get out of here. Had to find a way back.

Shaking her head in denial, she made for the door with hurried steps, ignoring his stunned look. Grasping the ceramic knob in her hand, she looked back over her shoulder and saw Rome Walker's shoulders sag with defeat. The furrows on his face reappeared; his eyes narrowed once more in resignation.

"I'm sorry," she said, and was surprised to find she meant it. "I truly am. But I can't stay here. I have to get home. Right now, I have to get home."

She yanked the door open and came face-to-face with Emily Walker. The little girl had been startled by the sudden appearance of Adrian and she blinked rapidly, clutching the broom in her tiny hands.

Adrian stared at the doelike eyes for a minute and felt herself being hypnotized by the sadness she saw there. This family needed help. They needed love and attention. But not from her, she thought frantically. Pushing past Mimi, she took the porch steps in a single leap and hurried across the carefully swept yard and away from the cabin, not daring to look back.

They needed help. But she wouldn't be the one to help them. She couldn't. Lord, she couldn't even help herself at this point.

Determined to get away, she broke into a stumbling run. The road hadn't changed and she watched the red dust billow up to cover her white sneakers. Sweat pooled behind her knees beneath the heavy denim of her jeans, and the white silk shirt fluttered as she ran. But she didn't stop.

She pushed herself on until the stitch in her side became a daggerlike pain. She dropped to her knees in an open field of grass and wildflowers.

Just how long she sat there, gasping and crying, she couldn't be sure. When her sobs finally
subsided, the sun shone bright on her damp
cheeks. She fell to her back and stretched out
on the ground, physically exhausted and emo-
tionally spent.

She tried to tell herself Rome Walker had lied
to her. His story had to be a fabrication. But she
knew it wasn't. What reason would he have to
lie to her? If she found out the truth, as she
surely would, he wouldn't stand a chance of getting her to stay. No, there was no reason he'd
be less than honest.

But the truth was even harder to believe and
she felt unable to deal with it at the moment.
For a long time she lay in the field, hiding from
the horrible, confusing reality. She tried to
block out what she'd seen and heard that morning. She racked her brain, trying to figure out
just what had happened the night before. Her
emotions vacillated between breathless panic
and blinding anger.

Hours later, she was calmer but no closer to
a solution. What if it were true? What if she
were truly in the past? How had it happened?

Rome said he was praying for a solution to
his problem when he saw the comet. She was
watching that same comet a hundred years in
the future, hoping it would be the answer to her
problem as well. A cosmic connection? A freak
accident of nature? Had they each made their

plea at the exact moment, somehow spanning the time barrier?

"No!" she shouted, shoving the wild red tresses out of her face as she sat up. "That's ludicrous! I'm a sensible, twentieth-century woman. I don't even like science fiction! I certainly don't believe in anything so ridiculous as . . ."

She couldn't even bring herself to say the words. She felt silly. There had to be another explanation. Something logical. Something reasonably sane.

A cold shiver started in her stomach and rippled out like waves on a pond until she was trembling all over. A breeze ruffled the tall strands of grass around her, carrying the scent of pollen and new growth.

She could walk to town and check out Rome Walker's claims. Even if it was a 30-mile trek, she knew she'd make it eventually. Of course, it would be dark by then and he'd mentioned panthers.

Funny, but she'd been afraid of two-legged predators last night. Now she found herself overcome with another kind of fear. She didn't know which she preferred.

At the same time, she strongly suspected she'd find exactly what Rome had described to her if she did go to town. She wasn't sure she could face seeing the Newhope he described right now. Besides, it would be the middle of the night. Even if she had a hope of finding employment, she'd have nowhere to go when she arrived.

Her head tipped toward the sky and she grimaced. Obviously a mistake had been made. Whatever had occurred to bring her here, it should never have happened. But how could she go about trying to fix things? The comet only appeared every 100 years. Did that mean that she was stuck here for good? Did someone up there realize the error they'd made?

She decided to tell him, just for good measure.

"I don't belong here," she whispered. "I don't know how I got here, or how I'm supposed to get home, but I promise you I won't stay stuck here. Somehow, some way, I'm going back to my own time. Don't think I won't," she warned, the tears filling her eyes once more.

Rome looked around the dinner table at the faces of his children. If possible, they looked sadder and more dejected than before Adrian Sheppard's arrival. Especially Emily.

Mimi had tried to comfort him after Adrian left, telling him they didn't need the other woman. She'd mothered him, her actions much too mature for a girl of only eight.

The oldness in her eyes tore at his heart. He pushed aside his plate, his appetite gone. He started for the back porch.

"Daddy? Did we do something wrong?"

Stopping, Rome felt the words cut through him. The small voice shook with an unspoken question. He tried, but he couldn't face his daughter.

"No, Mimi. We didn't do anything wrong."

The uncomfortable moment was interrupted by a knock on the door. Frowning, he went to see who was out this time of night.

He pulled open the door and took a startled step back. His eyes raked over the tall, slim woman standing on the porch, her eyes red-rimmed and swollen, her clothes looking even more disreputable than the last time he'd seen them.

"Miss Sheppard?"

She took a hesitant step forward, her chin going up a notch despite the fact that it trembled. He saw her swallow hard, her eyes going past him to the children. "If your offer is still open, Mr. Walker, I've decided to stay the month."

Chapter Five

Adrian refused Rome's offer of a meal, her stomach too unsettled to tolerate even the thought of food. Without question, he showed her to the bedroom, a tiny nook built off the main room. A narrow bed and a washstand were the only furnishings. Pegs attached to the wall held another pair of denim coveralls and a gray flannel shirt.

Rome quickly removed his meager belongings, ducking his head shyly as he fished out his long underwear from a small drawer in the bottom of the washstand. She started to tell him not to bother to clear the drawer. She had nothing to put in it. Glancing down at her ruined blouse, she knew she'd have to borrow something from Lorraine's trunk. Rome knew it, too, and after leaving to put away his own belongings, he returned with the trunk and set it at the foot of the bed.

"You'll want your privacy," he said, as though it was an order. She jumped and felt the edge of the lumpy, rounded mattress press against the backs of her knees. Nervously, she tucked her hands into the front pockets of her jeans.

Without waiting for her reply, he backed out of the room. Adrian turned to stare at the sparse room, the rough surroundings, and felt another wave of panic grip her. It's only temporary, she comforted her troubled mind. Only until I find out how to get back. I need food and shelter while I plan my next course of action. I'll get home soon. In the meantime, Rome Walker's house is the safest place in this strange, surreal world.

A sharp rap of metal on wood startled her and she whirled toward the opening of the room. A heavy quilt hung from one corner, and she saw Rome take aim with the hammer he held and drive a nail through the fabric into the wood frame overhead. He didn't meet her wide gaze as he lifted the opposite corner of the quilt and disappeared behind the raised cover.

He tacked the fabric into place with efficient strokes of the hammer, and in the silence that followed Adrian realized the room was now completely cloaked in darkness.

"Miss Sheppard?"

The powerful voice, even muffled through the quilt, sent a shiver up her spine. Though little protection, the fabric offered her an unreasonable sense of security.

"Yes?"

The quilt was pulled to one side and Rome entered again, carrying a lighted lamp.

"You'll need this," he said, setting the light on the edge of the washstand next to the pitcher. He frowned into the pitcher. "You'll probably be wanting warm water before you turn in."

There was a question in his voice, an uncertainty. Adrian was ill at ease in the small room. This man, tall and lean, seemed to fill the limited area. She couldn't retreat any farther, though his nearness discomfited her.

"If it isn't too much trouble."

"Not at all," he said, taking the pitcher as he once more pushed aside the quilt, disappearing beyond it.

Adrian sat gingerly on the edge of the bed, her thoughts in chaos. A rustling drew her attention and she lifted the edge of the thick comforter. A white sheet covered the mattress and she pushed that aside as well. The blue-striped fabric covering the mattress had come unsewn at one small seam and she pried the edges aside. Moss? She cringed. The mattress was filled with moss.

"Ugh," she muttered, standing. She glanced down at the lumpy surface and tentatively poked it with her finger. It rustled faintly, but all in all didn't feel too bad. Or maybe, she thought, she was simply so tired any soft surface seemed inviting.

"It doesn't have bugs, I assure you."

Once again she jumped at the sound of Rome's voice, deep and full in the close quarters. This time he carried a small stack of white cotton hand towels in one hand, the pitcher effortlessly in the other. Adrian could see a thin wisp of steam rising from the fluted rim.

"I beg your pardon?"

"The bed." He nodded toward where her hand still rested on the comforter. "I boiled the moss before I stuffed the mattress. It's clean."

She could only nod in response. Boiled moss? Funny, his reassurances brought her little comfort.

Setting the pitcher in the basin on top of the washstand, he carefully laid the towels on the shelf below. A puzzled frown drew his brows together and she watched as a flush covered his cheeks.

"The, um, the . . ." He pointed to the shelf and the flush deepened. "Well, the children needed it more than I did. But I can get it back if you don't want to go outside in the dark."

"Outside?"

Her confusion grew and she looked from his embarrassed countenance to the shelf below the pitcher.

"Why would I want to go outside?"

"Well, I mean—you may not *want* to, but you may *have* to. And if you'd like I can—"

The light finally dawned and Adrian gasped in shock. "No!" she nearly shouted. "I mean, no, thank you. I'm fine. I don't need . . . anything."

Nodding brusquely, he turned and left the room as though his heels were on fire.

"Oh my God," she breathed, slumping onto the mattress. An outhouse? It couldn't be. Fate could not be that cruel. She didn't even like portable toilets, and they at least had the barest amenities.

If she'd had any doubts about going home, they vanished like mist in the Southern sun. She could not stay here. Maybe not even for a month. Maybe not even for the night. She had to get home. Fast!

Another shiver of apprehension slid up her spine, raising gooseflesh all along her skin. This was a nightmare. It had to be. Maybe the falling space matter had hit her harder than she thought. Maybe it had knocked her out and she was having hallucinations. Could she be in some sort of coma-induced fantasy?

"Hah!" she snorted. I could certainly come up with something better than this if I were going to fantasize, she thought. And I swear, any fantasy I came up with would have modern plumbing!

As her mind chased disturbing thoughts

75

around in her head, she became aware of a soft droning sound. She sat up straight, straining her ears.

Rome's voice reached her, its warm tone settling her jangling nerves and easing the tension she'd felt tightening like a rubber band in the back of her neck.

He was talking to the children. A tenderness came through in his soft commands. From the words she could make out she knew he was helping them into their nightclothes, settling them on the small cots. Her heart slammed against her ribs and she pressed her hands to her chest.

She listened to the whispered prayers each child offered up, feeling oddly intrusive. She had no right to listen in on their private moments. She didn't intend to stay; she was only using them until she could figure out what to do.

This family, these people, were her only safe port in a stormy sea of strange and bewildering events. She clung to them like a shipwreck victim to flotsam, as a lifeline in a bizarre and confusing time she could not understand. It wasn't fair, though, she realized now. They had their own problems, and they saw her as some kind of solution. It wasn't fair to deceive them.

She knew she should go, leave them to find peace somehow without her. Coward, she thought, starting to tremble again. She didn't want to be alone in this strange world. She didn't know how to cope.

Lying on the bed, she curled into a fetal position and watched the shadows created by the flickering lamp dance on the planked walls. She wondered if she should extinguish the light. What was the danger of fire if it remained burning? Cowering, she knew she couldn't willingly douse the flame. For the first time in her life she was truly frightened, and she didn't want to face her uncertainty in the stark blackness of night.

"What am I going to do?" she asked the darkness. Somewhere in that field of flowers and grass, she'd accepted the fact that she'd traveled back in time. But still, just thinking of it fueled the fire of panic inside her. She carefully banked the helpless feelings and tried to think rationally.

The comet. It was the only answer to this bizarre mystery. But how could that knowledge help her? The comet wouldn't return for a hundred years. And what she knew of it was basic information she'd gotten from the newspaper article she'd read before going to the field.

Straining her exhausted mind, she recalled as much as she could. Unfortunately, most of the scientific info came from the British astronomer Edmond Halley in the 1700s. He compared the orbital elements of comets and successfully predicted when they would return.

Just my luck, she thought. He's dead. And I

don't know of any American astronomers in the late nineteenth century.

Suddenly she sat up. Maybe she didn't need an astronomer. They'd probably think she was a lunatic anyway if she went to them with her story. Maybe this had just been a freak occurrence. Was it possible she'd wake up one day back in her own time?

Was it possible? What was she saying? None of this seemed possible. But if time-travel was feasible, surely it could work both ways and send her home.

Until then, she didn't dare reveal the truth of her appearance to the farmers and merchants around here. They still considered comets as portents of calamity or important events, as Rome Walker had. No one would believe her.

She rolled to her back, still feeling uneasy in her skin. The crawling panic waited close by.

She needed to do something, anything, to keep from going mad with anxiety. But her only option was to go to town, and she didn't think she was ready for that yet.

Rome Walker was her only link to this world, she told herself. And she'd need him to take her to town when the time came. The Fable Comet wouldn't return for a hundred years anyway, she told her anxious brain. What harm could there be in waiting a while until she felt better able to face the shock she was sure to find in Newhope?

* * *

"You've gotta go, Daddy," Mimi urged insistently. She pushed at his arm as they stood by the back window in the house, peering out. Several yards away, he could see the partially open door of the privy. Mimi told him Adrian Sheppard had gone in search of the two-holer more than 15 minutes ago. It did seem a long time, but he certainly wouldn't go out there and ask her if anything was wrong. Just the thought brought a hot flush to his cheeks.

"Go," Mimi coaxed. "Somethin's wrong, I just know it. She was talking funny and stammerin'. I think she mighta been havin' a fit. I just know she's lyin' out there dead, or worse."

"She wasn't having a fit, Mimi. She was just confused."

"She was sure that," his little daughter replied. "Askin' about bathin' rooms and restin' rooms. It took me a full minute to realize she was askin' directions to the outhouse. But I ain't never heard it called a restroom. If I wanted to rest I sure wouldn't do it out there. You think that's what she's done?" she asked with horror.

"Of course not," Rome said absently, eyeing the small, square building where Mimi said Adrian Sheppard had finally gone. What could be taking so long? Was she hurt? Sick? Should he go out there?

He balked at the thought. They'd both been embarrassed last night when he'd tried to ask her about the pee can. What would she do if he came upon her—No, he'd just have to wait, and watch.

"Maybe a snake done come outta the hole and bit her right on her—"

"Toby! We'll have none of that kind of talk," Rome warned, silencing the little boy's enthusiastic imaginings. There weren't snakes in the outhouse. At least, none that he'd ever seen. Frowning deeply, he peered out the window once more.

"Why don't you go, Mimi? It wouldn't be so bad, you being a girl and all."

She glared at him with panic-filled eyes. "I ain't goin' out there," she told him emphatically.

Adrian stared in fascinated amazement at the catalog. Bloomingdale Brothers' Illustrated Catalog apparently sold everything from corsets to cookstoves. And if the missing pages told her anything, it was that the book served a dual purpose. She'd rushed to the outhouse, desperate for relief after a night of denying her bladder's persistent pleas. Somehow Rome Walker's reminder of her body's functions had recalled the fact she hadn't answered nature's call for some time. All night she'd fought the heaviness, refusing to even consider a trip outside in the blackest night.

By daylight, she couldn't put it off any longer. However, seeing the catalog had wiped every other thought from her mind and she couldn't seem to put it down. Leaning against the wall of the outhouse, she kept the door propped open with her toe, allowing fresh air and sunlight into the small building while she scanned the remaining pages of the catalog.

Fashions, dry goods, housewares. It seemed the brothers Bloomingdale dabbled in everything. Cigars, five cents. Ladies Dongola button patent leather shoes, one dollar. Dr. Price's delicious flavoring extracts. She turned page after page, captivated. This catalog could come in handy if she stayed around for long. It showed her accepted clothing, decorating tips. It even explained how some of the most *modern* appliances were operated.

However, if it remained out here much longer, she'd soon lose valuable reference material. And she didn't think removing it would go unnoticed. So she quickly scanned each page, desperate to imprint as much information in her mind as quickly as she could.

Twenty minutes passed and Rome's concern blossomed. What was taking so long? Behind him, Toby danced around, jiggling and holding himself earnestly.

"Dad-dy, I gotta go," he whined again.

"Mimi, get your brother the can," he said.

"No," Toby complained. "Don't want the can. I wanna go to the outhouse."

Rome glanced sideways at his son, the stubborn jut of his lip, and knew if Miss Sheppard didn't come out soon, it would be too late.

"All right, all right," he soothed. "Hold on a minute."

He did not want to go out there. There had to be another way. Toby sucked in his breath and tiptoed around in little circles.

"Okay, Toby. Hold in there, big fella." Resolutely, Rome opened the back door and stepped out onto the porch. Shading his eyes from the rising sun, he looked back at the three faces watching him from the doorway.

"Go on," Mimi beseeched softly, waving her arms as though shooing away a chicken.

Rome took another step and another. He walked out into the yard, shuffling his feet as loudly as he could.

Halfway to the little building, he stopped and glanced back. Three faces like a miniature totem pole, peered through the opening.

Clearing his throat, Rome cupped his hand to his lips. "Miss Sheppard?" he called softly.

When he didn't receive an answer, he cupped his hand again and called louder. "Miss Sheppard?"

A loud thump was followed by a frightened gasp, and the door of the privy swung open, then slammed shut.

"Y-yes?" a voice answered.

He could hear her through the small trian-

gular opening cut high in the side of the wall of
the outhouse. He directed his voice toward it.

"Is everything all right?"

"Yes, Mr. Walker," she called back primly.
"Everything is fine. I'll be out in a moment."

"That's all right," he shouted, backpedaling
toward the safety of the small cabin. "You just
take your time," he added, then cringed at the
awkwardness of his statement.

He strode back to the house and slammed
into the main room. Closing the door firmly behind him, he pointed to his middle child. "The
can," he said, brooking no argument. Without
another word, he crossed the room, opened the
front door, and strode right on through.

They were so uncomfortable with one another before, Rome thought; how would he face
her now? He'd obviously embarrassed her and
humiliated himself. Taking the long way
around to the barn, he yanked angrily on the
plank barring the door. Once inside, he fastened
the latch and buried himself in the ritual of
morning chores he felt comfortable executing.

God, how would this arrangement ever work
out? He needed a mother for his children; he
wanted a wife for himself. After a year alone, he
longed for the normalcy of a real family again.
And, he admitted, he ached for a woman's
touch. Hell, he'd settle for adult conversation.

Adrian Sheppard was odd, a puzzle. But she
was beautiful, and seemed decent enough even

though he didn't believe her story about being lost. She hadn't tried to hide her dismay at his house and he'd found himself anxious to set things right for her, to show her he could make the place nice once more with help.

She'd left them, certain she couldn't fulfill his requirements. But then she'd returned, her courage bolstered and her determination drawn around her like a shield. He'd seen her fear, and admired her bravery in facing it.

His heart told him she was perfect for them. He couldn't help wondering where such an odd, intriguing woman had come from, but he decided he was in no position to question a miracle. And even without the sign from heaven, Rome knew he would have recognized her as the answer to his prayers.

There was only one problem. Adrian Sheppard didn't see herself as their savior. Despite what she'd told him the night before, he knew with a certainty he couldn't explain that she wouldn't stay so much as the promised month.

She wanted to leave again. He could see it in her beautiful whiskey-brown eyes. His burdens weighed heavily on his shoulders this morning. To be offered a glimmer of hope, only to see it removed, was a terrific blow to the slender thread of optimism he'd managed to retain.

But how could he make her stay if she wanted to go? He knew he couldn't—knew even more he wouldn't. His situation was desperate, and no one deserved to be forced into the middle of it if they didn't want to be.

Since he didn't believe her story about being lost, he assumed she'd changed her mind once she saw the house, the children, the isolation they suffered out here, so far from town. He couldn't blame her for wanting to back out. She was probably from the city, where things were handy and convenient. She obviously regretted her decision to come at all and he wondered what had made her do it in the first place.

That was a question he would probably never know the answer to. But one thing he knew for sure. Whether she stayed a week, a month, or a year, he would not waste a moment of the time he had. He'd make the best of the assistance she'd offered as long as it lasted, and try not to criticize or judge her when she left. As she was sure to do.

Chapter Six

The baby sat on a tattered square of blanket, his fingers busily shaking a wooden stick with beads attached. The cots had been made up and the little boy, Toby, sat cross-legged on the far one. As Adrian came back into the main room, he looked up and glared at her, his bottom lip jutting out in an exaggerated pout.

"Where's your father?"

The boy only poked his lip out farther and intensified his glare.

Adrian tried again. "Is your sister around?"

She couldn't believe Walker and his daughter had just gone off and left her alone with the two smallest children. She didn't know anything about children. She knew less about farming and running a farmhouse. Going to the front door, she scanned the yard for any sign of her deserters.

The back door opened and Mimi came in, a basket under her arm. Adrian felt a ridiculous wash of relief at the girl's appearance. At least she wasn't alone with the helpless baby and petulant boy.

"Oh, am I glad to see you," she gushed. She hurried over and helped the girl with the basket, which was full of eggs. Adrian eyed them warily.

"Oh, Mimi, I think something's wrong with these eggs."

"My name's Emily," the girl said briskly, her gaze darting to the basket. "And there ain't nothin' wrong with them eggs."

"But they're—that is, they're odd-looking."

A heated stare was the girl's only reply. She turned her back on Adrian and went out the door again.

"Emily, wait," Adrian called, following the girl onto the back porch.

"What?"

"Do your chickens always lay brown eggs?"

Rolling her eyes, Emily plopped her hands on her hips. "Course not," she said, her tone indicating what she thought of Adrian's question. "Sometimes they're green."

"Green?" Adrian gulped down her revulsion. What was wrong with plain old white ones? she wondered. "Wait," she called, when the girl started down the steps.

Again Emily turned back.

"I think something's wrong with your brother. He won't talk to me."

"That's 'cause he's mad at you." Her eyes narrowed and she perused Adrian for a long moment. "Don't fret, he'll get over it soon enough."

"Emily."

The little girl met her eyes, but stood silent on the porch steps.

"Are you mad at me, too?"

The tiny shoulders shrugged and she stared down at her bare feet. "Nope. I ain't mad."

Adrian suspected that wasn't the whole truth, but she thought better of challenging the girl. Instead, she approached from another angle. "Something's the matter. Do you want to tell me what it is?"

The girl huffed and rolled her eyes again and Adrian thought she could quickly get tired of the irascible little girl's expression.

"Why would I want to talk to you? I don't even know you. And you don't know us. You don't know anything about Daddy, or me, or Toby or Eli. But I'll tell you somethin'," she said. "We don't need your help. We don't need anyone's help. I can take care of Toby and Eli. And I can take care of Daddy, too."

Without another word she turned and hustled across the expanse of yard toward a short, squat building to the far right of the house. Adrian watched her open an undersized, thick door and crawl through the opening.

So that was the way it was. Adrian went back into the house and sat down at the long table. Rome Walker had gone, who knew where, without so much as a good morning. Emily resented Adrian's presence in the house; saw her as an unwelcome interloper. And Toby was mad at her for God only knew what transgression. Her eyes went to the baby and a small smile tipped her lips.

"Hey, little fellow," she cooed, rising and going to kneel beside the baby. She lifted him onto her lap and cuddled him beneath her chin. "Are you at least glad I'm here?" she said. "Because if you're not then I'm afraid it's unanimous. I don't want to be here, and they don't want me here. What do you say, Eli?"

The baby giggled, reared back in an arch, and wet the only clothes Adrian possessed in the whole world.

Rome came out of the barn, a pail of fresh milk in one hand. Once Miss Sheppard—Adrian—got settled maybe he'd be able to give up the milking. Lorraine had always done that job, and recently Emily had volunteered. But she was still so small he feared her getting too close to the cantankerous cow. So he'd taken on the milking, as well as most of the other chores, and he'd been doing them every day since Lorraine first got sick.

As it was, Mimi did far more than a girl her age normally would. She'd even offered to cook, though he wouldn't even consider such a thing. Of course, he thought, rubbing his flat stomach, she couldn't do any worse than he had. His belly sincerely hoped Miss Sheppard could cook. His cooking left a great deal to be desired. Most of what he prepared the hogs wouldn't eat. But he and the children ate it, out of necessity mostly.

As he entered the house he feared his first encounter with Adrian Sheppard this morning might be uncomfortable after the scene at the outhouse. But as he came into the room he saw Adrian struggling with a naked baby, a diaper waving like a flag of surrender from her hand and a large pin clasped between her lips.

"Ug, mm i gad oo ee oo."

Rome stood framed in the doorway, the pail forgotten as he watched her juggle the squiggling infant. The front of her denim trousers was soaked, her thin blouse plastered to her midriff. He could see her breasts pushing out against the fabric as she raised her arms in an effort to catch the baby, who was climbing her shoulder like a mountain goat. For a moment he studied the figure outlined by the wet clothes and a surge of desire shot through him.

Clearing his throat—and his mind—he quickly set aside the milk and went to her assistance. "What did you say?"

She removed the pin from her mouth and

took a deep breath as he cuddled the tiny naked body. Her eyes softened as she watched his gentle movements, and the look she gave him stirred him.

Eli immediately put his fingers over Walker's lips so his question was almost as garbled as her words had been.

"I said I'm glad to see you." Adrian watched the dimpled buttocks settle into one massive palm as Rome hiked the baby on his hip, and she blinked away the tender feelings she'd been experiencing and raised an eyebrow.

"I wouldn't do that if I were you. He's dangerous enough when he has a diaper on."

Did he imagine the huskiness of her voice? he wondered. "I know," he told her. Was his tone equally as rough?

He took the diaper from her, went to the cot, and laid Eli down. With a few deft movements, he had the baby properly diapered. After planting a kiss on the chubby cheek, he set him back down on the floor to play.

"I'm sorry, I'm afraid I didn't do much baby-sitting."

"It won't take you long to get the hang of it." He glanced down at her wet clothes. "Maybe you'd better go change."

"I don't have anything else to wear." Looking down at the spreading spot, Adrian knew the point was moot. She would have to get out of the jeans and shirt.

"Didn't any of Lorraine's things fit?"

"I didn't try anything on. I was afraid. . . . "

He turned to look at her and she saw again the pain and bitterness around his eyes. The harsh lines flanking his mouth deepened as his lips turned down in a frown.

"Well, I thought it might make the situation more strained if I showed up wearing her clothes."

"Why would it?"

She shrugged. "She was your wife, their mother. You must miss her very much." She couldn't help wondering at that moment if anyone were missing her. A wave of self-pity hit her—there was no one who would even notice her absence for some time. All she had was Alex, and he and his family didn't exactly keep in touch with her on a regular basis.

"Clothes are just clothes; take whatever you can use," he said, turning around. "What's wrong with Toby?"

The boy still sat on the bed, but his attitude continued to worry Adrian. He now held one corner of the blanket in his hand and he was sucking his thumb.

"I don't know. He won't talk to me. Emily said he was mad at me, but I don't know why."

Rome seemed to understand and he went to Toby. "Come on, son, I need your help with the chickens."

Immediately, the boy jumped from the cot

and followed his father out the back door. Adrian looked down at the baby who was now busily playing with his toes as he reclined on his back.

"Everyone has something to do except me," she muttered into the stillness of the room. Eli gurgled. With a sigh, Adrian went into the curtained-off room and sank to her knees in front of Lorraine's trunk. In truth, she hadn't opened the trunk because she was afraid what she'd find this time. She didn't think she could take another shock like the Bible. But she had to have something to wear, so she slowly raised the lid.

On top of the pile of belongings she found a white tablecloth, the edges reminding her of the Battenburg lace tablecloth in her apartment. Once the cabin was cleaned up she thought she might get this one out and use it. For now, she pushed it aside.

Several doilies were carefully folded beneath the tablecloth, and beautifully embroidered pillowcases beneath those.

Again Adrian thought how the pieces would liven up the drab cabin.

Finally she found what looked to be several skirts of gingham and chambray. One, a light blue, reminded her of a western skirt she'd worn briefly during her stint as a waitress in a country-and-western bar.

She drew it out and held it up to her. The

waist would be about right, but the hemline hung way past her knees. She dug deeper and pulled out a sleeveless top which laced up the front. Adrian recognized it as a corset cover from the old catalog. It probably wasn't considered proper outerwear, but it would have to do. The only other things she could find were bulky, long-sleeved, high-necked blouses of thick, scratchy fabric which would be too hot even for spring.

Emily gasped, her flushed face draining of color. Rome turned at the sound, the plates in his hand all but forgotten. His eyes swept over the woman standing before him and a hard knot of surprise wedged in his throat. If he'd thought she'd looked odd when she arrived, it was nothing compared to this new appearance.

"Miss Sheppard?"

Rome tried to avert his eyes from the woman, but found it was impossible. He'd never seen anyone dressed, if he could call it that, as she was.

She wore a corset cover with no blouse over it, a skirt he thought he recognized except it was tied in a knot at her knees, white socks cut off at the ankle, and the strange pair of flat white shoes she'd arrived in. They looked like the little boats he carved for Eli and Toby.

Adrian glanced at the startled faces around her. "I hope you're not angry about the clothes.

You said it would be all right."

"You ain't even wearing a blouse!" Emily cried, with the innocence of a child.

Rome clasped her shoulder and silenced her with a look.

"But, Daddy—"

"Hush, Mimi. Of course we're not angry," he assured Adrian. "I told you to take whatever you could use. But, um, weren't there any blouses in the trunk?"

"Yes, but they looked hot and terribly uncomfortable." Seeing their faces she added, "However, if you'd prefer . . ."

"No, that isn't necessary," Rome cut in, desperate to keep her appeased. "Whatever suits you."

"But, Daddy . . ." the little girl wheedled.

"Mimi, serve up breakfast."

Adrian snapped out of the freeze their startled glances had held her in. "Oh, let me do that. If I'm going to stay a month I need to do something."

"A month?" Mimi turned from the fireplace where she'd been spooning scrambled eggs. Her face reddened and her fingers tightened on the long wooden spoon.

Adrian looked from the girl's angry expression to Walker's embarrassed flush.

"I didn't tell the children you were only staying a month," he confessed. "They've been through a lot, and—well, I thought you might change your mind."

96

Emily's furious gasp was followed by the familiar eye rolling, and Adrian felt her own anger swell.

"You had no right to do that," she told Walker hotly. "I made it clear I couldn't stay. As soon as you're free to take me to town, I'm leaving. You shouldn't have made the children think otherwise."

Emily came to the table then, carrying the plate of eggs. Adrian moved to assist her and the girl snatched the plate away from her and slammed the delicate china down on the table.

"Emily!" her father snapped. "Apologize."

"I won't!" the little girl snapped. "We don't need her here. Why don't you just take her to town right now? She ain't gonna be no mother for us. She doesn't even want to be here."

"Oh, Emily . . ." Adrian stepped forward, only to be stopped in her tracks by the hate in the girl's eyes.

"Emily, you go outside until you can apologize to Miss Sheppard."

"But I'm hungry."

"I said go outside."

"Mr. Walker, it's all right. The child needs to eat."

"Miss Sheppard, I'll handle this. Please stay out of it. Emily, go on."

The girl's eyes filled with sudden tears and Adrian felt her heart lurch. She took another step forward and the girl turned and ran out the

97

back door and across the yard.

All Adrian's instincts told her to go after Emily, comfort her. She watched until the racing figure darted out of sight behind the barn. Then she turned on Walker, nearly shaking with rage.

"You don't want a mother for your children. You want a maid. Someone to cook and clean and baby-sit. That child needed some love and understanding. And even if I don't plan to take on the job forever, would it have hurt to let me try to be her friend?"

Walker dug his fingers through his blond hair and sighed deeply. He shook his head dejectedly. Adrian thought he must be carrying quite a load to weigh down such broad, massive shoulders.

"I don't want a maid, Miss Sheppard. I need a wife, and a mother for my children. But I don't want them hurt any more than they already are when you up and leave at the end of the month." He looked up at her and along with the constant pain and bitterness she usually read there, something else burned. Love. He loved his children. It didn't matter that they were more a burden now than a blessing. He loved them deeply and he was willing to do anything—anything—to see them happy.

Adrian felt ashamed. She hadn't considered the children when she'd decided to stay the month. She had never thought what it would do to them for her to leave after so short a time. Guilt smote her.

"I'm sorry. I have no right to tell you how to handle your children. You're right. I shouldn't stay here. That'll only make things worse."

Immediately he straightened, his hand darting out to clasp her arm. "No, wait."

Fiery heat shot up her arm. The warmth of his fingers seemed to seep through her whole body. A ripple of awareness spread out from her middle, making her legs tingle.

For the first time she looked up into Rome Walker's face, not as a prospective employee, or as a refugee in a foreign world, but as a woman. A woman looking at a man. She swallowed hard.

The lines on his face made him seem sad and vulnerable and she felt an unreasonable need to ease his burdens. His eyes, which held only desperation, would be truly beautiful if lit by amusement, or desire. The shaggy blond hair fell around his face, adding an incongruously youthful appearance to the hardened features.

"Please stay. We really do need you, even if it's only long enough for me to get the seed in the ground."

She tried to pull away, but his grasp tightened. "I can't—"

"Just for the month. Even a month will help more than you could know. And you're right. The children need a woman in their lives, even if you're only offering friendship. Especially Mimi."

She met his gaze and saw that a touch of his despair had been replaced with hope. Some of the tension seemed to have left his features. Had she brought about the subtle change? She knew she had, and the knowledge filled her with a sense of power, a sense of worth she hadn't felt in a long time, if ever.

She'd been looking for a better, more suitable job. A position where she could make a difference. Here, she'd been offered a golden opportunity. She could touch these people. She could try to make a difference in their lives. And it didn't mean she'd have to give up her hope of going home. It was, after all, only temporary.

Smiling up into Rome Walker's anxious face, she slowly nodded. "I'll stay the month."

The lightness spread over his face. Smiling, he released a heavy sigh. His hand loosened on her wrist, but he didn't let go. Their eyes met. A tingle ran along Adrian's nerves, sending gooseflesh to cover her arms and neck.

She watched him, wondering what was happening. Her gaze went to the pale skin of her wrist where his dark fingers rested.

Surely he'd let her go now. Instead his hands followed the angle of her arm up to her shoulder. His fingertips traced the gentle curve exposed by the corset cover. He circled her throat tenderly.

"Thank you," he whispered, leaning closer.

Adrian stiffened. Was he going to kiss her?

Did she want him to? It would be misleading. Cruel, even. She wasn't planning to stay. She would never agree to be his wife.

Still, she found herself leaning toward him.

At the last moment, his hand fell away and he took a step back. "I should go and talk to Emily," he said brusquely, sidestepping her and going quickly out the back door.

Chapter Seven

The "kitchen" was a small stone building constructed of blocks of slate gathered, Emily told her, from a nearby ravine. It had a fireplace, the "real" stove Walker had told her about when she first arrived, and a long wooden worktable.

The stove was a black monster Adrian had always heard referred to as pot-bellied. She'd seen them before, but usually only as decorative pieces in modern homes.

She couldn't believe anyone had ever actually cooked on one!

"It's pretty dirty, but everything will look better after a good cleaning."

She looked back over her shoulder after his remark and saw the doubt register on Rome Walker's face. The man was trying so hard, she couldn't help but reassure him. "I'm sure it'll be fine."

She saw the lines around his mouth ease slightly and wished she could feel as certain as she sounded. Cooking had never been a great love of hers. Oh, she could microwave and defrost with the best of them, but preparing everything from scratch, and on such antiquated equipment, sent a frisson of trepidation through her.

Emily came in carrying a bucket, a cake of soap, and several rags that looked as if they'd been torn from an old bedsheet.

Her perpetual pout in place, she scowled at Adrian and dropped the things on the stone floor with a deafening clatter.

"I'll fetch the water."

"No, Mimi," Walker said, stopping her at the door. "I'll get the water and the wood. You stay here with Miss Sheppard."

He glanced from Mimi's stubborn expression to Adrian's apprehensive one. He considered intervening on Adrian's behalf; she seemed so lost sometimes. He wondered if the desire he felt for her could be trusted after the lonely months he'd spent with no one for company but the children and an occasional visiting neighbor. Would his attraction be this strong under different circumstances? He couldn't be sure, but he had to admit it seemed unreasonably potent.

Had he burned for a woman this way before?

He couldn't remember ever feeling such heat, longing. Guilt grabbed him by the throat and he swallowed hard. He couldn't recall a time when he'd ached for Lorraine with this much intensity.

Adrian caught his gaze and he thought he saw some of what he was feeling mirrored in her eyes. Was it just loneliness? Or would he have felt this way about Adrian Sheppard no matter where and how they met?

And why was his daughter being so cool to Adrian? He would have thought Mimi would welcome the help, and having another woman around the house. Could that be the problem? After a year of mothering them, did she resent Adrian's presence? If so, she would probably become more irascible if he forced her to accept Adrian.

He decided it would be better to let the females work out their strife alone. He turned and left them.

Mimi did no more than cut a harsh glimpse at Adrian before going to the stove and opening the little side door. With a hand-held whisk broom she drew from her apron pocket, she began to sweep out the dust. Adrian watched her, as much to see how the task was accomplished as to gauge the little girl's mood.

Finally, she saw Emily had no intention of acknowledging her presence so she took the broom and began sweeping the dust and settled dirt from the walls and floor of the kitchen.

When Rome arrived with water, he was surprised to see both Adrian and Emily working side by side to clear the kitchen of a year's worth of neglect. Neither spoke, or otherwise acknowledged the other, but they functioned as a team. He set the buckets of water down on the floor and silently stepped back out of the room.

Adrian collected the cleaning rags and picked up the cake of soap. It looked odd, sort of grayish tan in color. She wished for soap flakes, or better yet some strong spray cleanser. Shrugging, she carried the supplies to the table and then lifted a bucket of water.

As she dumped the cake of soap into the bucket, her nose detected a foul smell. She set the soap and cloth aside and peered under and around the table. Dirt and dust covered every surface, but she saw nothing that would cause the repulsive smell.

Again she put the rag and soap into the water and again the odor filtered to her nose, stronger this time. She sniffed, leaning closer to the table.

"Whacha doin'?"

She jumped, whirling to face the girl. "Something smells bad."

Emily came to stand next to the table. She lifted her button nose into the air and sniffed. "I don't smell nothin'."

Adrian sniffed again, her face moving closer

to the table, toward the scent. "How can you not smell it? It's terrible. It smells like . . ." She thought for a moment and wrinkled her nose. "It smells like something spoiled."

A now-familiar sigh drew her gaze toward Emily in time to see the blue eyes roll back in disgust. The stubby fingers took the soap from Adrian's hand and held it under her nose.

"Ugh, what is that?" she gasped, pushing the cake away.

"It's just plain old lye soap. Ain't you ever seen any?"

"Good Lord, it stinks. Why does it smell like rancid grease?"

Again the eyes lazily circled in their sockets and Adrian felt a surge of irritation. She was beginning to dislike that habit of Emily Walker's.

"Maybe 'cause that's what it is," the girl said sarcastically. "Ashes and tallow."

"Tallow?"

"Fat."

Grimacing, Adrian set the soap and rag aside. She lifted her hand to her nose and fought the urge to gag. "You wash with fat?"

"Course we do. What did you have where you came from, fancy store-bought scented soap?"

Adrian started to tell her yes, that was exactly what she'd had. But she held her tongue. She suspected Emily would not like to hear the truth.

"Oh, give it to me," Emily snapped. "I ain't too good to put my hands on it."

"No," Adrian said quickly, clutching the smelly soap once more. "I'll do it." She eyed the cake with revulsion and finally turned to look at Emily's tightened features. "Just tell me," she said. "You don't bathe with this stuff, do you?"

A wicked gleam came into Emily's eyes and she grinned for the first time all morning. Adrian groaned.

She held the soapy rag as far away as she could and began to scrub the table's rough surface.

"Emily, if you show me how to work the stove, I'll heat some of this water," Adrian said, finally breaking the tense silence.

Emily turned to stare at Adrian, her pale blue eyes wide and her rosebud mouth now forming a little round O. "Work it?"

Adrian knew immediately she'd made another mistake, but didn't know how to bail herself out without making matters worse. A full minute passed as she struggled with indecision. Finally, in desperation, she decided to take a chance. She only hoped it wouldn't backfire on her.

"Emily, I have a confession to make. They don't have stoves like this where I come from. I've never used one before and I don't have a clue how they work. I know you don't like me, and you resent my being here, but the truth is, I need your help."

The cool eyes narrowed, continuing to watch Adrian closely. Doubt, distrust, indecision, all crossed Emily's young face. The child was not yet used to hiding her emotions, and Adrian could see when her suspicion gave way to curiosity.

"You ain't never lit a fire in a stove before?"

Adrian shook her head.

"Where you been all your life? Did you have servants or somethin'?"

"Not exactly. But I'm not used to cooking meals this way."

Emily's expression grew more perplexed. "Then why did you tell Daddy you'd stay?"

Adrian thought for a moment. Why had she agreed to stay, even for a month? She told herself it was because she couldn't get to town before dark, even if she started at daybreak. And Walker's warnings about panthers had not gone unheard. But that wasn't the real truth, and she knew it.

Still, she shrugged her shoulders, not wanting Emily to know what a coward she'd been.

"I'm not really sure. Your daddy needs help real bad. And I feel sorry for you and your brothers," she hedged.

Instantly she saw the girl's spine stiffen. She should have known Emily would take offense at that statement. She wouldn't welcome pity;

none of them would. Knowing they didn't want charity and probably wouldn't accept it, she decided to be at least partially honest.

"No, that's not true. That isn't the real reason I stayed," she finally confessed. "I did it because I don't have anywhere else to go. I'm stuck here for a while, Emily. Your w—Your area is unfamiliar to me and I was terrified to be alone here. I'm not ready to face the reality of this place on my own."

She hadn't meant to say so much and she clamped her mouth shut. But then she saw the compassion in Emily's eyes and she couldn't stop the flow of words. "I always thought of myself as brave and resilient. But Alex was right: when things get tough I run away. That's not bravery; it's cowardice."

Suddenly it occured to Adrian how craven she'd become. She was clinging to a family of strangers, for heaven's sake. How depressing. She'd thought Rome Walker's children were to be pitied, but the truth was she was more pathetic than they were.

Tears rushed to her eyes and she turned away before Emily could see them. She made her way to a chair in a far corner and slumped into the wicker seat, not even caring that a layer of dust rubbed off on her skirt. Dropping her forehead against her palms, she felt the fear creep in again, tormenting her with the truth of her impossible situation.

A small hand came out and touched her arm. Without a word, Adrian grasped the fingers and held them in hers with a desperation she hadn't known she'd been fighting off. She needed to feel a human touch, needed to assure herself she was still alive and in the company of people not so different from herself. As long as she was alive, there was hope. And as long as there was hope she'd someday return home, she couldn't give in to the terror that plagued her.

"You all right, Miss Sheppard?" the hesitant voice queried, a hint of fear clearly evident.

Adrian forced a dry laugh and raised her head. She hugged the little girl to her, smelling the clean scent of her hair and skin. She closed her eyes and let the feel of the little body warm her chilled flesh.

"I don't know, Emily. I just don't know."

The little hand went to her back and patted it comfortingly. Adrian smiled despite her own despair. She raised her head and looked at Emily. "I know you don't want me to be your mother, and I can't promise you I'll stay after the end of the month," she told the girl, refusing to give the child false hopes. "But I could use a friend right now, Emily."

The wide blue eyes filled with light and her mouth turned up in the first real smile Adrian had ever seen on Emily's face. She patted Adrian's hand in a gesture older than her years. "Me too," she said. "You can call me Mimi."

Adrian's smile widened and she hugged the girl again. When she released her, they shared a smile.

"We'd better get to work," Adrian said, pushing out of the chair. "I've got a feeling I have a lot to learn."

The kitchen didn't exactly sparkle, but Adrian was pleased with all they had accomplished when she and Emily finally finished the chore.

She thought they had achieved a monumental amount, until she stepped out into the bright light of day and saw what Rome had managed in their absence.

"My word," she breathed, coming to a halt so fast Mimi slammed into her back.

The girl peered around her and stepped to the side. Her face split in a wide grin.

Looking at the long, tall wall which seemed to have magically appeared alongside the small cabin, Adrian shook her head. "Does your father always work so fast?"

Mimi beamed with pride. "He must want you to stay real bad," she said, unaware of the dismay her words caused Adrian.

The two walked over to where Rome stood, a hammer in hand and a board held firmly in place. Long, square nails stuck out of his mouth like spikes, but she could see the expectant gleam in his eyes.

"You've been busy," she breathed, truly impressed by the amount he'd been able to accomplish. He might not consider himself the best cook or housekeeper, but he'd make a hell of a construction worker. And shirtless, with his muscles outlined against his sweat-damp flesh, he'd even make the guy in the softdrink commercial jealous.

He gave the positioned nail one final whack and let go of the board. Removing the nails from his lips, he dropped them in the pocket of his coveralls.

"I'd been meaning to do this for some time. Had the materials in the barn. But with so much else to do I never seemed to find the time for this," he explained.

The wall connected to the cabin at one corner. It was supported by hugh planks propped at a 90-degree angle so it wouldn't fall forward, but Adrian thought it looked sturdy enough to stand on its own. Rome had done a wonderful job in an amazingly short span of time.

"I thought you were looking after the boys," she said, shaking off her bemusement.

He nodded toward the side yard and Adrian felt another silly grin cross her face. Mimi was standing next to a small pen made of chicken wire, her hands reaching over the top. Inside, the boys played with small wooden toys and several metal pots and spoons.

"A playpen. How ingenious."

"I figured you'd need a little help reining them

in until you get used to things around here."

Another pang of guilt hit her. He was doing a lot to make her brief stay as smooth as possible. She wished there were some way she could help him on a permanent basis but knew it would be impossible. She didn't belong in this time, much less this place. Still, she could do whatever needed doing for the next month and at least ease the way for whoever he finally married.

As she turned to look back at him, she caught his gaze. While she'd been watching the children, he'd been watching her. The heat in the teal depths seared her flesh and she felt the warmth of awareness blanket her.

What was he thinking? What did he see? An inept woman trying to bumble her way through an unfamiliar situation? Somehow she didn't think so. The way he looked at her made her aware of her femininity in a way she hadn't been for a long time.

And as the moment dragged on, Adrian became more and more conscious of his maleness. He was tall, taller than he'd first seemed with the burden of hopelessness weighing him down. His form was lean, probably from stress and eating his own cooking for too long, but his arms and chest hadn't lost any of the muscle mass which made him seem strong and broad.

His blond hair, badly in need of a trim, added that touch of boyish charm that took the edge off his otherwise serious demeanor. And those eyes. A woman could lose herself in those eyes, forget her troubles. Maybe even for a time forget the world around her. Forget that she didn't belong, that a different world awaited her.

Adrian felt that way at that moment. She could almost see herself going into his arms, their eyes meeting, their lips seeking each other's.

The thought snapped her out of the daze she'd been in. She took a hurried step back. Was she crazy? Had she hit her head too hard? What was she thinking? She would never, could never, stay in this place. She longed to go home, the sooner the better. Even her fear couldn't combat the desire to return home for long.

Rome must have seen the distance she'd put between them reflected in her eyes. He turned away and gathered the tools he'd been working with.

"I've still got to work the fields today," he said, not meeting her gaze. He fiddled with the hammer he held. "I'll be making up for lost time so it'll be late."

Without another word he strode away toward the barn. Adrian watched him go, a twinge of something twisting her insides. Rome Walker would find a woman to marry. He was a good man. And when he found the woman who would stay and fill the void in his life, he'd forget Adrian and her strange appearance.

The twinge grew into a pang. Jealousy smote her. The lucky woman. If the circumstances had been different, if Rome were from her time, she knew she'd fight to hold on to a man like him.

Immediately Adrian brushed off her wayward thoughts. She really had lost her mind. She barely knew Rome Walker. So what if he was handsome and gentle and good? So what if he possessed the qualities she'd always wanted in a man but had never been able to find? He was 135 years old! Or would be when she returned to her own time.

Which was exactly what Adrian would do. Somehow she *would* return to the future.

Chapter Eight

Adrian managed to prepare a supper of fried ham and burned biscuits her first night as Rome's temporary employee. She was thankful Rome hadn't shown up to eat any of it.

Thankfully, Emily had given up her sullen attitude, preening when she realized Adrian hadn't exaggerated her need for help.

She fed the children, set up a zinc hip tub on the back porch, and bathed each child despite their protests that it was not Saturday night and therefore they were not expected to be clean.

She scrubbed them from head to toe and dressed them in the odd nightshirts Emily provided. Then, with an unexpectedly full heart, she tucked them into their cots. She even managed a story, which seemed to please them, and

117

tears came to her eyes as she listened to their prayers.

Her heartstrings tugged as they asked God to look after their mama, and to help their daddy, who worked too hard. Then they surprised her further by adding her name to their list of well-wishes.

Afterward, she sank onto the bench at the table and laid her head in her hands. She'd never been so exhausted. But strangely, she couldn't remember ever having felt so fulfilled at the end of a day.

As darkness settled over the room, she stood and lit one of the candles atop the fireplace. It sat in a holder of hammered tin, the broad back reflecting the flame and illuminating all but the far corners of the small room. She went to the window and peered out, wondering where Rome had disappeared to. She hadn't seen him since he'd gone to the fields earlier.

The moon was full, casting its light upon the yard. Could he still be plowing? He'd spent valuable time this morning getting the new room started. That had probably put him behind and he needed to work late to make up for it. If so, he would be tired and hungry when he came in. She decided to repay his efforts by making sure he had a decent meal and a hot bath when he did return.

She went out the back door to the kitchen and quickly made a fresh batch of biscuits. This time she watched them carefully so they wouldn't get too brown. She fried some ham slices and heated a can of beans she found in the pantry. Carrying it all into the house, she positioned it around the fireplace so it would stay warm.

Then she went onto the back porch once more and set up the zinc tub. It was a cumbersome contraption that hung on a huge nail from the wall of the house. It looked more like half of a 50-gallon barrel than any bathtub she'd ever seen, but she considered it nothing short of a luxury under the circumstances.

She heard the sound of grass rustling in the distance. Tensing, she tried to see across the yard.

Rome's warnings of panthers came swiftly to mind. Having never even handled a gun in her life, she now wished for the knowledge. A rifle hung over the fireplace and she decided then and there she would ask him to show her how to use it.

"Evenin'."

She breathed a huge sigh as Walker's tall form separated itself from the shadows.

"Evening," she answered, feeling a flush of embarrassment creep up her neck. She waved her hand toward the tub. "I thought you might like a bath before you have your supper."

His eyebrows rose sharply and her flush deepened to crimson. Had she acted presumptu-

119

ously? Would he get the wrong idea? If he did, what idea would he get? She couldn't begin to comprehend what went on in this man's mind.

"Thank you. That does sound good."

She breathed a relieved sigh and felt a smile tilt her lips. "Good. There's hot water on the stove. I kept your food warm by the fireplace. I'll just go and check on it while you, um . . ."

She stepped back, reaching behind her to open the door. Twisting the knob, she nodded sharply. "I'll just go inside," she stammered nervously. "And check the food, across the room, at the fireplace."

After the incident with the outhouse, she didn't want any more uncomfortable situations between them. She thought she saw his mouth twitch as he fought amusement, but he only nodded in return.

Ducking into the house, she closed the door behind her and leaned against it. What would he think of her actions? Did she seem forward? Of course she must.

But she couldn't help it. She was a twentieth-century woman, for goodness sake. She couldn't expect to adjust to hundred-year-old codes of morality and behavior in so short a time. Although, she thought with a measure of pride, she hadn't done too badly.

"Even if I do say so myself," she whispered, going to the fireplace to dish up Rome's meal.

In fact, for a woman who'd never seriously

attempted domesticity she had to congratulate herself on having accomplished so much in one day.

It occurred to Adrian then that she had never thought of being a wife and mother as a real job. She thought of her failed marriage, and the reason for it, and regrets assailed her. She'd been so wrong, and Tate had suffered because of it. She'd wanted freedom, no restrictions. Always thinking a career would fulfill her more than a child would.

But after only 24 hours, she was having a change of heart. This had to be the most challenging job in the world. Any world, she added. She had the well-being of three children in her unskilled, and perhaps incapable, hands. Failure this time could be tragic. Even deadly. Sudden terror seized her.

The plate she held clattered to the tabletop and she quickly shot a nervous glance at the sleeping children. Their faces looked so angelic in repose. She felt again the tiny baby fingers Eli had placed over her lips when she'd told the bedtime story. She could smell the scent of his clean, baby skin.

Her success, for the first time, was imperative. Always before, she knew if a job didn't work out she could simply move on. No one had ever depended on her the way Rome and his children were beginning to. Filled with apprehension, she tried to push the troubling thoughts aside. She couldn't stay here. Eventually she had to face the rest of this world. And she had to find a way home.

"Adrian?"

She jumped, her gaze darting nervously to the back door. Rome stood there, his hair wet and slicked back from his forehead, his coveralls replaced with a rumpled pair of trousers and a much-mended flannel shirt. His feet were bare and she studied the long, narrow toes.

"Are you all right?"

She realized he'd caught her staring at his feet and she cleared her throat. "I'm fine. But you must be exhausted. Sit down and I'll get your supper."

She hurried over to the fireplace and dished up a plate of food. Carrying the whole tin of biscuits to the table, she set it all before him.

It felt oddly intimate to serve this man as though they were man and wife. Odder still to wait on a man at all. Being from the liberated generation, she would have thought the antiquated roles of male and female would go against her grain. Instead, she thought only of how hard he'd worked and how tired he must be after the work he'd done.

She even found herself pouring his milk and offering to get him some butter for his biscuits.

"That's all right," he said, stilling her jittery movements with a raised palm. "I don't expect you to wait on me, Miss Sheppard. It's enough that you're looking out for the children. For the first time since—well, since their mother passed on, I don't feel like I'm carrying the weight of the world on my back all alone."

She looked into the warm eyes, the color of the gulf on a clear day, and noticed a change in Rome Walker. Some of the tension, the strain, had gone from his features. Although the deep lines and grooves were clearly apparent, he did indeed look more relaxed.

A strange flutter started in her breast. Her heart beat like a Ping-Pong ball being volleyed back and forth. Pride blossomed inside her until she felt it flowering out to the far reaches of her extremities. Never had she felt such satisfaction in her accomplishments before.

She also noticed, with a surge of self-congratulation, that Rome had eaten every biscuit in the pan. He washed down the last of his meal with a final swallow of milk.

She could see the weariness of the day spreading over his face. A disturbing thought occurred to her then and she sat up straight.

"Mr. Walker, where did you sleep last night?"

His head came up sharply and his gaze locked with hers. She flushed again, reminding herself to temper her impulsive comments in the future. Undoubtedly it was not acceptable for a lady to question a man on his sleeping arrangements.

But Rome quickly recovered and pretended

there was nothing unusual in her words.

"In the barn," he said.

Adrian gasped. "The barn? Oh, that's terrible. You gave up your room and it never occurred to me you wouldn't have a place to sleep."

"It won't be for long. The new room should be ready soon enough. We can move you into it, and I'll put the children in there," he said, motioning to the room she now occupied. "I can sleep on one of the cots in here."

She eyed the short, narrow cots and a frown furrowed her brow. The sleeping arrangements would not be very comfortable for him. That thought reminded her of his first offer. He'd assumed the woman who answered his ad would agree to marry him. If that had been the case, he'd be sleeping in his own bed while he prepared the other room. Instead he was relegated to the barn.

It didn't seem fair, but Adrian decided there was nothing she could do about it. She knew she'd never get a minute's sleep if she had to stay in the barn. And she certainly had no intention of offering to share the bed she now slept in with him.

Just the thought sent heat rushing through her veins. Her skin felt hot, her breathing labored. She pushed away from the table and gathered the empty dishes.

"Can I get you anything else?" she asked.

He eyed her hasty departure with a raised

eyebrow, but only shook his head. "No, but that was good. Thanks."

"Well, I think I'll just put these in the dry sink until morning. I'm bushed."

She turned and hurried out the back door, the dishes clattering in her trembling hands. She dumped them into the sink and rested her fingers on the rim, trying to control her quaking. She had to get a grip. She'd been through a terrific shock, she reminded herself. It was only natural her senses would be alert and her nerves raw. And if she felt attracted to Rome Walker, that was equally understandable.

He was her shelter in a raging storm of emotions. A protector of sorts. It was perfectly natural she'd harbor romantic notions about him.

The rational thoughts settled her and she forced a shaky laugh. Of course, that was all it was. The way kidnap victims are drawn to their captors. The way people in life-and-death situations gravitate toward each other. Perfectly natural, she assured herself, placing a steady hand against her heart.

Relieved, she opened the door and entered the house once more. He looked up, hesitancy in his eyes. She forced a slight smile and saw him relax because of it. That realization offered her a feeling of confidence she couldn't remember ever having felt before. Quickly she brushed off the reaction as being a side effect of her trauma and fatigue.

"I think I'll turn in now," she said, escaping to the privacy of the curtained-off bedroom.

Once inside, she stripped out of the skirt and camisole and drew on a nightgown she'd found in Lorraine's trunk. It was a plain white cotton garment, similar to the gowns popular in her time. Except this one buttoned all the way to the throat and fell to her ankles. She refused to fasten the gown past her breastbone, preferring to leave the top three buttons undone.

She drew the covers back and climbed into the narrow bed. Turning her back to the other room, she tried to put thoughts of Rome Walker out of her mind. Instead she focused on her plans for the future.

A month wasn't such a long time, she told herself. It would give her a chance to get used to what had happened to her. She could plot her course so she wouldn't leave with any half-baked notions. Her impulsiveness had gotten her into trouble in the past. This time there was no room for error.

She had to find a way home, a way back to 1995. Someone, somewhere, must know a way to help her. She'd find them, no matter how long or how hard she had to search. But first she needed time. Time to collect her reeling emotions. Time to adjust to her new surroundings. All in all, Rome Walker's hardship was her good fortune. She could hide out with this family until she felt better able to confront this strange, bygone world.

*   *   *

Adrian planned to surprise Rome when he returned from the fields tonight. She looked down from the roof of the new room, the queasiness she'd felt when she first climbed up abating somewhat.

"You okay up there?" Mimi shouted.

Adrian waved the wooden hammer in response. She took one last look at the children on the ground. Eli played contentedly with a hand-sewn muslin puppy dog in the small pen. Mimi and Toby were busy pulling weeds from the garden behind the house.

She carefully positioned one of the wooden shingles and, removing a nail from between her lips, drove it into place. After working steadily for an hour, she was happy to see about three yards of the roof in place.

After two weeks of watching Rome work on the new room every morning, and then disappear into the fields until late at night, she'd decided he needed help. And nailing the small squares of wood in place seemed easy enough.

If she could finish the roof today, the room would be complete and he could slow down a bit.

She refused to analyze her disproportionate concern. Rome Walker was a man in need of help. She'd accepted his hospitality in order to bolster her courage before facing an unfamiliar world. The least she could do would be to ease his burden as much as possible. Besides, she told herself, adding another shingle to the growing number in place, staying busy kept her from dwelling on her bizarre and frightening situation.

Occasionally glancing over the side of the roof, she kept an eye on the children. After weeding the herb garden, Mimi took Toby by the hand and they went to the front yard. She could see the little girl instructing her brother where to sit. Then, as was her habit every day, she took up the broom and began to sweep the dirt into intricate designs.

Adrian still hadn't gotten used to seeing Mimi sweep the yard, but apparently Lorraine had convinced her daughter that a well-kept yard was a sign of good breeding and she'd turned the chore over to the girl before her death. Mimi took the job very seriously and each day she would whisk the yard into a pleasing configuration of circles and swirls. Despite the fact they had never once had a visitor that Adrian knew about.

From her position on the roof, she could see across the expanse of the Walker property. In the distance, almost beyond her range of vision, Rome continued his plowing. The 60-odd acres he planned to plant would be ready tomorrow if he didn't have to work on the new room.

Adrian forced her gaze away from the distant figure and returned to the task at hand.

She was just about to drive a nail into the last shingle when she heard Mimi scream. The strangled sound took her so much by surprise that she lost her grip on the roof and slid downward. Her hands grasped for a hold, her feet scraping the newly positioned shingles in an effort to stop her deadly descent.

The hammer, released from her grip in the first moment of her panic, slid past her, disappearing over the edge of the roof.

Adrian felt her feet slip over the last shingles. Her skirt had been pushed to her waist, her palms scraped raw. As she squeezed her eyes shut in preparation for the inevitable fall, she heard a rending of fabric. Suddenly she was jerked to a halt, her legs dangling in thin air. She quickly gained a foothold and looked down. The hem of her skirt had caught on a nail which partially rose above the shingle and stopped her from falling.

With her heart in her throat, and Mimi's screams still ringing in her ears, she scrambled up the incline, carefully grasping the edges of the shingles as she went. On the other side, she clambered to the ladder and climbed down.

Rushing around to the front of the house, she scanned the yard for Mimi. Seeing the girl next to the playpen, she rushed forward.

"Oh, Adrian," Mimi cried, tears flowing down her cheeks. "Do something; he's choking."

Adrian whirled toward the baby, lying flat on

129

his back, his face blue and his eyes wide but blank. She ripped the wire from the ground and shoved it out of the way so she could kneel beside Eli.

"Eli!" She jerked the baby up in her arms. "Eli, come on, darling!" She positioned him carefully and placed her hands on his abdomen. With several quick, upward thrusts, she tried to dislodge the object.

Mimi cried out and tried to pull Adrian away from the baby. Toby stood off to the side, tears streaming down his face. As Mimi struggled to remove Eli from Adrian's hold, Toby began to cry in earnest.

Adrian shrugged the girl away and repeated the maneuver. Again Mimi cried out.

"I'm not hurting him!" Adrian shouted, jolting the baby once more with her clasped fists. "Mimi, trust me."

The blue eyes looked up into hers and for a moment they cleared.

Eli still had not taken a breath, and whatever was lodged in his throat had not come up. Desperate, Adrian opened his jaws and pushed her finger between the tiny blue lips. She felt around in his airway until she located the obstruction. But she couldn't get hold of it. And she didn't dare force her fingers down his small throat any farther.

"Come on, darling," she cried, turning him upside down and applying three short, sharp thrusts between his shoulder blades. She laid him down once more and again tried to dislodge the object choking him.

This time she felt a whoosh of air follow her upward thrust. She turned the baby around and fished in his mouth with her finger.

"I've got it!" she shouted, drawing a black button from his mouth. She looked down, and her heart slammed against her chest. He still wasn't breathing!

She laid him on the ground and compressed his chest three times, then covered his nose and mouth with her lips and tried to blow life into the still little body.

Again and again she performed the procedure, deaf to Mimi's shouts of dismay and Toby's constant sobs.

Finally Eli gasped sharply and coughed. She lifted him in her arms and rubbed his back to encourage him to breathe on his own.

Tears of relief flowed down her own cheeks as she heard him begin to cry. As his pitiful weeping quickly rose to high-pitched wails of displeasure, Mimi and Toby rushed toward them.

"He's all right now," she said, laughing at his howls of anger. "He's going to be just fine."

She cradled him in her arms, unaware she was crying harder now. Relief crippled her and she knew she couldn't stand on her own at that moment. Never had she been so grateful for her

131

training as a nurse. She might have collapsed at her first emergency in the hospital, but she hadn't stopped to think for a moment when she'd seen Eli in trouble.

She'd done what needed doing, and he was alive. Alive and kicking, she thought, laughing through her tears. Mimi and Toby gathered close and she held her arm out to them. They rushed into her embrace and she held all three children as their tears stopped and they quieted down. She rocked gently, offering comfort to ease them through the traumatic moment.

Adrian realized something in that instant, and she felt the knot of fear return to her throat. She choked down the panic that accompanied her realization and tried not to let the children feel her trembling.

They wouldn't understand, and she couldn't explain to them. How could she, when she didn't understand herself? All she knew was that these children had come to mean more to her in the past two weeks than she had dreamed possible. Holding them, feeling their trust and gratitude, filled her heart to overflowing.

God, she loved them. It had only been two weeks. Fourteen short days. And already she wondered how she'd ever be able to leave them when the time came for her to go.

Chapter Nine

When she felt her legs would support her once more, Adrian gathered the children up and went into the house. As she opened the front door, she took a moment to eye the little cabin. It was cleaner than when she'd arrived, but otherwise hadn't changed. Adrian realized the change was in her.

Somehow the place had grown on her. The cozy welcome of its fireplace, the rugged table hand-made with loving care. Even the quilt hanging over her door, a symbol of Rome's attempt at her comfort.

She felt the peace of the place settle over her as she crossed to the cots.

Mimi and Toby followed close on her heels. They wouldn't let go of her skirt hem. She couldn't blame them. She wished there were someone at hand she could cling to. She hugged Eli closer. Together they all sank down on the nearest cot. She pushed into the corner, making room for Mimi and Toby. Rocking the baby, she felt another wave of terror close over her and she had to assure herself Eli was all right.

Positioned with her back to the wall, she laid the baby on her chest and gently soothed him to sleep. Mimi curled next to her thigh and Toby draped himself over her feet. Within minutes the children were all sleeping off their close encounter with disaster.

Adrian let her hands continue to roam the baby's soft skin. Her fingers played over his back, gently moving up and down, to his dirty little toes and chubby thighs. A wealth of affection and unexpected contentment swelled in her breast. She leaned her head back and savored the feel of the children all around her.

For the first time in her life Adrian knew how it felt to be a mother. Funny, she'd never longed for a home of her own. And children? God, what an irony that she only discovered all this now.

She'd been happy in her small apartment with its carefully decorated interior and assortment of inexpensive knickknacks. Odd, but she could barely remember why the place had meant so much to her. None of it could compare to the rush of joy she felt seeing Eli's toys scattered over the wood floor, waiting for his return. Smiling, she let her eyes drift shut.

*   *   *

Rome pushed open the door and stopped to stare. Gathered on the cot like a duck with her ducklings, Adrian and the babies slept. Arms and legs sprawled in every direction so he couldn't tell where one body left off and another began.

He'd never known Adrian to nap during the day, and for a moment he felt a trickle of fear creep up his spine.

Then, her eyes opened and she offered him a warm, sleepy smile. Her full, pink lips formed his name on a sigh and he felt a jolt rock his world. God, she was beautiful. He'd become accustomed to her wearing the corset cover without a blouse and the shortened skirt. Even the odd-looking shoes didn't register as curious any longer.

They were all a part of this fascinating and remarkable woman. And he realized with a start he liked every quirky facet of her. Adrian Sheppard had penetrated the hardened shell of despair he'd carried around for so long. As he watched her with his children it was like the bright morning sun coming up to chase night's darkness away. He suspected she could rid his life of the final shadows of grief and despondency.

In a short span of time, he'd gotten used to having Adrian Sheppard in his home. Her enthusiasm and vivacity drew him like livestock to the watering hole. Finding it more and more difficult to stay away from her, he couldn't stop the feelings of warmth and desire she evoked. Seeing her this way only further stirred his passions.

She held her finger to her lips and gently tried to extricate herself from the pile without waking anyone. Tenderly she laid the baby on the pillow and rubbed his back a few times.

"Daddy," Mimi said, looking up drowsily. "Oh, Daddy, Adrian saved Eli's life. She was wonderful," the girl whispered before closing her eyes and going back to sleep.

Rome felt the room shift as Adrian came toward him. He could see the lines of tension and fear still evident on her lovely face. His heart slammed against his ribs as he saw tears come to her eyes.

"Adrian?"

Without a word, she stepped up to him, and his arms automatically reached out for her.

"The baby choked on a button, Rome," she whispered against his chest, not even aware she'd used his name. His hold tightened.

Rome stiffened. He shot a hasty look at his youngest son and saw the little chest rising and falling steadily. The baby didn't seem affected by his close brush with death. Breathing a ragged sigh, Rome pulled Adrian closer to him. "I thought he was going to die. I've never been so frightened in my life. I'm sorry, but I just need you to hold me for a minute."

"Thank God you were here," he whispered against the flaming red hair he'd ached to touch. Letting himself go, he furrowed his hands into the tresses and drew them up to his nose, inhaling the sweet scent of woman.

Her arms went around his waist and he tipped her head back, letting his mouth close over hers. They kissed desperately, with the ferocity of two people trying to affirm life.

When they finally drew apart, they were both breathing hard. Rome longed to lift her in his arms and carry her to the bedroom, but she carefully collected herself and stepped back out of his embrace.

"I'm sorry," she breathed, wiping at the tears on her cheeks.

He crossed his arms over his chest, trying to erase the emptiness he now felt. "I'm not," he confessed, holding her gaze and gauging her reaction.

The bright brown eyes widened with surprise and, he thought, a hint of pleasure. Then she took another step back.

"No, we can't do this," she said. "I can't be what you need. A month, that's all I can stay."

He felt the heaviness settle on his shoulders once more. Didn't she feel what he was feeling? Couldn't she see how right it all seemed? He longed to shake her, kiss her, make love to her, until she vowed to stay with them. But he felt sure that would only frighten her off.

"All right," he said, his lips pressed tight. "I won't push you. Thank you for what you did for Eli, though. I'll never forget it."

Adrian stared at the man before her and felt a longing she'd never known. More than anything, she wanted to go back into his arms. His embrace had felt so wonderful, so right. And it had quickly gone from a need for comfort to pure, raw need. Never had a man moved her as much with a mere kiss. Even now she could feel the heat of his mouth on her lips. She wanted more. She needed to explore the emotions he brought out in her.

But she didn't dare. She would leave in two weeks, hopefully to return to her own time. Complications like the feelings Rome Walker aroused in her had no place in her already complex situation.

"You haven't told me what you're doing home in the middle of the day," she said shakily, trying to change the subject.

Still a bit peeved, he couldn't help teasing her. He grinned. "I decided I was tired of sleeping in the barn."

Purposely he let his words take root for a brief moment. He saw her eyes widen, her mouth open slightly in shock. "I came back to finish the bedroom," he added.

A wave of relief swept Adrian and she felt an answering smile tip her lips. So he thought he could bait her. Well, she'd just have to remember to repay him for that bit of mischief.

"Well, you've wasted your time, Mr. Walker," she told him haughtily. Motioning to the front door, she quietly went out. Rome followed.

"The roof is already finished," she announced, waving her arm elaborately.

He climbed the first few rungs of the ladder and surveyed her handiwork. With a gleam in his eye he gazed down at her. "So you were tired of me sleeping in the barn, too, huh?"

A flush covered her cheeks and she bent to retrieve the hammer she'd forgotten in all the earlier excitement. Pretending great interest in the tool, she averted her eyes. "Don't flatter yourself, Mr. Walker. I was just passing the time."

He threw back his head and laughed. Then he descended the ladder and reached for the hammer she continued to rub between her fingers.

"Um, I've never wished I was a hammer before, but right now . . ."

She looked down to see her long, slim hands gently caressing the smooth wood. With an embarrassed huff, she thrust it toward him, catching him in his stomach.

He clutched the hammer—and his middle—and laughed again. But this time he had to force the amusement. There was nothing amusing about the feelings her action had caused in him. His loins were tight, his heart pounding. He did long to feel her fingers moving over his body the way they had the wood of the hammer.

"All you have to do now is knock a hole in the main wall of the cabin for a doorway, and we'll be all set."

"We'll do it as soon as the children wake up. Sort of like a celebration," he said.

Adrian smiled at him and quickly turned and walked back into the cabin.

Rome reached up and touched his mouth, surprised to find himself smiling broadly. How long had it been since he'd felt so good? When had he last laughed that way? He couldn't remember. Somehow it didn't matter. Adrian Sheppard brought out feelings in him he'd never felt before, not even with Lorraine. He waited for the guilt to hit him again, but all he felt was a deep satisfaction.

And in that moment he knew he didn't want her to go, ever. Running his hands over the still-warm wood of the hammer, he felt his passion stir.

So what if she wasn't the best cook in the world? Neither was he. Besides, she'd more than proven herself capable with Eli today. If she seemed a little awkward with the children, that was only natural. The tension would pass as they grew used to one another.

Again he wondered where such a remarkable woman had come from. Immediately he dismissed the thought. What did it matter now?

Already the house looked better, he had to admit. The children smiled more, except when she insisted on bathing them each night. He left each morning with the comfort of knowing his children were in good hands, and looked forward to coming home in the evenings. Beauty, compassion, inner fire. What more could any man ask for?

Adrian Sheppard possessed all the characteristics of a fine wife and mother, even if they hadn't been the qualifications he'd thought he wanted.

"Somehow," he vowed, "I've got to make her stay."

Each child was allowed to wield the small hatchet once, making a cut in the rough planks of the wall. Then Rome carefully widened the opening until it was big enough for a doorway.

Adrian and Mimi prepared supper while he completed the task, and after they ate Adrian readied the children for bed while Rome moved the furniture into place.

The children were so excited at the prospect of sleeping in a real bedroom, they could barely fall asleep. Adrian couldn't blame them. She kept going into her new room, smelling the scent of new wood and marveling at Rome's careful workmanship.

"It's not much, but I'm glad you like it," he said, coming up behind her.

141

Adrian jumped and turned to meet his gaze. "It's lovely. Really. I've never seen anything so fine."

Of course that wasn't the whole truth, she had to admit. She'd seen elegant skyscrapers and elaborate architectural displays. But the truth was, they couldn't compare to the rough-hewn, wooden bedroom she stood in.

They held neither the love nor the care Rome had put in this one. They seemed cold beside the warmth of knowing he'd driven every nail, split every board by hand. Never one to pay much attention to the construction industry as a whole, she felt a new respect for the men and women who put homes together with their hands.

What a feeling of accomplishment it must bring to know you were able to live in something you built yourself. Just knowing she'd participated, in a small way, in the birth of this room suffused her with pride.

She grinned and held out her hand. Rome took it in his and drew her to stand beside him.

"You done good, Mr. Walker," she joked, nodding her head firmly.

"So did you, Miss Sheppard." He tugged her closer and placed a kiss on her temple. Adrian felt the rush of awareness race through her like a brush fire. She stiffened, but didn't try to draw away.

"So did you," he repeated, his words a sigh against her hair.

Adrian slept in her new room that night, when she finally managed to sleep. The sound of Rome's steady breathing, the shifting of the children in the next room, filled her heart with emotions she couldn't name.

What had she been missing? How could she not have known how rewarding it could be just to be a wife and mother? She'd always considered that occupation as somehow old-fashioned. Certainly not the thing for a modern woman of the 90s. Well, the 1990s, anyway.

Now she had to readjust her misconceptions. She enjoyed being a mother to Mimi, Toby, and Eli. At the end of every day she felt a pride in her accomplishments that she'd never felt with any of her other jobs.

Could it be she'd been a closet sexist all this time, never giving credit to the women who stayed at home and cared for families with the same passion and zeal she'd put into each of her occupations?

This job was tough, tougher even than the month she'd spent training as a lineman for the electric company. The stakes were high, the chance of defeat good.

But she thought of Eli's happy laughter as he played with his food at the dinner table. She remembered Mimi's shy good-night kiss and Toby's blanket trailing as he went off to bed. As she sat on her moss-stuffed mattress in the new

143

wooden room, she couldn't help smiling through a sheen of tears.

Damned if the perks weren't the best she'd ever enjoyed.

Chapter Ten

The smell of bacon and coffee woke Adrian the next morning. She couldn't get used to waking without the aid of an alarm clock, and this wasn't the first time she'd overslept.

Rolling out of bed, she donned a lacy robe that matched the gown of Lorraine's she'd borrowed. Barefoot, she padded into the main room of the cabin.

Rome already had the children dressed and sitting at the table. He served them eggs and bacon, biscuits, and milk.

"You cooked breakfast?" she said, brushing the tangles of hair from her face. He looked back over his shoulder and grinned.

"Sure. Who do you think did all the cooking before you came along?"

Adrian didn't tell him she hadn't thought that much about it until now. She remembered Mimi saying that first day that she served up all the meals. Her only thought had been to relieve the little girl of the heaviest chores as soon as she could.

But she'd soon discovered Mimi was not like children of the twentieth century. She was more mature, capable. The two older children had regular chores they did each day, and even Eli toddled along, scattering chicken feed or ferreting out hidden eggs in the henhouse.

Everyone on the farm had a job to do, and they all did it without complaint. Adrian thought of Alex's children and shook her head. They wouldn't know how to clean their own rooms, much less sweep the yard or gather herbs from the garden.

"It smells good," she said, pouring herself a cup of coffee.

Breathing in the aromatic steam, she frowned. In fact, it smelled much better than the brew she'd been serving. The eggs looked better, too. Hers either came out runny and undercooked or rubbery and too done. And the bacon was fried to crisp perfection.

It bothered Adrian that Rome Walker had been able to prepare such a delicious meal when she struggled to make her offerings barely passable. Of course, she wasn't used to the heavy iron pots and pans or the unpredictable wood-burning stove. She told herself she'd get the hang of it soon.

The cup stopped halfway to her lips and she glanced around the table at Rome and his children. The truth hit her then, and she sucked in a sharp breath of pain. She wouldn't be with them long enough to get used to anything. In less than two weeks, she'd be gone. They would be on their own once more, and she would be adrift in an unfamiliar and antiquated world.

After taking a calming sip of Rome's delicious coffee, she sat down at the table. Maybe she shouldn't leave. At least not for a while, she hurried to add. She could stay on, give Rome time to find proper help. And, she had to admit, give herself enough time to adjust to what had happened to her and what she would be facing when she left the farm.

Then she thought of her realization the day before. She was already half in love with the children. Glancing up, she met the teal gaze Rome directed her way. More than half in love with them, and their father, she had to admit.

She couldn't deny it any longer. She was falling in love with Rome Walker. His tenderness and concern for his children, his strength to have withstood the last months of work and worry without becoming hardened or resentful, his warm touch and soft stare all tugged at her heart in a way nothing else ever had.

And the children. She scanned the three little

faces and felt another, stronger pluck at her heartstrings. In two short weeks she'd come to love them. Their welfare and happiness meant more to her than her own.

Acknowledging that, how could she leave them to fend for themselves again? How could she just turn her back and walk away?

Though they were not hers in blood, she felt for them all the responsibility and devotion she thought a real mother must feel. And not having ever felt anything so strong in her life before, she didn't know how she could deny the feelings now.

Her eyes went to Rome once more. He sat next to the baby, dishing tiny bites of egg and crumbled biscuits between the full, pink lips. The muscles of his upper arm flexed each time he raised his hand to Eli's mouth. The sleeves of his worn long johns stretched tight.

He hadn't yet shaved and a rough stubble, darker than his hair, covered his strong jaw, giving him a rugged, unkempt look. Adrian's stomach contracted and her thighs tingled with arousal. He looked, in fact, like a man just risen from a night's pleasure in bed.

His expression held sleepy contentment and more peace than she'd ever observed on his face before. Was she the reason for the lightness in his eyes? The missing lines of tension and despair?

The thought was intoxicating. Her blood

raced as though she'd downed a glass of hard liquor in a single swallow. She could feel the beat of her heart against her ribs as it raced out of control.

Suddenly she realized the noise she was hearing wasn't coming from her erratic pulse. It was coming from outside. The children looked up, excitement in their eyes.

"The rolling store," Mimi called, jumping to her feet and racing for the door.

She rushed outside, little Toby close on her heels.

"The rolling store?" Adrian asked.

Rome smiled and lifted the baby from his chair. "Get dressed, Adrian," he told her. "We've got some shopping to do."

Adrian didn't waste any time stripping out of the nightclothes and donning her favorite light blue skirt and white lace camisole. She thrust her feet into her sneakers, ran a brush quickly through her hair, and tied it back with a ribbon.

She hurried onto the porch, gasped, and stopped at the edge of the steps.

"My word," she breathed.

A wagon sat outside the yard on the trail of red dirt leading to the house. It was as old-fashioned a rig as she'd ever seen, with a real canvas cover and wooden, spoked wheels. Two horses stepped lively as the man at the front directed them to a stop.

He pulled back on a lever beside his planked

seat, and jumped down.

"Howdy, Walkers," he called, shaking Rome's hand and tousling Mimi's hair. The little girl beamed up in adoration.

"You folks are looking mighty fine, I see," he added, taking the baby from Rome's hands and tossing him into the air with rough but steady hands.

Adrian cried out, but Eli only laughed out loud. Her exclamation brought the peddler's attention to her and she saw his eyes go wide beneath bushy black brows.

"Well, now, who do we have here?" he asked, passing the baby to Mimi. He took a step toward the porch, and Adrian found herself looking to Rome for assistance.

"Rome, you sly dog. Someone answered that advertisement you put out. And what a beauty she is, too, you lucky old cracker."

"Miss Sheppard isn't here in answer to my ad, Harp," Rome clarified. "She lost her way and ended up at my place by mistake. But she's agreed to stay until month's end and we're sure glad to have her."

Always the salesman, the peddler turned back to his wagon. "And I've got just the thing to make her stay more comfortable," he said, nodding to Adrian.

Rome laughed and stepped to the porch to lead Adrian toward the odd store. "I thought you might," he said, winking at her.

Adrian walked to the wagon, her mouth agape at the assortment of wares hanging from every surface of the canvas and wood.

Harp lifted the flap covering the back of the wagon and waved Adrian forward. She took a hesitant step, glancing back at Rome. With a nod, he coaxed her to look inside.

What she saw took her breath away. Furniture, clothing, tools, and implements of every shape and description were stuffed into the wagon. A rocking chair with a petit-point cushion, a bolt of lacy fabric, and what looked like a huge triangle of rusted metal caught her eye.

"It really is a store," she said, awed.

The men laughed, and Rome stepped up behind her to peer over her shoulder. "What do you think, Adrian? See anything you'd like?"

"Me?" she gasped. "Oh, no. I couldn't."

"It's all right," he whispered, his words for her ears alone. "I told you I wasn't rich, but I do have some money put aside. And now, with you helping out, I'll be able to get this season's crops in on time, so we're actually doing fine."

"Can I have something, Daddy?" Mimi asked.

Rome glanced down at the three exultant faces watching him hopefully. "Sure, Mimi. Y'all pick yourselves something."

The children apparently knew just where to go. They scrambled into the wagon and went for a row of barrels lining one side of the interior. Rome laughed.

Chubby hands disappeared into the first barrel and came up with long, hard sticks of peppermint. The next barrel had nuts and the next fruit. Harp picked up a piece of stiff paper and rolled it into a cone, folding the bottom so it wouldn't unroll. It formed a container and he handed each child one. Mimi, Toby, and even Eli began to fill their cones.

"Come on, Adrian, you must want something. The house is practically bare. And now, with the extra room, we need some more pieces."

"You want me to pick out furniture?"

"Furniture, fabric for curtains, whatever you like. How about a new dress?"

Adrian looked over at the concoction of pink satin he fingered. The neck was lined with stiff lace and the bodice was form-fitting. The waist seemed incredibly narrow, the skirt wide and cumbersome. She cocked an eyebrow and studied the garment.

"No, I don't think so," she said, despite the fact she'd seen the peddler eye her strange outfit with surprise and curiosity.

"How about a chair, then? You could use a rocker to sit in in the evenings."

"That's one of a set," Harp spoke up, lifting the rocking chair and setting it down in front of Adrian. "One for each of you."

Adrian pictured herself and Rome sitting in front of the fire at night, the children tucked into their beds in the next room. She knew she had no right to dream such things, but she found herself nodding her head.

"They're lovely. They would look nice in front of the fireplace."

"There you go," Rome coaxed, taking the chair Harp handed down. "Now, how about curtains?"

"Curtains?"

"Yeah, those windows are surely bare. Some of that lacy stuff would make nice coverings."

Adrian didn't know how to sew a stitch without a machine and she didn't see anything resembling one in Harp's wagon. But she did see some polished horseshoes, and an idea occurred to her.

With a smile, she bit her lower lip and turned to Rome.

"How much money do you have?"

He seemed to know what she was thinking and he smiled. Waving his hand toward the wagon, he said simply, "Go to it. I'll tell you when to stop."

For more than an hour Adrian plundered the wagon's precious offerings. She picked out matching kerosene lamps with rose-colored globes, a quilt for Mimi's cot, and another length of fabric to use as a divider between her cot and the boys'. She found a small round table which was scarred on top and which Harp threw in for nothing.

To the growing pile she added the two rockers, the length of lacy material, and four of the horseshoes. Rome eyed the last with a mixture of doubt and hesitancy, but he didn't stop her.

Gathering courage, she took a basket of oranges, several apples, and a cone filled with nuts. Ribbons and dried flowers followed, as well as two large embroidery hoops and a carved wooden shelf.

At the last minute, she spotted a small wooden bird and her breath caught. Hand-painted, the figurine looked lifelike. Harp saw her admiration and quoted a figure which seemed extreme compared to the other items she'd purchased. She knew the amount to be extraordinary and she set the bird back in its place with a shake of her head.

"That's enough," she said, satisfied with the collection of items she'd chosen.

"Take the children in the house," Rome said, lifting the youngsters down from the wagon, their treasures clutched in their hands. "I'll settle up with Harp and then bring this stuff inside."

Adrian herded the children toward the porch, her mood light and excited. She couldn't wait to get started on her projects. She took one last look at the fabulous rolling store.

It suddenly occurred to her the peddler might be going into town. For a full minute she considered asking him if he could take her along. But she'd seen the way Rome looked at her and the words died on her tongue. He wanted to please her. He was trying so hard to make her happy here. And she'd promised him a month. She wouldn't go back on her word.

Besides, this was her chance to really help him. Up until now, Mimi had been more help to her father than Adrian had. But Adrian knew she could fix up the cabin, make it presentable. Before she left, she could at least make sure the Walker family had a pleasant home.

With a twist of pain, another thought occurred to her. Another woman might find his home more welcoming after Adrian wrought her changes. His wife, when he found one, would benefit from the decorating ideas Adrian had. Another woman would share the coziness of the cabin, rock beside him in the matching chairs.

With a small shock, Adrian realized she was jealous. Jealous of a woman that didn't yet exist in Rome's life, but whom Adrian knew soon would. For he had to have help and when she left he'd be forced to find another to take her place.

The green-eyed monster rose up to thrust a knife of pain through her chest. Adrian knew with a certainty she could no longer ignore that she didn't want another woman to replace her in Rome's life.

Chapter Eleven

Later, as Adrian unloaded the carton of goodies Rome had brought inside, she felt a warmth steal into her chest and she placed a hand lightly over her heart.

Beneath the lacy fabric and the polished horseshoes she found the wooden bird she'd admired and rejected because of the cost. She also found a box of scented soap, and several candles which, unlike the tallow ones, had a pleasant smell.

A tear threatened, replaced by a wide smile. Rome was such a wonderful man. She could see him out the back window, plowing relentlessly despite the fact it was Sunday. He never took a day off. She learned from Mimi that he'd already been to the fields that morning before coming in to prepare the breakfast. He seemed tireless in her eyes, but she knew he couldn't go on carrying the majority of the burden alone.

With a firm resolve, she decided she would rise when he did in the mornings so she could prepare him breakfast before he went to work. It seemed the least she could do.

With Mimi's help, she began to put the house to rights. They put the quilt on Mimi's bed, hung the matching fabric down the center of the room to allow the girl a measure of privacy, and set the scarred little table beside her bed. With a scrap of gingham, Adrian made a make-shift cover for the table. After adding a round doily, she had to admit the room looked cheer-ful and feminine, and not too shabby consid-ering she couldn't sew a stitch.

Mimi showed her delight by throwing herself into Adrian's arms, laughing and crying. Wip-ing away a tear of her own, Adrian shrugged off the emotions.

They nailed two horseshoes over the wooden frame of each window and, by draping the lacy fabric through the loops, fashioned a scalloped valance. The ends hung down the sides and Adrian tied them back with lengths of ribbon.

Then she covered the embroidery hoops with fabric and lace and tied a bow atop each one. With the dried flowers added, they made attrac-tive wall hangings. She hung the matching lamps on the wall and centered the small shelf between them. The bird figurine looked beautiful set on a white embroidered doily on the shelf.

She gathered the tablecloth from Lorraine's trunk and put it on the table, adding the basket of arranged fruit and nuts as a centerpiece.

With the leftover fabric, she and Mimi draped the bottom of the dry sink and covered the kitchen shelves of canned and jarred food in the pantry.

The soap and scented candles she placed in the drawer of the washstand in her room, to be enjoyed later.

When Rome decided to call it a day and come to the house, Adrian could clearly see he was stunned by the cabin's transformation. She'd even swept and scrubbed the wood floor of the main room until it shone.

The cabin looked quaint and charming when he stepped through the back door. Smells of nut bread and something tangy met Rome's nose. The children were washed clean and ready for bed, and Adrian looked lovely with her hair curling around her face and a rosy flush on her cheeks.

"What do you think?" she asked cautiously.

Rome couldn't stem the flow of desire that coursed through him. He looked around and felt he'd come home for the first time in nearly a year. He knew at that moment that he wanted Adrian for his wife, and not just because he needed her help. He admired her for her quick adjustment to him and his children, more so because he suspected she didn't know the first thing about being either a wife or mother. He hungered for the feel of her in his arms, and had ever since the first moment he'd held her after Eli's near brush with death. And he desired her as a woman. As he'd never desired another in his life, not even Lorraine.

For a moment he battled the feelings of betrayal that thought caused him. After all, Lorraine had been a good wife and mother and he had loved her. But the simple truth was he'd never ached for her the way he did Adrian. He'd never lain awake at night and longed for her touch, not even before they were wed.

He struggled with his need until he could speak normally. "Everything looks real nice," he said.

She beamed. Actually glowed with pleasure, and he felt himself hardening at the sight of her in the revealing camisole. Again he wondered at her strange choice of garments. One would have thought she didn't know how inappropriate her attire was. But he'd chosen not to antagonize her with demands that she don something else. At first because he didn't want to anger her and possibly drive her away.

Now, however, he found he liked her costume. He enjoyed seeing the curve of her neck, the softness of her shoulder. He caught himself glancing at her shapely calves beneath the shortened skirt, and her trim ankles in the odd socks.

Everything about her intrigued him, Rome had to admit. From the terrible way she cooked, as though she'd never used a stove before, to the stories he heard her reciting to the children each night. Stories about flying machines, and boxes that could write, add, and balance figures for you just at the touch of a few keys.

Ships that traveled to the moon, telephones without cords or wires, and an interesting device that showed moving pictures on a little glass screen all came alive as she spoke. Of course, he knew such things didn't exist, and he wondered at the effect her tales would have on the children. But then he realized she had a very vivid imagination and he wholly approved of offering the kids an opportunity to expand their minds with the impossible fantasies.

Despite her lack of domestic skills and her unusual exploits with the children, Rome knew he would miss her terribly if she left. Just the thought of taking her into town and returning without her left him coldly bereft. Could he convince her to stay? She hadn't said a word to indicate she'd changed her mind about going.

Perhaps she needed more from him than subsistence. Maybe she needed a hint of his true feelings. If he tried to woo her, she would see he wanted more from her than a loveless marriage to ease his burdens. She'd realize how he truly felt about her. And just maybe, if he were lucky, she would decide she loved him, too.

After the children were asleep, Rome invited Adrian to walk outside with him.

"Excuse me?"

"Walk out. Take a stroll," he said, indicating the front door. He saw her brow furrow and thought he'd moved too quickly. But then she surprised him by pushing out of the rocker.

"Sure, that sounds good."

He opened the door and held it for her to go ahead of him. As she stepped onto the porch, she stared up at the diamond-studded sky. Frogs gurgled and crickets chirped in a cacophony of night sounds. The leaves rustled lightly in the warm breeze.

With the moon no longer full, the area seemed cloaked in shadows. The March nights were still cool, but not cold, and she enjoyed the breeze rippling across her heated skin.

When had she grown so warm? Cooking the meal? Or thinking about Rome as they shared the food?

He took her elbow lightly in his palm as they stepped down from the porch. She felt a thrill ripple along her nerve endings, quickly warming her again. She considered pulling away, just to see if the flush came from his touch alone, but she knew she didn't want to lose the closeness of the moment.

"I was surprised to see the cabin looking so good," he said, his eyes forward as they slowly meandered across the red dirt of the yard. "I don't know when it's looked so nice."

She felt a quiver of pride straighten her spine. "It turned out even better than I'd hoped," she admitted, unable to keep the hint of pleasure from her voice. She felt an unexpected gratification at having redone the house. It warmed her to think she'd made the place a haven for Rome and his children.

She couldn't plow fields, or at least she didn't think she could. And she wasn't much of a cook. But it seemed she wasn't half bad as a mother and housekeeper. Two jobs she'd never tried before but found surprisingly rewarding now.

"I'm glad you're here, Adrian."

Again, he didn't look at her as he spoke and she got the feeling he wanted to say more but was hesitating. They came to a stop beneath the overhanging branches of an oak tree, and Adrian rested her back against the contorted trunk.

Her eyes met his in the darkness. She felt more than saw his gaze on her face. A breath of a breeze brought the scent of warm skin to her nostrils.

He leaned closer and she could feel the heat of his body reaching out to her. His breathing quickened and the moment drew out until Adrian was sure he meant to kiss her, touch her.

"The children like you a lot, Adrian," he whispered.

She nodded, then realized he couldn't see her well and mumbled, "Yes, I like them a lot, too."

"You've done a wonderful job taking care of them."

Again she nodded. This time a lump formed in her throat and she couldn't manage a verbal reply. Fearing she knew where the conversation was heading, and not wanting to face such a difficult dilemma at the moment, she took a step away from the tree.

Rome's hand came out and stopped her. Apparently he could see her better than she'd thought. His hand landed unerringly on the curve between her neck and shoulder, his palm cupping the soft skin.

"We'd like it very much if you would stay with us, Adrian," he said, his voice low and rough. For a man with a booming presence, it strained him to whisper. But whisper he did, like a trainer soothing a frightened horse.

His fingers moved slightly, brushing along the vein in the side of her throat. The rough tips plucked strings of awareness within her and she felt her eyes slowly drifting closed. She knew he was waiting for a response, but she found it impossible to concentrate on his question.

"*I'd* very much like you to stay," he added.

Finally she focused on his words and tried to make her voice strong. "I can't stay, Rome. I'm sorry. But it's impossible."

"Nothing's impossible," he told her staunchly. "We can work out some arrangement."

Still his fingers danced seductively along her flesh and Adrian had to force her brain to work.

"I swore I'd never remarry," she murmured, tipping her head to brush the back of his hand.

Suddenly his fingers stilled, growing hard against her neck. A chill swept her and she realized he'd taken a hasty step back. Eyes fluttering open, she tried to see his face in the dark.

"Rome?"

"You've been married?"

She blinked, trying to catch the tail of the conversation that seemed to have zipped past her.

"Married? Yes, I've been married. It was my biggest failure to date, and believe me, you'd know how bad that was if you knew a little more about my life."

"What happened?" She heard the frigidity creep into his words.

"Happened? The usual. We grew apart." She didn't want to tell Rome about her marriage. Not now, not the real truth.

Though it happened nearly five years ago, the divorce had been difficult for both of them. Not so much because of any great love she and Tate shared, but because they'd once been friends. Friends who got tired of waiting for the right person to come along and chose instead to settle for the next-best thing.

Only second best had never been good enough for either of them, and their marriage had proved no exception. Not only had she lost her husband, a fate she could have easily withstood, but in the end she'd lost her very best friend. A much harder blow.

"It's over now anyway," she said, breathing a tattered sigh. "I'd rather not discuss it."

"He's . . . gone?"

"Gone?" Adrian barked a short laugh, thinking exactly how far "gone" Tate was now. This crazy trip through time had put a span between them that far outmeasured mere emotional distance. "Yeah," she told Rome. "He's gone, all right."

She wished she could say good riddance and forget the whole deal. But she sometimes still missed Tate the friend. And now more than ever her guilt ate at her.

"You could always try again," Rome said, shocking her from her musings. She bristled at the very mention of matrimony.

"No, I would never do that to anyone again," she vowed, laying her hand atop his. "Especially someone I liked," she added, only half kidding.

He held her a moment longer, then released her. She felt the loss of his touch and wrapped her arms around herself to ward off the sudden chill.

"We should get back," she said, stepping from under the tree.

Rome didn't answer, but fell into step behind her as she headed for the front door. It struck her then that they would sleep under the same roof tonight, and every night from now until she left. It hinted at an intimacy she hadn't felt before. They would be almost like a real family, sharing the limited confines of the little cabin.

The chill dissipated and she felt heat on the back of her neck. She wondered if Rome were watching her, staring at her back as she preceded him.

Inside, the rockers seemed to beckon to them. A real couple would sit before the fire at night, he whittling or reading, she supposed, the wife mending or sewing.

The picture brought her a measure of comfort she hadn't felt since this wild four-ticket ride began. With a snort of self-derision, she shook off the fanciful notion. You don't even know how to sew, she chided herself.

Still, she found herself going to the far rocker. Her hand caressed the smooth wooden arms; her eyes lingered on the carefully stitched seat.

"They look real homey," Rome said, close behind her.

She turned sharply and her eyes locked on the front of his shirt. He was wearing the flannel, and the top two buttons were undone. She realized it was because one of them was missing.

"You've lost a button." The words escaped before she could catch them. What a terrible thing

167

to say in answer to his praise.

He looked down, and a grin tipped his full, inviting mouth. Inviting? Where had that thought come from? His mouth was normal, nothing special, she told her careening emotions. Two lips, a slight touch of dampness, a hint of color. Her breath caught painfully in her chest and she tried to look away. Nothing special, she repeated to herself firmly.

"Yes, it seems everything has gone to rack and ruin since Lorraine died. And I can't manage a needle even a little."

"Oh," she breathed, seeing the question in his eyes. Her mind shouted a warning. *You cannot sew!* But Adrian ignored the pesky voice of reproach. Before she could tell him she didn't know one end of a needle from the other, she opened her mouth and volunteered to mend his shirt.

Eyes wide, Adrian wondered where the crazy offer had sprung from. She started to withdraw the proposal, but Rome's wide grin stopped her cold.

His eyes were smiling. Those poor, tired, weary eyes looked fresh with hope and happiness. She couldn't disappoint him now. How difficult could one little button be? Her dry cleaner replaced hers all the time.

Reluctantly, she returned the smile and went to her room to fetch the sewing kit from Lorraine's trunk. As she stepped out of her room, she froze.

Rome had taken down the straps of his coveralls and removed his shirt. His bare chest gleamed in the soft glow of the dying fire. The denims hung precariously at his narrow hips, fastened only by the two brass buttons on either side.

He noticed her disturbed frown, and cleared his throat nervously.

"Beg your pardon," he blustered, shoving the shirt at her quickly. "I'll go and put on another shirt."

"No," she said. Too quickly? She clutched the flesh-warmed shirt to her, and Rome's masculine scent drifted up to tease her nose.

He watched her grip the fabric, an odd light in the blue-green eyes now. Adrian thought absurdly that his eyes were indeed mirrors to his soul. Unlike most of the men she knew, who were masters at hiding true emotions or summoning bogus ones when the moment suited, Rome's true feelings were always reflected in the teal depths.

She was touched by the confidence that thought stirred in her. Her last vestiges of defensiveness slowly seeped away. A trust she'd never felt with another man filled her. A faith she hadn't known was missing until now.

"No," she repeated, this time with more assurance. "It's warm in here. You're all right the way you are. This'll only take a minute," she babbled, fingering the coarse material.

He nodded, readjusted his straps over his naked chest, and settled in the rocker across from her.

Her eyes locked on the muscles of his arms as he rested his hands on the chair arms. They flexed and twitched slightly beneath the tight, tanned skin. She gulped and watched the veins outlined beneath the smooth flesh.

Yes indeed, it was warm in here. And getting hotter by the minute.

Chapter Twelve

Adrian sucked the tiny pinpoints of blood from her finger and smiled. She'd done it. She'd sewn the button on without much difficulty, and Rome had been delighted by her efforts. Such a small thing. Yet it meant something to him.

Oh, she felt sure he could have managed the task himself easily enough. Even Mimi probably could have done as well. But nevertheless, a swell of gratification filled her. Every duty she'd attempted here had been a success. Well, her cooking was nothing to brag about, but it was edible. Her attempts at decorating had been pleasantly appreciated. And she'd taught herself to sew, a little. So far, she thought ironically as she donned Lorraine's white, ruffled nightgown, she was better at this job than any other she'd previously undertaken.

Settling between the freshly washed sheets, she curled on her side and huddled in the bed. The ropes creaked and the moss rustled. She was even getting used to the strange mattress. In fact, she rather liked it.

Tomorrow, she had decided, she would get up and help Rome with the morning chores. Telling herself she shouldn't care so much, she remembered the way some of his despair had been lessened with her meager assistance earlier.

Placing her tender fingertip to her mouth once more, she sighed and slipped off to sleep, a small smile playing on her lips.

The sun still slept. Daylight seemed distant. But Adrian had been listening for the rooster's crow and she'd unmistakably heard it 15 minutes earlier.

"Well," she said, glancing out the back window of the small cabin, "he must see something I don't."

She scanned the darkness but saw not a hint of light on the horizon.

Still, she dressed and went to the kitchen, where she put a pot of coffee on to boil the way Mimi had shown her. She quickly mixed the ingredients for biscuits and slid them into the stove she'd stoked to life.

She was beginning to get a feel for the stove.

It would never be her friend—she was no Betty Crocker—but she'd finally managed to quit burning everything.

A quick look into the larder told her they were almost out of ham and bacon. She'd have to ask Rome about their meat supply.

"Since I assume there isn't a supermarket in the area," she mumbled, missing even that small advantage.

When the biscuits and coffee were done, she collected a jar of peach preserves and a crock of butter from the pantry shelf.

Dipping her finger into the smooth, yellow butter, she sighed and rolled her eyes in pleasure. Cholesterol be damned, there were some definite advantages to being stuck on a farm.

Hands and arms full, she made her way back to the house. She caught her breath as she came in the back door and nearly dropped the jar of jam.

"Adrian."

Rome stood in front of the fireplace, a pair of snug denim trousers riding low on his hips. He was barefoot, shirtless, and the most desirable figure of a man she'd ever seen in her life.

He took a step toward her and her eyes dropped to his fly. Only three of the four buttons had been fastened, the top one left undone to reveal a trail of dark, wiry hair leading below the waistband.

She swallowed hard, wondering what had

lodged in her throat. She thought it might be her heart. It didn't seem to be in her chest any longer.

She gazed down his long, slim legs encased in the form-fitting fabric, to his slender feet. The tops were lightly sprinkled with fine brown hair, the toes narrow and long.

She'd never thought of a man's feet as seductive before; she'd never thought much about them at all. But seeing Rome's sent her sluggish heart into overdrive and she knew it had settled in her breast again when she felt it slam against her ribs.

"Adrian?"

She snapped to attention, meeting his eyes. The concern there brought her wild ruminations to a shrieking halt.

He took the coffeepot and pan of biscuits from her ineffectual hands and set them on the edge of the grate in the fireplace.

Adrian carefully set the butter and preserves down. Searching frantically for something to say, she remembered the dwindling pork.

"We're nearly out of ham," she blurted. "And bacon, too."

Slowly he turned, rising from a squatting position. His movements were unhurried, graceful. A small pop came from his knee joint and Adrian thought it a very cozy sound to hear in the morning.

A flush crept over his neck. "I was about to

wake the kids," he told her, motioning behind him.

"Oh, why don't you let them sleep in a little later this morning? It won't hurt them, and I can handle whatever needs to be done."

Rome shrugged. "All right. If you like."

For a moment she felt pleased that he'd given in to her wishes, just as if she were an important part of the family. Only she wasn't, she reminded herself quickly.

This wasn't her life. And this wasn't her home. And she'd do well to remember that before she did something foolish. Like agree to stay.

A wave of panic swept over her. Had she actually been considering staying? No, she told herself. That was ridiculous, absurd. She meant to leave this farm—and this world, if that was possible—at the first opportunity. And nothing would change her mind, she firmly resolved.

"What are you doing up so early?"

Glancing over her shoulder, she saw him push his arms into the flannel shirt.

"I thought you could use some help with the chores. You've been doing most of them alone, except the small ones the children do each morning. And then you put in a full day in the fields." She shrugged and turned back to the table. "If you show me what to do I'm sure I can take a few of them off your hands."

He lifted two plates down from the shelf over

the fireplace and set them before her. She jumped, startled, as his hand brushed past her shoulder.

Stop this foolishness, she admonished herself. Collecting her wits, she gathered two china coffee cups and matching saucers and poured them each a helping of the hot brew.

Then she set the pan of biscuits on a hot pad in the center of the table and motioned for Rome to take a seat.

Silence ruled as they drank their coffee and each meticulously buttered one of the flaky biscuits.

Rome swallowed three in succession. Adrian nibbled at hers.

"Digger's gonna bring another hog on Tuesday."

Adrian sucked a clump of warm dough down her throat and had to wash it down with coffee. "A hog?"

"Yeah, you said we were out of pork. We don't usually use so much but since you seemed to favor it over the chickens, I bought another one."

"Chicken? I haven't seen any chicken in the smokehouse, or the larder."

A grin split his face, but he rubbed a hand over his mouth and wiped it away. "Adrian, the yard is full of chickens, haven't you noticed?"

She sat up, a disgusting theory forming in her mind. "But those are for laying eggs. Aren't they?"

He nodded and she sagged with relief. It was short-lived, however, as he added, "Among other things."

Pushing aside the rest of her breakfast, she cringed. She'd offered to help, but murder wasn't in her job description. Then and there Adrian decided if there was any killing to be done that was one chore Rome would have to do himself.

"Are you sure you want to help me?"

She looked up, into his eyes. "Do I have to assassinate anything?"

He laughed and shook his head. "No. But I'd sure appreciate you taking over the milking and a couple of small tasks if you're up to it."

Thankful she wouldn't be called upon to talk one of the chickens into committing suicide, she eagerly agreed to milk the cow, though she'd never even seen one up close.

"Good. We'll get started as soon as you're finished."

She eyed the remains of her biscuit and grimaced. Pushing up from the seat, she met his gaze. "Ready when you are."

"Don't let them intimidate you," Rome called, a chuckle in his voice.

Adrian shot him an angry look through the wire fence and turned back to the stampede coming at her.

"Here, chicky, chicky, chicky," she soothed,

reaching into her apron and gathering another handful of feed. She tossed it with a sweeping motion the way Rome had shown her. But the crazy birds just ran right over the feed and kept coming toward her.

"No," she said nervously, waving her hand. "Back there. I threw it over there." She tried to shoo the chickens away, but they just kept closing in until they had her surrounded.

"Rome?"

"Don't show fear," he told her, laughing in spite of his efforts to remain supportive.

"Ow, hey, cut that out." Adrian danced backward. "Rome, that one pecked me," she called out indignantly.

His mirth escaped and he bent forward, holding his middle as he fought the wave of hilarity. "They know you have more feed in your apron. They're just trying to get it."

"But you said not to throw it all in one place. You said they wouldn't all get fed unless I scattered it evenly over the coop."

"That's right. But they're stupid chickens, Adrian. They don't know why you're keeping it from them."

Another beak attacked her ankle and she screamed, jumping to the side. A pile of corn fell from her apron like sand from an hourglass and she watched her attacker devour half of it. "They're not as dumb as you think, Rome. I think they have a strategy."

"Go on, Adrian. Close your eyes and step forward. They'll get out of your way, trust me."

She could still hear the masked humor in his voice and it chafed her pride. Doing as he directed, she pressed her eyelids shut and took a bold step.

A raucous cackling erupted and she felt feathers float past her face. Her eyes flew open and she saw the indignant hen flurry away, still raising a commotion.

"Hey, watch it," Rome shouted in mock exasperation. "That one's dinner."

"Rooooome, yuk!"

Adrian hurriedly distributed the remainder of the feed, carefully sidestepping the fowl. The hen she'd stepped on looked up at her and she studied the tiny face, the beady eyes void of intelligence, and her heart went out to the doomed creature.

There were definite disadvantages to living on a farm, too, she reminded herself.

Next came the milking.

Adrian followed Rome into the dark interior of the barn. As they stepped inside, he stopped and turned back.

"Better cover your hair," he said, dragging a kerchief from his back pocket and handing it to her.

She reached for the bandanna. "Why?"

"Spiders, flies, maybe even mites. We have pigeons in the loft, you know."

Adrian quickly wrapped the kerchief around her head and tied it at the nape of her neck. She blanched as Rome went into the barn.

Slowly walking along behind him, she imagined all manner of creepy crawlers coming out from the corners to initiate the new recruit. So intent was she on searching the darkness for multilegged critters, she plowed into Rome's back when he stopped.

"Umph." She stumbled back and he reached to steady her. "Sorry," she mumbled.

The rasp of a match was followed by light as Rome lit a lamp and turned up the wick.

"There, that's better. I'm used to the lay of the place; I don't usually need the lamp until I get to Wendy's stall."

"Wendy?"

"The milk cow."

Now then, Adrian thought. That's more like it. An animal with a name. Someone she could get accustomed to without fear of facing it down a dinner table. Wendy, such a nice name, too.

"Why do you call her Wendy?" she asked, following him down a narrow corridor between stalls. Only two were occupied, she saw. One held the horse she'd seen him use to pull the plow. The other a scraggly looking cow.

" 'Cause you don't want to be downwind of her when she lifts her tail," he said.

Adrian stumbled to a halt and Rome glanced

back over his shoulder and grinned.

"Very funny." Drolly, she rolled her eyes. So much for befriending the cow.

"Isn't this Wendy?" she asked when he walked past the stall with the cow.

Rome stopped and looked at the shaggy creature. "That?" he asked, a look of amazed disbelief on his face.

She nodded, already certain she'd made a mistake.

He stopped, lifted the light, and quirked his eyebrow. "*He* is not a cow, Adrian. *He* is a bull."

"Oh," she breathed, tipping her head to the side and catching a glimpse of his equipment. "Yep, he's a bull, all right."

She heard Rome's muffled laughter. This time she couldn't blame him and she found herself chuckling as well. In the far stall she heard a low bellow.

"That," Rome said, stopping at the gate and lifting the latch, "is Wendy."

Adrian approached cautiously. She peered over the slats of the gate. Big doe-brown eyes looked up at her. Long lashes fluttered as the animal blinked against the harsh glow of the light. A damp black nose twitched as Wendy caught Adrian's scent. Her brown-and-white hide quivered in greeting. Immediately a bond was formed.

"Oh, she's so cute," Adrian said.

Rome just chuckled and shook his head.

Adrian reached out her hand and Wendy sniffed her, snuffling her wet nose against Adrian's palm.

"Ugh."

Taking a stool down from a nail on the wall, Rome set the pail he carried beside the cow.

"Come on," he said.

Adrian eyed the cow and hesitated.

"What's the matter? I thought you said she was cute."

"She is cute. But don't you think we should get better acquainted before I—well, you know, get personal?"

This time he managed to keep a straight face, barely. Clearing his throat, he waved Adrian forward. She took a small step into the stall.

"Wendy, this is Adrian. She's going to milk you this morning. Adrian, this is Wendy. She hasn't been milked since yesterday morning and she's anxious to get it over with."

Cutting Rome a snide glance, she eased up to the cow. "Very funny," she mumbled, reaching out to lightly touch the coarse hide. As her hand fell gingerly on the cow's flank, the long tail whipped around and slapped her hard.

Adrian jumped back, shrieking. Rome gave up trying to contain his amusement and laughed out loud.

"Don't tickle her, Adrian. She'll think you're a fly to be swatted away. Put your hand firmly on her side, like this. And give her a little pat."

She tried again, this time tapping Wendy solidly. The cow let out a deep bellow and Adrian smiled.

"I guess she likes that?"

"Yeah, she likes it. Now, come here and I'll show you how to milk her."

"Me?"

"You."

"But I thought maybe I'd just watch this time. You know, take it slow."

"Come on. I'll be right beside you."

Adrian eyed the cow, whose hooves now shifted in anticipation. Rome moved the stool closer. He stepped back and motioned for her to sit.

Swallowing hard, she eased up to the stool. Gathering the hem of her skirt close to her legs, she carefully sat down. Wendy sidestepped and Adrian lunged back, tipping the stool. Rome grasped her shoulders and steadied her.

"Put your shoulder against her here and press. Let her know where you are."

Adrian did as he instructed.

"Now rub your hands together. She doesn't like cold hands on her teats."

Looking over her shoulder, Adrian raised an eyebrow. "I can't say I blame her," she told him with a saucy grin. He chuckled deeply and shook his head.

She felt his body press against hers as he knelt behind her. His warmth seeped through their clothing and enveloped her. The morning chill evaporated.

His arms came around her and she sucked in a shaky breath. The firm muscles pressed against her upper arms. She could feel them flex as he took her hands in his.

Leaning into her, he eased her closer to the cow.

"Put your fingers at the top of the teat, like this," he whispered next to her ear.

Adrian almost forgot the reason for their closeness. Thoughts of cows and milk flew out of her head. She lavished in the heat Rome radiated, closing her eyes and soaking it in. She memorized the feel of his chest, broad and firm against her back.

Watching their hands drift toward the pink nipples, she stared hard at the contrast. His were rough and dark, hers soft and white. His long fingers covered her thin ones. Heat spiraled through Adrian and she sighed, leaning back further.

Just then, Rome eased their hands down the length of the teat and white liquid shot into the pail with a loud ping and a whoosh.

Adrian sat straight, her eyes going wide. "Oh, look," she cried, "we made milk!"

Chapter Thirteen

Rome tossed his head back, closing Adrian tighter in his embrace, and laughed.

"Well, actually, the cow made the milk. We just coaxed it out of her."

Blushing with both pride and chagrin, Adrian giggled. "I know, I've just never seen it happen like that in real life."

With his hands still clasped around hers, he looked down into her upturned face. His eyes studied her closely and she saw the flame of passion blaze to life. A current of awareness shot through her and she seemed to suddenly fill with wanting.

How easy it would be to reach up, press her lips against his. His full, wet mouth tempted her. His eyes told her the move would not be unwelcome.

She longed to go into his arms, to lose herself in the hypnotic teal gaze he fastened on her. Swallowing hard, she forced her attention back to the warm, spotted belly of the cow.

"You're a very unusual woman, Adrian Sheppard," he told her. "When are you going to tell me exactly where it is you're from? You've got to know I'm about eaten up with curiosity."

The husky tone of his voice told her curiosity wasn't the only thing eating at him. The warmth of his breath on her neck sent a shiver of heat down her spine.

"I thought men liked women to be mysterious," she breathed, forcing a lightness she was far from feeling to the words.

He didn't answer, but she heard his exasperated sigh behind her. Still, he didn't question her further.

They continued the chore, working in harmony, but suddenly Adrian felt trapped in his embrace.

Rome was getting too close, too inquisitive. Their emotions were becoming involved. Pretty soon he'd start demanding answers. Up to this point he'd been so glad to have her help he hadn't bothered to press her about her background, her reasons for coming to the farm or, later, agreeing to stay.

Sometimes she saw the query in his blue-green eyes, and a flicker of apprehension would sear through her. But he'd never before voiced his wonder. She couldn't let him too close. Feeling vulnerable and alone could make her slip up. And wouldn't he be horrified if she blurted the truth in a moment of weakness?

Desperate or not he'd probably load her up and deliver her into town posthaste. No one wanted a delusional woman tending their children. He'd think even Mimi a better alternative.

Forcing her voice to sound normal she said, "I guess that wasn't too bad for my first effort. What do you say, Wendy?" she teased, lightly patting the cow's flank.

She heard Rome clear his throat and felt a moment of panic, thinking surely now he'd demand answers. Instead he reached past her and gripped the bucket by the curved metal handle. She felt a chill replace the heat of his body as he rose to his feet. "You did fine," he said.

Afterward, Rome showed her the springhouse, a small squat building built of slate over a shallow stream of water. It was surprisingly cool inside and he showed her how the milk could be kept by putting it in a crockery jar tied to a rope and lowering it into the stream.

"It also comes in handy during the summer when you want a cool wash," he said, his voice unusually coarse.

Adrian watched the small, mischievous smile curve his mouth and her body responded by

187

sending gooseflesh over her skin. She rubbed her arms and studied him for a moment. Was he flirting with her? That was a new side to Rome Walker. One she hadn't chanced to see before. Had he been too mired down with hardship to show this lighthearted mien before? And why should he bring it out now? she wondered suspiciously.

They left the cool interior of the springhouse and he accompanied her around the other outbuildings. They bypassed the smokehouse and the outhouse, which she'd already become familiar with. And still cautious after her earlier attack, Adrian carefully skirted the chicken coop with its raised, slanted henhouse.

The final building was a toolshed. Rome mentioned it in passing but didn't offer to show her the interior. Adrian assumed that meant she wouldn't be needing anything from that small wooden edifice.

"That's about it," he said, leading her back to the house. "Toby likes to collect the eggs and toss the feed. You can let him keep doing it, just watch he doesn't get in over his head."

"I'm appalled that child is better at feeding those wretched birds than I am, but I won't argue if he pleads to be allowed to continue."

"Mimi is still a mite small for the milking, but she'll be wanting to learn soon enough."

A frown creased his brow and a shadow doused the light in his eyes. "Of course, you'll be long gone by then, I suppose."

Fighting a wave of sadness, she forced a nod. "I suppose," she murmured.

"Well, I'll leave you then. You sure have been an immense help to us these past weeks, Adrian. But I've still got a ways to go today," he said.

With a small smile, he strode across the yard to the toolshed. She watched him disappear and still she remained standing on the back porch. The sun had finally decided to grace the morning sky and she went into the house and poured herself another cup of coffee. Bringing it back out onto the porch, she watched her first sunrise on the farm.

It was a beautiful sight, more enchanting because of the vastness of the open spaces. She could see the view without the distortion of high-rise buildings and blacktop roads reflecting like endless dreary mirrors.

Here, the colors were the pure, radiant copper of a new penny, the blushing beauty of cerise, and an emblazoned yellow like the finest gold. It stirred her soul like nothing she'd ever experienced before.

"Oh, Lord help me," she prayed. "I'm really in love with the man and his land."

And she knew it was true. Adrian had readily admitted her fondness for the children. This was more difficult, more sobering.

She saw qualities in Rome she'd never found

in the men from her time and social station. Things like a love of earth, and an untouched benevolence. Something few people could understand when they came from cities or large towns where they punched clocks and drove slick cars.

The farm had a magical essence, as if time slowed to a crawl. But not the dragging, clock-watching lag that made you crazy. Rather, as if you lived by the sun's chronometer and not man's.

She sipped her coffee and watched as Rome led the horse to the toolshed. He disappeared inside once more and came out, pulling the heavy plow close enough to harness the animal in place. She saw him pause a moment to gaze at the sky. When he looked back at her, they seemed to share the timeless moment.

Then he hitched the horse in place and climbed into the small metal seat atop the plow. With a companionable wave to Adrian, he spoke to the horse and they were off.

Adrian stood on the porch another minute, her heart heavy and her mind troubled. Then with a resigned sigh she turned and went inside.

Rome held the copy of *American Agriculturer* in front of his face, watching Adrian over the top of the magazine. After a strange but filling meal of something she called "soo-flay," she'd gathered up everything she could find that was missing buttons and she'd been reattaching them ever since.

He wanted her to put aside her sewing now that the children were in bed. He'd come to the conclusion Adrian had grown attached to the children. Still, she wouldn't agree to stay. That could only mean one thing. She wasn't interested in him.

He couldn't claim the same. Quite the opposite. He'd grown more and more fond of her with each day, each encounter. There was only one answer, if he hoped to keep her. He'd have to instigate his plan to court her and, hopefully, win her heart. If she came to feel something for him, surely then she'd stay. If it were possible. For the first time he wondered if there was something in her past, maybe something to do with her marriage, that prevented her from agreeing to his proposal. If so, it might be difficult to win her over.

But that was his plan, meager though it seemed.

However, his ploy appeared in danger of defeat before he'd even had a chance to try it. Why was she so intent on sewing those buttons?

Rising, he went to the fireplace. "I think I'll have another cup of coffee, Adrian. Would you like one?"

She didn't look up. "No, thank you. I've had enough."

He frowned. Deciding to take the bull by the

horns, so to speak, he came up behind her rocker and gently laid his hands on the back. Her fingers slowed to a halt.

"How about a stroll? We could walk off that wonderful supper you prepared."

Looking over her shoulder, Adrian narrowed her eyes and stared up at him. What on earth was he going on about? She'd never known him to be so talkative. Usually he was a man of few words. Besides, the souffle she'd made for supper had fallen when she'd removed it from the oven and she knew it had been far from wonderful eating the egg-and-vegetable mixture after that.

Could he be leading up to more questions? Had he decided now to continue the conversation she'd aborted in the barn that morning?

"No, thank you. I need to finish up here, and, quite frankly, I'm beat. I can't remember when I've done so much in one day."

Rome winced. Of course she'd be tired. She'd been up since before dawn, helping with the chores. He'd progressed so far due to her assistance that he was nearly ready to put the seed in the ground.

Taking his seat once more, he picked up the magazine. Adrian went back to her task.

"Maybe we could just talk," he said, rustling the pages he held.

She paused, and he thought he saw a brief flash of panic in her eyes. "Talk?"

"Yes, you know. Get to know one another."

Again her eyes widened and this time there was no mistaking the alarm.

"I don't think—"

"Daddy!" Toby called.

Adrian breathed a tremulous sigh and quickly put aside her sewing. She jumped from the rocker before Rome could respond to the little boy's call.

"I'll see what he wants," she told him, turning and hustling from the room.

He watched her go, frowning deeply now. All of a sudden she didn't seem tired. In fact, she'd leapt from the chair as if the seat had caught fire beneath her.

She came back into the room and hurried to the door. "He just wants a drink of water," she explained as she hurried past him.

Minutes later she returned but didn't sit again. Instead she stood anxiously behind the chair, gripping the back.

"I really am tired. I think I'll just go on to bed now."

"Wait," he said, quickly getting to his feet. He saw her move back. Not a full step, just a fraction, but enough that he couldn't miss the movement. "Is anything the matter?"

"No, nothing at all. I'm just tired. I've got to get up early tomorrow, too, if I'm going to take care of the chores by myself."

He stepped forward. Adrian stepped back. No

furtive moves this time. She was no longer trying to hide her discomfort.

Again he advanced. Again she retreated. Her thighs met the edge of the table and she glared over her shoulder to see what had stopped her progress. He took the opportunity to move in closer. When she looked back, she gasped. He was right in front of her.

"Did I tell you how much I appreciate all you did today, and since you've been here?"

"Y-yes, you did."

He nodded. "Well, I want to make sure you know how grateful we all are."

"That's very nice," she whispered, leaning back until her spine bent.

Rome pressed his advantage while she was trapped and unable to run. "I wish there was some way I could show my appreciation."

"Your thanks are sufficient."

He shook his head. "No. I mean *really* show my appreciation."

His hands came up to cup her shoulders. Adrian couldn't move. She knew he was going to kiss her and she wanted to stop him. If he touched her she'd be lost. She'd admitted to herself she was falling in love with Rome Walker. But she wasn't ready to let him see her true feelings. One kiss, though, and he'd surely know.

At the last minute she rolled away, ducking beneath his arm and skirting the edge of the table. She looked up and her breath caught in her throat.

Relieved, she pointed a trembling finger to the curtained doorway of the children's room.

Rome followed the direction of her gaze and saw three pairs of eyes peering around the edge of the blanket.

"Are you gonna kiss Adrian, Daddy?" Toby asked guilelessly.

Mimi rolled her eyes and poked him with her elbow. "Shhh," she hissed.

"All right," Rome said, dragging his gaze from Adrian to his children. "Everybody get to bed." He shooed the kids behind the curtain and turned back. "I'll only be a minute," he told Adrian.

She watched as he lifted Eli in his arms, and then the cover fell back in place and she was alone in the main room.

What was going on? If she didn't know better, she'd think Rome was trying to seduce her. Thank heavens the children interrupted. A relationship between her and their father could only lead to heartache. She couldn't stay here, not for Mimi and Toby and Eli. Not even for Rome. And to admit her love for them now wouldn't make the situation any easier. Her mind made up, she scrambled to her room and closed the door Rome had hung just last night.

She sat on the bed, clasping her trembling hands together. Thank goodness for the door. He wouldn't dare come looking for her if it was shut. She could relax now. The precarious moment had passed. Whatever he'd been planning had been thwarted.

She felt the tension in her belly unwind a notch. Slowly she unclenched her fists. Her escape had come not a moment too soon, either. Already she could feel the mounting desire Rome's nearness had caused. Another second and she'd have been in his arms. Irrevocably in his life.

Stretching out on the bumpy mattress, she closed her eyes and took several calming breaths. How could this have happened? After all these years she was finally in love. In love with a wonderful, caring man. A man who, despite his obvious pique at the moment, seemed to have unlimited patience when it came to dealing with his children. A man who worked 14 to 15 hours a day without complaint, and who had a distinct and unfailing love of the land.

And she couldn't have him. No way. Not even a glimmer of hope. They were as far apart as their separate worlds. She belonged in her time; he obviously belonged in his.

And never the twain shall meet. Only they had met. Their worlds, their lives, had collided. For some unknown reason she'd been brought here. An obvious mistake, but a fact nevertheless.

And now she'd gone and fallen for the man and his children. Fallen hard, if the weight of her heart was any indication.

Though her body was exhausted from the amount of work she'd done since rising, her mind refused to shut down. She lay still, thoughts playing tag in her head.

Yes, she cared for the Walkers. All of them. But that didn't change anything and she'd do well to remember that fact. At the end of the month she'd go into town and face the reality of her situation. She'd begin her trek to discover how she'd come to be here and, hopefully, how to get home.

Her time here would be nothing but a fantastic, unreal memory.

She would go home eventually. Even without any proof to substantiate her optimism, she knew she had to believe in that probability. It was the only thing keeping her sane at the moment.

She would go home, and Rome would go on to find the wife and mother he so desperately needed. And if that knowledge brought her jealousy and pain, she knew she'd learn to live with it. The feeling would pass once she was back in her own world, her time here resembling nothing more than a bad dream from which she'd awakened.

She comforted herself with her thoughts, but deep inside she knew the truth. She'd never forget Rome or his children. And, as dreams went, this one wasn't turning out half bad.

Chapter Fourteen

As she stared down the row of freshly turned dirt, Adrian groaned. Her back had never hurt so much. Her shoulders ached.

Everyone on the farm was needed in the fields now if they were going to get the seed in the ground. It was a tiring job, but the more people they had doing it the sooner it would be done.

Even Mimi and Toby carried small sacks and filled each tiny hill before pushing the dirt back into place. To them it was more fun than work.

Rome had the toughest job of all. He walked along, a huge wooden bucket with a thick leather strap slung over his shoulder so he could water each individual plant, baby Eli in a harness on his back.

For three days they'd done naught but drop

the pellets of corn and cotton and rice into the ground. And Adrian had worked right alongside the family the whole time. They now shared the morning chores and the cooking and cleaning up. Until the planting was done there would be no diversification of duties.

Today, Rome promised her, they would complete the task. She looked forward to the end of the dreadful ordeal. But at the same time, she found a certain odd sense of accomplishment in it. Knowing what you sowed today would be reaped tomorrow, and so forth.

When she left the farm, something of herself would stay behind in the seeds she had planted. And since those plants would go on to produce more seeds, the cycle would continue. Again she thought about how timeless it all seemed.

And again she knew how much she would miss it all when she left.

She thought back over the past weeks and smiled through her exhaustion. Rome's children had more spirit than any youngsters she'd ever encountered. Alex's children had always been busy with Little League or video games.

But Mimi spent her time trying to learn how to cook and run the household, something Adrian knew she was woefully inadequate at teaching. Toby adopted more critters than one boy should be acquainted with. Then there was Eli, junior Houdini. That child could disappear faster than Adrian could say jackrabbit. The first time she'd been frantic, running to the fields to fetch Rome in a panic. Eli had been sleeping, blissfully ignorant of the uproar he'd caused, beneath the dry sink.

Ahead of her she saw the tiny kitten trailing behind Mimi. She'd really been duped by that one. Obviously certain her chosen pet wouldn't be allowed in the cabin, Mimi had pretended to see a mouse, frightening Adrian out of a year of her life. Then Mimi informed her that the little kitten who'd been born to the barn cat would be just the thing to rid the house of the infestation.

Adrian had gone promptly to Rome with the plan. He'd smiled, apparently wiser about such things than she, and agreed to take the kitten into the family.

Toby tried hard to be good, even volunteering to keep an eye on Eli while Adrian hung out Monday's wash. Unfortunately, his patience had been strained trying to keep the toddler on the porch so he'd solved his dilemma by nailing his brother's diaper to the wood slats.

Unhurt, but furious, Eli let out a shriek that caused Adrian to drop the sheet she was hanging. In her hurry to get to the porch she stumbled over the laundry basket and dumped the entire load onto the ground, trampling it beneath her feet.

She would have scolded Toby if she'd known the trouble, but instead she tried to pick the baby up. It seemed he'd suddenly grown extremely heavy. By the time she figured out why she couldn't lift him, she'd torn a hole in his diaper. Eli, thoroughly amused by her attention, giggled wetly.

Unable to find fault with Toby's ingenuity, she began to chuckle. Pretty soon, Adrian and all three children were sitting on the porch laughing. That was how Rome found them, and the look on his face stopped her cold.

One look. One brief glance. The endearing teal eyes had spoken volumes. He felt relief, happiness, joy. A sense of home and family had returned for Rome and his children, and she was the catalyst.

That night Adrian realized something momentous. Something that caused her to sit up in bed with a shock. She'd finally found a job she loved. Maybe she wouldn't have been content to hold those positions in her time, but here things were different. A mother was called upon to be cook, doctor, teacher, and counselor. A wife to be gardener, agriculturer, and part-time veterinarian among other things.

Never had she been so fulfilled. Each day brought new and interesting experiences. Funny, she'd had to travel back in time a hundred years to find something she really enjoyed and now that she wanted to stick with a job, she wouldn't be allowed to.

Though the thought of staying here appealed to her at the moment, she knew it was impossible. She had problems in her other life that had yet to be resolved. She had a brother she loved. Besides, she couldn't let a freak accident decide the course of her life. No, she'd have to find some way to get home, back to her own time. And she'd have to do it soon.

Of course, once there she'd be right back where she started.

This place wasn't exactly fun and games, she reminded herself. She'd never forget the encounter with her first chicken dinner. Unfortunately, the meal was still walking when she first made its acquaintance and that was where the trouble began.

But Rome was patient. She was learning his wealth of endurance seemed endless.

He'd offered to show her how to wring the bird's neck, but she'd turned green at the very idea so he'd taken it out behind the barn and performed the task alone. Then came time to boil and pluck it. Adrian took one look and began to cry. Again he'd completed the job without complaint. Finally he'd brought the naked fowl to her ready, he said, for dressing.

"Sorry," she'd mumbled, still unable to forget its beady, insipid eyes watching her. "I don't have anything that'll fit her, I'm sure." And, clasping her hand over her mouth, she'd run around the side of the porch and lost her breakfast.

Her reaction to Digger's appearance with their hog, still alive and walking on a rope leash, was similar. Rome took one look at her stricken expression and paid the man extra to dress the hog away from Adrian's sight.

But Adrian wasn't ready to give up just yet. She still had a little time left here, and she intended to continue helping Rome and the children in any way she could.

She reached the end of her row and methodically made a half-circle to go down the next row. That row had been done and she stepped to the next. It, too, was seeded and covered. Stretching her bent back, she looked up. Mimi and Toby were coming to the end of their rows and Rome was going along behind them, ladleing water from a bucket over the tamped dirt.

He looked up and their eyes met. A weary smile tipped his full lips. He came to stand beside her. A rain barrel had been set at the front of the patch they were currently working and he dumped the remainder of his water into it and set the bucket aside.

"We're finished?"

"We're finished," he acknowledged, some of his fatigue vanishing in his relief.

"Oh, thank God," she whispered, coming up behind him and unstrapping a sleeping Eli. She cuddled the baby and rested her chin on top on his bonneted head.

Toby and Mimi, not so tired since they'd

napped earlier after the noon meal, were running along the rows holding hands and turning circles.

"I've never been so tired," Adrian confessed, handing the baby back to his father.

Rome took him. "You did real good, Adrian. I thought you'd give out after the first day, but you didn't. You stuck in there, working right alongside me until the last." His free hand came up and curved along her jaw.

She fought the urge to rest her face in his big, warm palm. She wanted to close her eyes and indulge in the feel of his strong fingers against her cheek. More than that, she wanted to go into his arms and rest her weary body against his broad chest. Instead she let her eyes drift to Eli.

Rome was having none of that. He lifted her chin and met her gaze. "You've been a helpmate to me, a mother to the children. You're more than I hoped for when I placed that ad. More than I dreamed possible when I saw that shooting star. Adrian," he said, his face coming closer to hers, "don't you see—"

Toby and Mimi crashed into his thighs, knocking him off balance and into Adrian. He tried to grab her, but he still held the baby. She flailed her arms, trying to regain her balance. Finally, after what seemed an extended moment in time, she tumbled backward. Right into the rain barrel full of ice-cold spring water.

205

Mimi and Toby froze, aghast at what they'd done this time. Rome's eyes flew wide, his jaw dropping. Eli came awake at the commotion, saw Adrian sitting in the barrel, and pointed his pudgy finger.

"Baff," he cooed, jumping excitedly in Rome's arms.

At the baby's observation, Mimi began to chuckle. Adrian scowled. Rome and Toby delayed their humor as long as possible. But soon they, too, lost the battle and began to laugh.

The icy water rolled over Adrian's tired muscles. The chill soothed her aching hands and shoulders. Splashing her hands, she doused the trio shaking with mirth before her. Shrieks and wails of protest went unheeded as she began to kick her feet and slap her palms against the surface of the water.

Rome handed the baby to Mimi and came at Adrian with his hands held out in front for protection against the frigid drops raining down on him. She squealed and tried to get away, but her position in the barrel afforded her no balance and she flopped helplessly.

He reached down and scooped her from the water, catching her against his chest. She grasped him around his neck and the children clapped their hands in delight.

Rome's eyes went to the front of her camisole. Looking down, she could see that the fabric was all but transparent when wet. As the slight breeze caressed her nipples, they rose to peaks. She heard Rome's indrawn breath.

Then his eyes drifted up to her face and their gazes met. She could see desire turn his eyes a deep turquoise. Her heart slammed to a halt, then raced so fast she could feel it pounding against her ribs.

His head came down. His eyes continued to watch her. His lips reached for hers. For the first time Adrian didn't think before acting. She wanted Rome's kiss, longed for it. She'd waited, hoping the attraction she felt would eventually subside. But it had grown, taking on a life of its own. And now she wanted a small measure of what she knew she could never wholly have.

His lips were warm and firm, his hands strong against her back and legs. His heart beat faster and she could hear its rapid staccato as he gathered her close.

She forgot everything in his embrace. There was no room for doubts or worries. There was only pleasure, real and intense.

Her hands slid up the back of his neck and she ran her fingers through the long, thick hair at his nape. She tugged gently and he deepened the kiss, pressing her lips apart, searching, demanding. The mating of their tongues sent shivers of desire through her. She never wanted to let him go.

"Daaaaddddddyyyy."

Rome slowly pulled back, his grin no match

for the ones Mimi and Toby wore. Even baby Eli smiled, blowing tiny bubbles of spit as he jumped excitedly.

"Last one to the stream is a lily-livered, yellow-bellied, egg-sucking dog," Rome shouted.

Adrian barely had time to register his battle cry before the children scattered, shrieking and running hell-bent-for-leather down the slope to the stream.

"Now, where was I?" he asked, his grin turning devilish.

"Rome," she cried, wiggling in his arms. "You can't let them go to the stream alone. Especially the baby."

"I know. Quick, let's finish what we started before I have to run and catch them."

He bent toward her but she squirmed out of his arms. The moment of harmless abandonment had passed and she knew it would be dangerous to prolong their embrace. She scrambled to the ground and gathered the hem of her sopping skirt up in her fist.

"Last one to the stream . . ." she shouted, and turned and darted ahead of him.

They raced to the water, laughing and stumbling. The children were sitting beneath a tree, discarding their outer garments.

Rome yanked his shirt from the waistband of his trousers and ripped off his boots, first one then the other as he danced from foot to foot.

"Better turn your pretty head, lady," he

warned. "I'm shucking these britches."

Adrian whirled around, clasping her hands over her eyes. Mimi and Toby laughed and teased as they ran into the icy water.

"Great day in the morning," she heard Rome shout.

When she looked back, he was waist-deep in the shallow stream.

"I'm glad your head was turned," he said, shivering. "I mighta been embarrassed, this water is that cold."

She flushed crimson and he laughed again. "Rome Walker, you are scandalous!" But Adrian couldn't help giggling naughtily. This was yet another side of Rome Walker she had never seen. His many layers were vastly different, yet each one was endearing in an unspoiled way.

Rome had changed much in the last two weeks. Gone was the despondent, defeated man she'd first met. In his place was a strong, sensitive, funny man with more heart than any man she'd ever known. And then, as she watched him lift his arms and gather a toddling Eli into his damp embrace, her love blossomed.

No longer could she ignore what had been happening. She'd become a part of this family. Against her better judgment she'd let them into her heart. A bond had formed between her and this little group. A tie not easily severed. Not without a great deal of pain and anguish, she thought on a shaky sigh.

Oh, she'd made a terrible mistake. She knew that with a dead certainty. But the laughter of the children drowned the pounding of her racing heart and eased her distress. Yes, she'd erred. But it was too late to worry about that now. For better or worse she loved the children. And the man. And she wouldn't change that to spare herself a second of anguish later.

With her resolve firmly in place, she kicked off her shoes and tugged off her wet socks. With a wild yell, she plunged into the stream and joined the festivities.

Chapter Fifteen

Lying on the bank of the creek, Adrian let the warm sun dry her skirt and soothe her jangled nerves. Rome lay beside her, the baby napping on his chest.

Toby and Mimi played at the shallow edge of the water, and the sounds of their happy voices drifted to Adrian's ears like an angel's song.

Content. She'd been searching for a word that would sum up her feelings, and as inadequate as content sounded she found it fit. Her heart was at peace. Her soul seemed to have accustomed itself to this place, this time, these people.

Glancing sideways at Rome, she felt a tug deep inside her. He looked so serene now, the signs of fatigue and stress all but invisible as he sought repose on the soft, warm bank.

She longed to reach out and touch the smooth skin of his forehead, to soothe the final vestiges of sadness from his brow.

Wiggling her bare feet into the tufts of velvety grass, she stretched her arms over her head and sighed with deep satisfaction. For a moment, one brief span of time, all was right in the world. Even if it wasn't *her* world.

Her mind continued to drift on a cloud of comfort as the sun dipped low on the horizon. Rome stirred and rolled his head in her direction. She met his gaze and for a minute they stared at each other in silence. Something deep and intense flared between them. She felt it. His eyes told her he felt it, too. The moment dragged out. Adrian was afraid to move, not wanting to break the bond that held them.

Eli made a small squeaking sound and his little body twitched. His arms and legs stiffened as his head came up and his tiny mouth opened wide in a huge yawn.

He looked around, saw Rome and then Adrian, and broke out in a smile.

Rome laughed. Adrian felt her heart melt like chocolate in the sun.

"Hey, fella," Rome whispered. "Have a good nap?"

"No nap," Eli said with a pout. "I seep good."

Adrian reached for him and lifted him from Rome's chest. "You sure did, Eli."

"Time to round up the prunes and get them to the house. It's getting late."

Adrian nodded, gathering Eli close to her chest as she rolled to her knees and then stood. Rome called to the two children in the creek and they moaned and groaned but plodded out as he directed.

As they turned toward the house, she saw Rome stiffen. He lifted his hand against the fading sun and squinted.

"What is it?" She scanned the horizon, seeing the outlines of several figures coming toward them. "Rome?"

"Company," he said, his tone telling her he wasn't expecting anyone and didn't know who it could be. They started forward slowly.

As the visitors came closer she saw the tension leave Rome's shoulders.

"Who are they?"

"The Hansons."

At her frown he offered a small smile. "Our nearest neighbors," he clarified.

"Neighbors?" Adrian gasped and looked down at her bare feet, hopelessly disheveled skirt, and the still-damp camisole.

Rome lifted his hand in greeting and the neighbors, who seemed more and more like a crowd the closer they came, increased their stride.

"Hello," they called.

Adrian counted two adults and then her eyes

went to the shorter members of the group. One, two, three, four, five! The Hansons had five children.

"All boys," she whispered, somewhat in awe.

"Yep. Five boys," Rome confirmed with a grin.

The two groups met and the children immediately separated into clusters of two and three. The Hansons' children seemed to range in age from about 12 down to a child about Toby's age.

"How are you?" Rome asked, gripping Mr. Hanson's hand. Adrian smiled shyly at his wife.

"We can't complain," Hanson said, his voice laced with a Swedish accent.

"It's good to see you. What brings you over?"

Hanson exchanged a glance with his wife and she smiled. "We finished our planting today. So Ella cooked up a big feast and we loaded the boys into the wagon and came over. Thought we'd sleep in the wagon tonight and tomorrow we'd all pitch in and help you get your seed in the ground.

Ella had been eyeing Adrian closely, but without rancor. Adrian offered a hesitant smile, and the woman's face immediately broke into a huge, crooked grin.

Rome shifted and cleared his throat but when he spoke his voice was hoarse with emotion.

"Berg, that's really good of you. A couple of weeks ago I didn't know how I was going to manage. But the truth is, we finished our planting today, too."

The man's face showed his surprise. Rome put his hand to the small of Adrian's back and she took a step forward.

"This is Adrian Sheppard. She's been helping me out for a few weeks, so I was able to get into the fields on time. Adrian, this is Berg and Ella Hanson and their boys, Albert, Johann, Manny, Erik, and Burr. In order from the tallest to the smallest."

"How do you do?" Adrian said politely.

Ella grinned again and Adrian / saw her crooked, overlapping teeth. But her smile was nice, and certainly welcome.

"So good to meetcha," the woman said, her voice thick with a surprising cockney accent. Adrian thought she sounded just like Eliza Doolittle in the play *My Fair Lady*.

"Adrian," Berg Hanson crowed. "A good Swedish name." He reached out and pumped her hand hard.

"Is it?" Smiling, Adrian endured the jarring greeting.

"So," Hanson said, puffing his chest out. "We didn't come all this way to go home. Instead of working, we will celebrate."

"That sounds like a great idea," Rome said. "Come on, let's go to the house and we can visit."

"I brought food," Ella told Adrian. "I hope

you're not offended. We didn't know Rome had a . . . someone helping him."

"Offended? I'm thrilled," Adrian assured her. "I'll be the first one to admit a little of my cooking goes a long way. It'll be nice to eat someone else's for a change."

They followed the men across the yard to the back porch. The women sat on the steps while Rome and Berg went to look at the newly planted fields. Adrian watched Rome walk away, pride in her heart. She'd suspected he was a truly good man from the first moment she met him. The Hansons' generous offer seemed to prove it. They had gone to a lot of trouble to help him out.

Ella reached for the baby and Eli settled on her lap, playing with the watch pinned to her bodice. Her brown hair had several streaks of gray and her face showed signs of premature aging, but when she smiled even her uneven teeth couldn't detract from the simple goodness Adrian recognized in her.

"So how long have you been with Rome's family?" Ella asked. She jiggled the baby and made little kissy sounds with her lips. "If ya don't mind me askin'."

"A couple of weeks."

The woman looked up. "Don't look so alarmed. I'm not here to make any judgments. I think it's a good thing Rome has help, and I can see ya care for the lot of them."

216

"Yes, I do."

Ella smiled and Adrian could see the lines on her face deepen. Laugh lines. That was a good sign, wasn't it?

A few moments of silence passed and Adrian looked away. She caught sight of her bare feet and remembered she'd left her shoes at the creek. She tucked her toes beneath her, suddenly embarrassed.

Ella saw her timorous movements and took a long look at Adrian's clothing.

"I must look a mess," Adrian mumbled, crossing her arms in front of her chest in a vain attempt to cover the diaphanous top. Ella wore a long-sleeved, high-necked blouse much like the ones Adrian had seen in Lorraine's trunk. Her skirt covered everything but the tips of her shoes.

"I suppose I should explain my outfit. . . ." Adrian stammered, not sure how she'd accomplish such a task.

"Don't worry none about that," Ella said. As she leaned closer, her eyes sparkled with mischief. "Don't tell no one I said this, but I sometimes wear Berg's trousers when we're working the fields."

Adrian warmed to the woman instantly. She hadn't been lonely in the time she'd been with Rome and the children. But she realized now she'd missed having another female to talk to. If she had to live in this place and time permanently she would want someone like Ella for her neighbor and her friend.

"And I don't mind you knowing, he rather likes it when I do. I suspect Rome hasn't made any objections to your garb, either."

Chuckling, Adrian shook her head. "No, now that you mention it, he hasn't." Adrian hadn't given a thought to her choice of clothing since that first day. She'd opted for comfort then, choosing the tops and skirts she'd wear. But as she recalled, Rome had never offered a word of complaint.

"Shall we set up a table for the menfolk?" Ella pushed to her feet and juggled Eli on her hip.

Adrian nodded, following the woman to the back of the wagon parked in the yard. Beneath checked cloths and several cotton towels were bowls of vegetables, pies of several varieties, jars of corn relish and tomatoes, and even a basket of perfectly fried chicken. Berg hadn't been joking when he'd said Ella had made a feast.

Adrian's mouth watered at the sights and smells that greeted her as they unloaded the wagon. The men arrived to carry the table out the back door and set it up beneath a shade tree.

The children rushed forward, eyes wide, excited at the assortment of treats spread out. Soon they were all seated on blankets on the ground, their plates full and laughter ringing through the branches overhead.

The sun set and the children began to drift off

to sleep one by one beneath the stars. Berg brought out a mouth harp and played a lively tune. Rome tapped his toe to the music and Adrian and Ella clapped their hands.

Then the older Hanson handed the instrument to his number-one son, Albert. The boy played a slow, sweet melody and Berg and Ella danced to the soft notes.

"Adrian?"

Looking up, she saw Rome standing beside her, his hand held out. She gently removed Eli's head from her lap and settled the sleeping baby on the blanket.

She took Rome's hand and he helped her to her feet. They walked out into the open and he carefully drew her into his arms. She loved the feel of his hand on her waist, the strong fingers warm and assuring. He gripped her other hand and drew it close to his chest. She could feel his heart beating. Closing her eyes, she laid her head against his shoulder and swayed with the movement of his body.

How long they danced together, barely moving, she didn't know. It could have been hours. It seemed like minutes. She never wanted him to release her.

But Albert soon tired and he lay down on the blanket and fell asleep, the harp still in his hand.

Berg and Ella called out quiet good-nights and made their way, arm in arm, to the back of the wagon.

"We should get the children in the house," Adrian whispered.

She collected Eli and he carried Mimi. Toby woke up and begged to be allowed to sleep outdoors with the Hanson children, so Rome left him on the blanket.

"Will they be all right?" Adrian asked, biting her lip as she glanced back at the sprawled bodies littering the yard.

"They'll be fine. Berg will hear the slightest noise and I'll be in the barn if anything comes up."

Bending to place Eli on his bed, Adrian looked up. "The barn?"

Rome tucked Mimi's cover around her and met Adrian's curious glance. Even in the dimly lit room she could see the flush covering his cheeks.

"I think it'd be best if Berg and Ella think I've been staying out there."

Thinking it an unnecessary precaution, Adrian nevertheless nodded. She suspected Ella knew Rome had been sleeping in the house. And Adrian felt certain the woman thought nothing untoward about it. But she could understand Rome's discomfort. After assuring themselves the children were asleep, they walked back into the kitchen.

"I really like your neighbors," she told him.

"Yeah, the Hansons are good people. Ella helped me out quite a bit with food and such after Lorraine died. Of course, she had her own family to look after and they're a handful."

"Yes, I noticed. I don't know how she manages to take care of them all."

"Oh, I don't know. You've taken on three small children and you've managed all right."

His praise suffused her with a warm glow of pride. She ducked her head shyly. "Yeah, I guess I haven't done too bad at that."

"You've been wonderful, Adrian," he told her, taking her by the shoulders. He leaned down and pressed a tender kiss on her lips. When he lifted his head she could see the spark of arousal in his eyes. "I really enjoyed myself today for the first time in a long time. Thank you."

She smiled her pleasure and reached up, giving him a soft kiss on his cheek. "I had a good time, too."

Clearing his throat, he stepped back. "Well, good night."

"Good night, Rome."

He turned and walked to the back door, glancing once over his shoulder. He held her gaze for a long moment, then left the house. Adrian touched her lips and felt the heat of his kiss lingering there.

The Hansons pulled out of the yard early the next morning. The children shouted to one another as they drove away. Ella waved, looking back several times as Adrian and Rome stood in the narrow, dirt road.

It had been a good visit, but it had left Adrian unsettled. Ella's comment that morning had gotten her thinking, and her thoughts continued to swirl in a storm of indecision.

Rome's neighbor asked Adrian if she planned to stay with the Walkers permanently.

"Permanently?"

"I thought, that is, you an' Rome seem . . . close."

Yes, they did seem to be getting closer with each day. She'd been unable to offer Ella a response and the woman had apologized for imposing, obviously embarrassed at Adrian's reaction.

Again Adrian felt the sting of guilt. What right did she have to ingratiate herself into this family when she didn't plan to stay?

Rome had gotten his crop into the ground. He could make do without her now. She should think about leaving. It was time to stop running from the problems she'd left behind in her world. Time to begin her search for a way home. The first step of her journey would be the hardest. She'd have to go into town and confront a very different Newhope.

And even though the thought filled her with numbing panic and the pain of loss associated with leaving Rome and the children, Adrian knew the time had come.

Chapter Sixteen

Staring out at the rain, Adrian wondered how their joy could have turned to despair so quickly. It had only been two days since they celebrated the end of the planting with the Hansons.

Now, after 36 hours of nearly nonstop rain, they were in danger of losing the whole crop. Already some of the low-lying acreage had flooded, the precious seeds washed away in the torrent.

"More coffee?"

Turning away from the disheartening sight, she accepted the cup Rome held out. He looked so tired. Every hour he went into the sodden fields to assess the damage. With each inch of rain she knew his anxiety increased tenfold.

She'd never questioned him about his finances before. She hadn't felt she had the right. And maybe she still didn't. But somehow she had to try to help ease his burden. The tendency had become second nature to her in the past weeks.

Looking at his teal eyes, their joy doused now, she felt her heart wrench. "Isn't there anything we can do?"

He just shook his head. "No one could have predicted this." Raking his hand through his hair he scanned the skies, searching for a break in the clouds.

"Are you—that is, how will you stand if the crop is lost?"

He shrugged. "I might be able to get more seed: I still have enough money for that. But it'll be a late crop. Probably won't do as well."

"The money you spent on the furniture and accessories . . . ?"

Quickly he shook his head, reaching out to lay his hand on her shoulder. "Won't matter one way or the other. As farms go, ours is better than some. But most farms, and farmers, are cash poor and land rich. I'm no exception."

He set his coffee aside and led her to the table. "I have two hundred and sixty acres. We can generally produce whatever we need to survive, so what money I do make, about four or five hundred dollars a year, goes for staples, the pork Digger provides, clothing, and occasional extras. Sometimes we have to replace equipment, but not very often. As long as I can get a crop, at least enough to feed us all and bring in enough for taxes, we're not in danger of losing the place. Things'll be tight, but we'll be all right."

He placed his hand over hers and she looked up. Some of the disappointment had gone from his eyes and a small smile tipped his mouth.

"If you hadn't shown up when you did, it'd be a different story. Without at least a partial crop we wouldn't have enough to exist on. We won't go hungry, at least, thanks to you."

She swallowed hard and shook her head. "I didn't do anything, really. I just happened to be in the wrong place at the right time."

"Yes, I've figured that out."

She quirked a brow in question and he grinned. "I didn't believe you when you said you were lost. There didn't seem to be any reason for your presence here except in response to my advertisement. I assumed, wrongly it seems, that you changed your mind at the last minute and didn't want the position. But I've come to realize I was wrong."

"How?"

His eyes narrowed and he studied her closely. "You were horrified at the thought of being a wife and mother. As though you'd never considered the possibility. I thought it was the children who'd frightened you, but it wasn't."

"No," she admitted, remembering her first re-action to Rome and his family. She'd thought they were poor beyond anything she'd ever seen. But in truth, they were no better or worse than any other farmer in their time.

"You really were lost."

"Yes."

He watched her face tense, saw her eyes dart away.

Tipping her chin up with his finger, he met her anxious gaze. "I think I began to realize that when you came back that evening. I'd never seen such fear or panic in another person's eyes before. I didn't know where you were going or where you'd been, but it looked as though you suddenly needed us as much as we needed you."

"Yes," she whispered, the feel of his strong fingers against her jaw reassuring. She longed to lay her cheek in his palm and close her eyes, drinking in his warmth, his sanctuary.

"You must know I've been wondering about your appearance here ever since. Not one to look askance at a blessing, I didn't dare ques-tion you deeper. But your clothes, your confu-sion, the way you fled. I'm still burning, Adrian," he said, his fingers gently tracing her cheek. His eyes turned a deep turquoise; his lids lowered heavily. Then he cleared his throat and broke the spell which held them. "I'm burning to know all the answers."

Her eyes widened and she leaned back, turning her face away from him. She saw the flash of disappointment in his eyes, but she forced herself to ignore his magnetic pull. She could not tell him what he wanted to know. Ever. And she had been a fool to let things go so far. Of course he would want to know more about her the closer they became. God, she'd been crazy to let her guard down, even for a minute.

Rising, she went back to the window. Her heart slammed against her ribs and she gasped, throwing her hands up against the imperfect glass.

"Oh, Rome," she cried. "No."

He rushed to the window and she heard him muffle a curse. More than an inch of water now covered the entire field. The ground had absorbed all it could, and yet the rain showed no sign of letting up. A hot sting of emotion clogged her throat, and tears rushed to her eyes.

"It's not fair," she cried. "We worked so hard. And now it's all gone."

His arms came around her and together they watched the torrent continue mercilessly. She huddled in his embrace, feeling more dejected than she ever had in her life. All his hard work, all the sweat and effort was being washed away before her eyes.

"Shhh," he soothed. "It'll be all right. I told you, we'll be fine."

But Adrian could hear the worry in his tone. He had promised to take her to town at the end of the month when he went in for supplies. If he held to his vow, and she had no doubt he would, he'd be right back where he started. No crop, no one to mind the children. And with time running out now the situation was even more critical. How could she leave them?

How could she not? She didn't belong here. She had to get home somehow. And she knew that meant going to town. Staying here, on the farm with Rome and the children, she knew she would never find her way back to her time.

Savoring the tender strength of his embrace, she battled her feelings. She cared for Rome and the children now. She couldn't leave them knowing they had no one to help them. At the same time she was truly frightened, fearful of being stuck in this time forever.

Slowly she became aware of a change in his embrace. His arms tightened; his body stiffened. The hands which had soothed her now stroked softly. Shivers of response feathered along her spine. The movement of his fingers seemed to tug at something in her stomach, causing it to tighten and clench.

Lifting her head she caught him studying her profile. She perused the dark-skinned face, the sun-kissed hair which always seemed in need of a trim. Her fingers reached out and wove through the unruly curls lying boyishly against his neck.

"What will you do if I leave you?" she asked,

desperate to know he would be all right, needing the comfort of his assurances.

"It'll be hard, but we'll manage," he said, the
half-truth of his statement evident in the reflec-
tive turquoise pools.

She tried to draw away, but he clasped her to
him. Her breasts crushed against his chest, he
braced her. "Don't turn away. Look at me." She
did as he bid and he smiled. "We'll miss you,
Adrian. But we'll make it. You have to do whatever you have to do. I accepted that your presence here might be temporary. I won't lie to
you: I prayed for more time. But I won't hold
you here with words or emotions."

Again tears sprang to her eyes. He smiled and
touched a fingertip to the drop in the corner of
her eye. "Don't cry," he said. "I've come to de-
pend on your smile."

She offered him a weak attempt and he nodded. "That's it."

"I'm not going to go," she told him, surprising
herself as much as Rome. He blinked, a wild
glint of excitement flaming to life in his hot
glance.

She held up her hand. "Not until you can get
another crop in the ground. Not until I know
everything will be all right after I'm gone."

The illumination dimmed, but didn't completely dissipate. He nodded. "I'm glad," he said,
lowering his head for a sweet kiss.

Their lips met and lingered, softly exploring,

gently seeking. It had been so long since Adrian had felt such pleasure, such heat. She drew closer; his hold tightened. The fierceness of his hug told her he'd missed the feel of another soul in tune with his, too.

"Did you mean it?" he whispered, drawing back a fraction, just enough to speak softly against her lips. "You'll stay longer?"

She nodded, and his mouth closed over hers once more. He bent, swept her into his arms, and carried her into her bedroom. Lowering her gently to the bed, he followed her down, never releasing her from his kiss.

They tugged and rolled, fingers fumbling with buttons and ties. The corset cover she wore parted down the front, exposing her breasts. He swooped to kiss one rose-tipped nipple and she arched in response.

It had been too long, much too long for either of them to go slowly. Their clothes fell away beneath trembling hands. Soon they lay naked atop the coverlet.

Rome kissed her once more, roughly and desperately. He lifted his head and let his gaze sweep down her body. Adrian felt no shame. She took the opportunity to discover the muscles and planes of his form.

Fingertips touched, soothed, searched. Palms lingered and examined, as though memorizing the shape and feel of skin and sinew.

Adrian was filled with wanting. She grasped

his buttocks and dug her nails lightly into the flesh. Rome groaned, fitting his hands over her breasts, lifting and molding them in his grasp like a sculptor.

Drawing one taut, aroused peak into his mouth, he slid his hand down between their sweat-damp bodies. He found the site of her burgeoning desire and let his fingers delve and caress her to unbearable heights.

Crying out with fulfillment, she wrapped one leg behind his knee and strained to get closer. He answered her need with a swift, sure thrust.

"Rome," she moaned. "Oh, Rome, yes."

He repeated the movement and she cried out again. Each time she called his name, Rome's passion soared. She was gasping and making little mewing sounds between thrusts, and the sound of her pleasure drove him mad with desire. He clutched her waist, holding her in place, and plunged into her deeper and harder.

She responded by gripping his shoulders as though holding on for dear life. Again, her actions left him crazed with flames of fervor. He couldn't get enough. He wanted to touch every inch, stroke every curve.

His hands found her waist again and he looked down into her eyes. Their gazes locked as their bodies moved in rhythm to their racing heartbeats.

Adrian felt the building tension grip her core and spread out. She tried to hold his stare, but as her body spun in a whirlpool of ecstasy, she could only throw her head back, squeeze her eyes shut, and give in to the uncontrollable spasms rocking her.

Rome's hands came up and he gently palmed her cheeks, forcing her gaze back to his. As he allowed himself release, he held her stare. The moment bound them together, locked them in shared harmony.

She cupped his face and together they rode the flood tide of sensation to complete fulfillment.

As their hearts slowed to normal and the salty sweat cooled on their bodies, Rome rested above her. But before his weight could grow too heavy, he slowly withdrew and then, propping himself on his elbows, entered her once more.

Adrian could feel the evidence of his unsated desire growing within her again. This time he went slowly, drawing out each movement until she bit his shoulder to keep from crying out her sweet agony.

The nip of her teeth inflamed his ardor and Rome struggled to keep the pace slow. He continued to hold back until she raked her fingernails down his back and over his buttocks once more, sending him into a tailspin and setting off an explosion of passion.

They came together again, sweeter, slower this time. She answered the call of his body with a shuddering response and he let go, driving into her deeper than ever before. She opened her mouth and he swallowed her cries with a tender kiss.

Adrian could barely breathe. Spots danced before her eyes and she feared she might faint. Why had she never known it could be like that? She clutched Rome's shoulders and released a ragged sigh.

Was it because for the first time in her life she was truly in love? She'd already admitted she loved Rome. There could no longer be any doubt of that.

And it was true she'd never felt this way about a man before, not even her husband. Especially not Tate, she thought, once more wishing they'd never ruined their friendship with marriage.

This was the way it was supposed to be, she thought. Sex was nice, and could be a needed release. But it could never compare to making love.

Rome moved to her side and drew her body into the curve of his, fitting them together like two spoons. She snuggled closer, settling her bottom against his lap. He groaned and his hand cupped her breast.

She could feel his hot breath fanning the strands of hair over her ear. His heart slowed to normal, tapping a staccato rhythm against her spine.

This was love, she acknowledged with a mixture of joy and pain. She'd finally found the elusive feeling. Only to have it elude her again?

She couldn't stay here.

Could she?

Despite the way she felt in his arms, she didn't belong with Rome.

Did she?

Could this bizarre voyage through time be fate? She'd discarded that notion earlier because of the unresolved problems she'd left behind in her world. But the possibility came back to haunt her now. Had someone, somewhere, in their infinite wisdom sent her here, knowing she belonged with Rome? Was such a thing even possible?

Or was she rationalizing because she knew, deep in her heart, that she never wanted to leave him now?

Chapter Seventeen

The sun shone down strong and relentlessly. Moisture from the sodden fields hung in the air like a blanket. Adrian followed along beside Rome as he checked each freshly turned row for damage.

"How bad is it?" she asked, biting her lip as he bent to examine the ground.

He rose, brushed the dirt from his hands on his coveralls, and plowed his fingers through his hair, staring out across the horizon. "It could have been worse. We've lost about half the crop in all."

She gazed out over the acreage, some places still puddled from the rain. "Half," she whispered, turning to him. He reached for her and she went into his embrace. "I can't believe it."

Their night of passion amid the rumble of thunder and flash of lightning had brought them a closeness that belied their short association. Adrian let the strength of his arms comfort her as they surveyed the damage.

"I'll have to go into town Saturday for supplies. I'll pick up more seed then." He saw her worried frown and gently took her by the shoulders, turning her to face him. "We can replant what was lost." He looked at the flooded furrows. "It could've been a lot worse."

She offered him a small smile and he pressed a quick kiss against her lips. The touch brought a rush of sensations, remembered feelings from the exquisite hours of love they'd shared.

His eyes darkened and she knew he was fighting the urge to take her in his arms and repeat the slow, drugging process.

"We'd better wake the children," he said, letting his hand slide down her arm until he clasped her fingers in his. "There's a lot to be done today."

She kept her hand in his as they walked slowly back toward the cabin. The companionable silence they shared seemed natural somehow. Adrian felt as though they'd experienced a lifetime together, instead of one night.

Again her thoughts came back to taunt her. Had she been sent here to find Rome? Was she meant to stay with him? How could she?

She studied his profile, so strong and defined.

236

God, she loved him. Her heart ached at the sight of his clean-shaven jaw and the pale lines fanning out from the corners of his eyes. She reached up and took his arm in her hands, reveling at the feel of his corded muscles through the tight sleeve of his shirt.

"What do you say we wait a little while longer before we wake the kids?" she said, offering a silent message with her eyes.

A brief flash of surprise crossed his face and he gazed down at her. After a moment a wicked smile tipped his lips. "What do you have in mind?"

"A nice quiet place somewhere, alone. Before we have to start the day."

"The children are getting spoiled since you took over the morning chores. They sleep later and later every day."

"One more won't hurt, then, will it?" She offered him a suggestive smile and he grinned in return.

"Nope, I reckon not." With a swift motion, he bent at the waist and hefted her into his arms.

Adrian laughed as he juggled her in his embrace, pretending to lose his grip only to catch her closer to his chest.

"Ah, a quiet place. Let me see." He twirled her in a circle, pretending to search for just the right spot. Adrian laughed and clutched his neck tighter.

Finally he strode toward the barn, and Adrian

waved her feet in the air. She felt so free, so good. On what might have been the worst day of her stay here, they were both still able to find happiness.

Dear Lord, this had to be right. It felt too good to be wrong.

He pushed open the barn door with his foot and Adrian pressed herself closer to his chest. He responded with another kiss, this one hot and long as he continued toward the ladder leading to the loft. He set her at the bottom of the ladder and gave her bottom a light swat.

"You go on up. I'll get a clean blanket from the tack room."

She scrambled up the rungs and reclined on her back against a pile of hay next to the open window. She could see the house from her vantage point and knew they'd be able to hear the children if they should wake up and come outside.

Rome's head appeared over the floor of the loft and he grinned. Tossing the blanket to her, he continued to stand on the ladder as he removed her shoes and socks. Lifting her ankle, he placed tiny trailing kisses along the arch of her foot.

Her toes curled, and heat spread up her legs. His lips found the back of her knee and desire swept her. Instead of sating the longing she'd felt, their night together had only whetted her appetite for his touch.

"Have I told you how much I like the way you tie your skirt up that way?" he asked, climbing into the loft to kneel over her.

"You do?" she murmured, straining to hear his words over the roar of her heart pounding in her ears.

"Yep. I love watching you walk, the fabric swirling around your bare calves."

"Ummm."

His lips continued to feather lightly up her legs and over her thighs. His hands slid along her legs, opening them to his seeking, searching mouth.

Adrian couldn't resist his urging. Through the thin silk of her underwear she felt the heat of his breath on the most sensitive part of her. His fingers grasped the edges of her panties and he lowered them.

"I'm uncommonly fond of these drawers you wear, too. What did you call them last night?"

"Bikini panties."

"Oh, yeah. Panties. Ummm. Nice." The scrap of silk and lace vanished beneath his ministrations. His head dipped and Adrian sucked in a raw breath as he laved her intimately with his tongue.

She'd never felt anything so wonderful in her life, and she gripped his shoulders frantically as she opened more fully to him. Her head spun and blasts of white heat whipped through her.

She cried out his name and her nails dug into

his flesh through the fabric of his shirt. Her pulse pounded; her muscles trembled. She even imagined she could hear bells ringing.

The pinnacle of sensation raged through her. Suddenly her nerves locked in spasms of fulfillment. Bright points of light danced before her eyes as she cried out her pleasure.

Her senses slowly drifted into focus once more, and again she heard the unmistakable ring of bells.

The sound grew louder, and despite her attempts to ignore it her mind sent a warning through her. Lifting her head, she squinted up at the roof of the barn. It wasn't just her reaction to Rome. She *did* hear bells.

"Rome?"

Fighting her frustration and the passion still rocketing through her, she called his name again and shook his shoulder. When he still didn't respond she grasped his head and lifted him away.

"Rome. I hear bells."

His dazed expression finally cleared and he gazed up at her. Tipping his head to one side, he listened for a moment. Then his eyes shot wide and he scrambled over her.

She felt the rush of desire surge to life once more as his weight settled atop her, his denim-clad thigh rubbing erotically against the exposed petals of her womanhood. Then, with a disappointed sigh, she realized he was only trying to get a look out the window.

"That isn't bells, Adrian, it's traces. Quick, fix yourself," he said, his voice a harsh whisper. "Someone's coming."

"Here? Who?"

She fumbled through the hay, searching for her abandoned underwear. They were nowhere to be found and she rolled to her hands and knees and crawled frantically around in circles.

"I don't know. I can't see them clearly from up here. But I'm sure it isn't anyone I know."

Finally successful in her search, she rose to her feet and, hopping on one foot at a time, hastily donned the panties.

"Oh," she cried, pulling a stiff twig of hay from the silk.

Rome grabbed the hay, tucked it into his teeth, and grinned. "Come on, darlin'," he teased, preceding her down the ladder.

They left the barn just as the wagon pulled to a stop in front of the house. A woman, outfitted in a modest black skirt and fitted traveling jacket, slowly closed her matching parasol and stepped down from the wagon with the help of the driver.

Rome recognized the man from town and called a greeting. Wilbur, as Rome called him, nodded a curt response but ducked his head as though unwilling to meet Rome's eyes as he hefted a trunk from the back of the conveyance and deposited it beside the woman.

The elegant blonde opened her reticule, drew out some coins, and paid the man before turning to watch Adrian and Rome approach from the side of the yard.

Adrian studied the shining blond hair, fashioned into a loose topknot on her head. Her thin face was milk-white and unblemished. The eyes narrowed further as Adrian and Rome drew near.

"Yes, can I help you?" Rome asked, removing the hay from his lips and tossing it aside.

The woman smoothed the folds of her skirt as the driver climbed back into his rig, tipped his hat, and hastily drove away.

Adrian shared a look of bafflement with Rome and he shrugged his shoulders.

"Actually," the woman said, her voice warm with greeting, "I've come a great distance to help you, Rome. I know it's been nine years, but I can't believe you don't remember me."

Her eyes—blue, Adrian saw now—studied Adrian with open curiosity. They swept the corset cover, the shortened skirt, and fell to her tennis shoes with a look of shock and dismay.

Rome met Adrian's raised eyebrows and shrugged again, taking a tentative step forward. He perused the woman standing expectantly in front of his home, the sharp tip of her parasol twirling in the dirt at her feet.

"I'm sorry," he said, shaking his head. "Do I know you?"

"I should hope so," she blustered, her gloved hand going to her chest in a gesture of consternation. "You invited me here."

When no acknowledgment was forthcoming, she reached into her reticule and drew out a folded sheet of paper. Opening it, she held it out before him. "You asked me to be your wife," she breathed, cutting a pointed look at Adrian.

Adrian gasped, her hand flying to her lips. She choked back the stunned words that flew to mind and turned to Rome.

The look on his face told her he was riffling his memory for a clue to the woman's identity. He reached out slowly and took the page waving before his eyes.

As he quickly scanned the writing, Adrian saw the color drain from his face. His shock and confusion were instantly replaced with stark dismay. She saw recognition dawn and fear pooled in her stomach. Cold foreboding chased away the last traces of their heated embrace.

"Rome?"

Instead of answering, he faced the blonde. "I don't understand. I wrote this nearly a year ago. I never received a response."

She waved her hand casually. "Oh, well, I wrote you to say it would take a while to settle my affairs. Oh, my, don't tell me the letter was lost in the post. No wonder you look so surprised. But of course you had to know I wouldn't refuse such a heartfelt plea."

His eyes narrowed, but he blinked away his shock and nodded. "I see," he said, his voice hoarse and frazzled.

Adrian shifted and he met her dull gaze. "Adrian, I'd like you to meet Winifred Norton. My sister-in-law."

"Your sister-in-law?"

Adrian heard her own thought spoken aloud by the beautiful woman in black. She blinked and focused on the pouty pink lips as they parted in surprise and then pursed in displeasure.

"According to that letter I'm more than your sister-in-law, Rome. I'm your fiancee."

"But, Winifred—I mean—it has been a year."

"As I said in my letter, which I realize now you didn't receive, I simply needed time to get organized before rushing to your aid."

Rome seemed unable to comprehend what was going on. Shock dilated his pupils, making his stare look farcical.

In her dazed confusion Adrian watched him, thinking he looked like a dashboard dog with his vacant stare.

"Rome?"

He snapped out of the dumbfounded spell and placed his arm possessively around her shoulders in a show of support. Adrian wondered if he were reassuring her or himself.

"Winifred, I had no way of knowing you were coming. My situation has changed."

Adrian could see Winifred's lips tighten. The dim blue eyes widened with alarm. "But you invited me, Rome Walker," she gasped. "Are you telling me you're already married? That I've come all this way and now I'm not welcome?"

She had them there, Adrian thought. And Rome could never throw the woman into the street. He had asked her to come, and besides, she was family.

She looked up and saw the same thoughts registered in his eyes. He offered her an apologetic shrug.

"I'm sorry," he said, taking a step toward his sister-in-law. "I didn't mean to be rude. I'm just so surprised. Of course you're welcome here."

Winifred tugged her gloves off, not meeting Rome's stare for a long minute. Then she looked up and the apprehension had magically disappeared from her face. She smiled and Adrian thought again how beautiful she was.

Still, something in her cool eyes made Adrian suspect at least a measure of her apparent fear had been feigned.

"Wonderful," Winifred said, stepping forward and taking his arm. "I just can't wait to see those darling children and shower them with all the love I have in my heart for Lorraine's precious babies. Just the way my poor, beloved sister would have wanted me to."

Chapter Eighteen

Winifred's words hung between them like a challenge. Adrian could see Rome didn't know what to say.

What could he say? He'd asked the woman to leave her life in the city and travel a great distance to become his wife.

At the same time, Rome couldn't have anticipated her intentions. Winifred must have known he couldn't wait for her indefinitely. Why had she taken nearly a year to show up? And what would her appearance mean to Adrian and Rome now?

The fact was, she was here now and they couldn't continue to stand in the yard silently surveying one another. Adrian felt some sort of action needed to be taken. Swallowing her apprehension, and the fear that rose in her at Winifred's arrival, she forced a smile.

"Won't you come inside, Winifred?"

Rome seemed to snap out of his stunned disbelief. "Yes, yes, of course. Come in."

"Thank you," she said, releasing her breath on a sigh. The look she gave Adrian was full of questions. Obviously she didn't miss Rome's deference to Adrian. Considering Winifred's reason for coming here, Adrian couldn't blame her for being curious.

However, perhaps because of her own tenuous position, Winifred didn't ask uncomfortable questions, for which Adrian was glad.

"Where are the children?" she asked, as she passed Adrian and proceeded into the house.

"They're still sleeping," Rome answered.

Winifred stopped in the doorway and turned back to face the bewildered pair behind her. "Asleep? At this hour of the morning? Well, I can see I've arrived just in the nick of time. Lorraine would never have tolerated such slugabeds."

She swept regally into the small front room and stopped short. Her small eyes widened and she gasped as she scanned the place.

"Oh, my!" she exclaimed, clutching her chest. "No wonder you were in such a state of despair. Look at this place."

Adrian felt a flush cover her cheeks and she lowered her head.

Rome saw her shame and anger flooded him. He took a step toward Winifred. "Adrian has been working on the house ever since her arrival. She's really done a wonderful job of fixing the place up."

His sister-in-law quirked a brow at Adrian and he could see the inquiry. He knew she must be interested in Adrian's presence, but she continued to hold back her questions.

"Well, I'm certain you did the best you could," she hurriedly added, forcing a smile for Adrian.

Adrian noticed the strange lack of warmth in her eyes despite the contrite expression and she wondered if Winifred had intended to insult her. She dismissed the uncharitable thought, passing it off as another example of her weak self-confidence.

"No matter," Winifred said. "I'll have everything back to normal in no time."

At Winifred's words Adrian's head snapped up and Rome saw the fire in her gaze. He could see she'd been hurt by Winifred's unthinking remark and he squeezed her hand to offer her a silent show of support.

Winifred had taken him by surprise with her unexpected appearance. But now he'd recovered from the shock of finding he had a fiancée he'd known nothing about. She was Lorraine's sister and he couldn't be outright rude to her. But there was no way he'd ever marry her. Not now, not when he loved Adrian so much. He would have to tell Winifred his decision as soon as possible.

But how? He did ask her to come, even if it was in a moment of weakness. He'd been drinking and thinking of their impossible situation when he'd received a brief letter from Winifred responding to his telegram informing her of Lorraine's death. Although he'd never thought the two women very close, she'd sounded truly pained at the news of her sister's death and she'd offered her help should he ever need it.

Still in his cups, he'd written back and made his offer. He couldn't even remember the exact wording of that long-ago missive now. Or why he'd thought she would take him up on it. He still couldn't believe she had.

Almost immediately he'd realized his mistake and he'd been truly thankful when she didn't respond. But apparently she had. Here she was now, prepared to marry him and raise her sister's motherless children.

However, next to Adrian the idea of kissing Winifred's lips left him cold. Her thin, lithe body held no appeal for him, especially when he thought of Adrian's curves.

He couldn't help comparing this woman to the memory of his wife. Lorraine had been thin, in a fragile sort of way. But she'd been loving and generous. Winifred resembled his wife, with the same blond hair and blue eyes, but something seemed amiss. Her smiles seemed forced, her pleasantness exaggerated.

Rome looked at the two women now standing in his home. If Winifred suffered in comparison to Lorraine, she all but vanished into oblivion next to the radiant glow Adrian exuded. Adrian's wild red hair caught sparks of fire from the light, and her vivid brown eyes shone with energy. She looked so appealing in the camisole top and altered skirt, so alluring. Winifred's stylish outfit mirrored her precise manner and befitted her personality.

He didn't know how, but he would have to tell Winifred her trip had been in vain. He would never be able to abide by the decision he'd made nearly a year ago in his grief and despair following Lorraine's death. He would never marry her sister.

"Well," the object of his thoughts queried, "aren't you going to wake my niece and nephews so we might become acquainted?"

"I'll put coffee on," Adrian said, scooting across the room to the back door. She gave Rome a reassuring smile, pulled the door open, and hurried outside.

"Yes, of course. Please have a seat."

He looked around as she did, seeing only the dining table with the benches, and the two rocking chairs flanking the fireplace. She paused, then started for one of the chairs. Rome watched her settle into Adrian's chair and he fought the pain he felt seeing her in it.

He'd come to think of their evenings as cherished times. He and Adrian would sit in the rockers and talk, or he'd read and she'd do mending. Just the memory could warm him. Seeing Winifred in Adrian's place sent a cold arrow through his chest. She could never take Adrian's place, either in his home or in his heart.

He left his sister-in-law sitting in the rocker and went to wake the children. With Mimi's help he dressed the boys in their nicest clothes. His daughter, informed of their aunt's arrival, donned a soft blue bibbed dress. The garment was a bit snug, and too short, having been made for her over a year ago. But it was her nicest dress and she insisted on wearing it to look her best.

"How long will Aunt Winifred be visiting?" she asked.

Rome's face tightened and he shot a glance toward the curtained doorway leading to the main room. "I don't know for sure," he said. "We'll just have to wait and see."

He offered Mimi a small hint of a smile, but he couldn't help wondering just how long Winifred would be with them. How would he tell her she was no longer needed here? He had no desire to hurt the woman. She was family, but more than that she'd come a great distance to help him.

Still, he couldn't help resenting her appearance in their lives at this particular moment in time. In all honesty he knew it was because he wouldn't have a moment alone with Adrian as long as his sister-in-law was in residence. And already his desire for Adrian threatened to consume him.

He took Mimi and Toby by the hand and lifted Eli onto his hip. Together they went through the curtained doorway to the main room where Winifred waited. He saw her eyes narrow at the children, her nostrils flare, and for a moment he thought she was going to say something insulting. He felt his spine grow rigid.

Then she pushed out of the chair, came forward, and forced her lips into the semblance of a smile.

"Oh, my darlings," she cooed, kneeling to offer Mimi and Toby a hug. The children looked to Rome and he nodded once. She took their stiff little bodies into her embrace and squeezed them once before releasing them. Without another word or gesture she stood and held out her arms for the baby.

Rome handed Eli over, and he saw her settle the infant expertly in her arms.

"What beautiful children," she said, her compliment sounding somewhat strained. "But the poor darlings look like street urchins. When was the last time you had a new dress, sweetheart?" she asked Mimi.

Rome saw Mimi's glance fall to the skirt of her dress and she clutched it in one small fist. His mouth tightened. "Not since their mother died, Winifred. There has been no one to sew for them."

"Oh, my. The poor little things. But what about your, um, guest?" Her eyes widened in innocence but he could see the question there. She was waiting for him to reveal Adrian's position.

Rome thought of how Adrian had taught herself to sew a little. She'd improved her mending so much she'd just last night mentioned trying to make some new things for the children. He'd agreed to pick up all the things she'd need when they went to town. But he couldn't explain that to Winifred. She would wonder, as he did, how Adrian had managed to reach maturity without being taught something as simple as stitchery.

He was saved from making a reply when the back door opened and Adrian came in carrying the coffeepot. She set it on the table and collected three cups from the shelf.

She motioned Winifred toward the table. "You must be exhausted after your trip. Did you travel out here in the dark?"

Adrian could have sworn she saw a faint blush rise on the woman's cheeks before she quickly answered.

"Oh, indeed," Winifred said. "That man, Wilbur somebody, wanted me to wait until this afternoon. But I couldn't wait another minute to get here and hug these precious babies." A handkerchief magically appeared from the cuff of her blouse and she dabbed her eyes. "If only I could have been here for poor Lorraine."

Adrian shifted uncomfortably. She flushed, embarrassed to be a witness to the tender scene. She couldn't bear to look at Rome, to witness the effect Winifred's words had on him.

"I was about to go and get breakfast when you arrived," Rome said stiffly. "If you'd like to sit and have a cup of coffee you can get better acquainted. . . ."

"Nonsense. I didn't come here to burden you further. Just point me in the direction of the kitchen. I'll have a fitting breakfast prepared in no time."

"Don't you want to rest a bit first, Winifred?"

"I told you, I came all this way to help you raise my dear sister's motherless children. And that is exactly what I plan to do. I didn't come here to be waited on by—by anyone," she finished, her eyes darting toward Adrian.

Her voice was syrupy sweet, without a hint of censure. But Adrian noticed the sideways glance Winifred cut in her direction. Still, no one offered any explanation for Adrian's presence in Rome's home, and Winifred didn't press the matter.

When no one moved to direct her, Winifred only smiled and raised one perfectly arched eyebrow. "The kitchen?"

Adrian was the first to snap out of the dazed hold Winifred seemed to have thrown over the group. "Certainly," she said, setting aside the dishcloth she'd twisted mercilessly in her nervous grip. "I'll show you where it is."

The woman gathered up her skirts and smiled engagingly at Rome as she went out the back door.

Rome watched them go, thankful to at last be out of the woman's presence for a minute. She unnerved him with her honeyed smiles and willingness to help. She seemed determined to ingratiate herself into the household, despite the fact he no longer needed her assistance.

And every minute she stayed here would make it that much harder when he told her his offer no longer stood.

Adrian came back into the cabin then, a look of bemusement on her face. Mimi ran to her side and grasped her hand. Rome thought he'd like to do the same.

"Well," Adrian said breathlessly. "That was quite a shock."

"Why is Aunt Winifred cooking breakfast, Adrian?" Mimi asked, looking up into Adrian's timorous gaze. "She's a guest, isn't she?"

Adrian didn't know what to say. How could she answer the child? Was Winifred a guest? Or was she now the woman of the house? And where did that leave Adrian? She looked to Rome.

"Yes, of course she's a guest," Rome hastened to assure them all. "She's just here to get to know you children." He continued speaking to Mimi but he never took his eyes off Adrian.

She nodded and offered him a small smile, realizing he needed reassurance as much as she did in that moment.

Her eyes swept the small house she'd come to think of as home and her chest tightened around her racing heart. If only she had been in a position to accept Rome's proposal when she first arrived. If she were his wife, there would have been no doubt of her place in his home. But she couldn't marry him then, any more than she could now.

Marriage was the one failure she'd taken personally. She'd vowed never to do it again. Besides, she couldn't be sure she'd stay here in the past, and marrying Rome would have been unfair.

But now she felt a wedge being driven between her and this family she'd come to love. When had she become so possessive of them? At what point had she begun thinking of these children as her children?

She looked at Rome. She couldn't, wouldn't, imagine him married to Winifred. The pain of that thought cut through her like a saber. When had she begun to think of him as her own?

"I'd better clear my things out of the bedroom," she said, knowing somehow that she was being displaced in more than just the physical way.

"What? What are you talking about?" Rome asked, blinking away the last of his shock. "Why should you move your things out of the bedroom?"

"Winifred is going to need a place to sleep. And I can't see her sleeping on the cot by the fireplace or in the barn. I'm afraid you're going to have to move back to the barn and I'll take the cot in here."

Already he was shaking his head. "No. Absolutely not. She is the one intruding, not you. She'll just have to make do with the cot. I'm not asking you to give up the bedroom I built for you."

She smiled and stepped closer to him. "You didn't ask me. I volunteered. Besides, she was the one invited, remember? If anyone is intruding it's me, not her."

Rome grasped her arm and pulled her close to his chest. She could smell the sun-warmed scent of his cotton shirt, feel the heat of his grip on her flesh. Her heart answered the need in his eyes; her stomach fluttered with unfulfilled desire.

"I don't know why Winifred came here now, after all these months. But don't forget, Adrian, she isn't the one I want."

His words sent a frisson of pleasure along her nerves. Gooseflesh pebbled her skin. She touched his arm and tried to steady her own trembling. "For whatever reason, she's here now. You can't just toss her out."

Lifting her hand, she drew away. It was difficult to let him go knowing another woman waited close by, ready to claim him as her own. But she forced another smile. "I'll go get her room ready."

Adrian left him standing still, the children clustered around him like refugees in a storm. Indeed, they were all being buffeted by this new twist. No one knew what would come of Winifred's arrival, but Adrian was certain of one thing. The woman wouldn't just turn around and go back where she came from. She'd come all this way to marry Rome and help raise Lorraine's children. Adrian suspected she wouldn't give up her plan easily.

Chapter Nineteen

Adrian awoke the next morning to the sound of bustling activity around her. She rolled over on the cot, wondering how Rome had ever slept on the miserable thing. Or maybe it was her doubt and indecision that had kept her awake most of the night.

She looked up at Winifred, standing on a stool to remove the fabric of the makeshift curtains from the horseshoes. "What are you doing?" she asked.

"I'm removing this ridiculous parody of window dressing. I declare, I can't believe my sister had the bad taste to actually hang the things."

Sitting up on the cot, Adrian smoothed her tangled hair away from her tense face. "I hung them," she said, glaring up at the woman on her perch.

Winifred clapped a hand to her cheek. With an embarrassed flush she whispered, "Oh, my, I didn't mean anything, really. I'm terribly embarrassed. I'll leave them if you like."

"No, go ahead, take them down," Adrian said, again wondering if Winifred's comments were as innocent as she made out. "They were only temporary," she murmured.

Winifred smiled apologetically and turned back to the window, removing the last of the fabric valance.

"Well, the fabric is truly beautiful. Don't worry, I can have proper curtains stitched in no time."

Knowing it would be useless to take offense, Adrian rose and went to the table. "I'll start breakfast."

"Oh, that isn't necessary," Winifred called brightly over her shoulder. "It's been done. I woke the children and fed them over an hour ago. They're out attending their chores."

She stepped down, turned to look at Adrian, and widened her smile. Still, Adrian couldn't help but notice the lack of true warmth in Winifred's eyes. She told herself she was being ridiculously suspicious, no doubt out of petty jealousy.

"If you're hungry the remains are being kept warm on the stove outside," Winifred informed her. "And if you truly want to help out, the dishes have yet to be done."

Adrian resisted the urge to scowl at the woman's saccharine tones. Irritable and tired from her sleepless night, she went onto the back porch and pumped water into the basin to wash her face. She cleaned her teeth, straightened the rumpled camisole and skirt she'd chosen to sleep in rather than bother Winifred for the nightgown she'd forgotten to collect, and pulled on her sneakers.

She scanned the yard for Rome and the children. She could see Rome in the fields, busily trying to save what he could of the damaged plants. But the children were nowhere to be seen. She started across the yard.

When she reached Rome, he looked up and smiled. "Good morning," he said.

She felt ridiculously like blushing. His eyes perused her face as though he hadn't seen her in a while and his interest warmed her blood and sent it racing through her veins.

"Good morning. Why didn't you wake me?"

His smile died and he glanced into the rising sun, squinting. "I wasn't allowed in the house."

She'd turned to follow his gaze, but at his words her head snapped back and she stared at him. "What?"

He chuckled, though the sound held little humor. "Winifred doesn't think it's proper for me to come into the room where you're sleeping."

Adrian could tell he was repeating the woman's admonition word for word. She felt her irritation grow.

"I ate breakfast in the kitchen," he told her, poking at one soggy plant with the toe of his boot.

"I see. Why didn't *she* wake me up, then?"

He shrugged, but something in his expression told Adrian Winifred had had more to say on the matter. She blew it off, thinking it was just another example of the differences in their codes of morality. She couldn't understand Winifred's thinking any more than the woman could have understood the twentieth century if she found herself in the reverse of Adrian's position.

"Where are the children?"

His frown returned. "She put them to work cleaning out the barn." He grinned and tapped her nose. "Claims it's a real mess with all those cobwebs and hay strewn everywhere."

He was trying to lighten her mood with reminders of their stolen moments of pleasure in the loft. But the unsettled feeling Winifred had brought with her arrival continued to disturb Adrian.

"Even Eli?" she asked.

Rome nodded. "She said it's never too early to teach children responsibility." At Adrian's frown he added, "He seemed pleased to be included."

"I see." She did, only too well. Winifred had arrived with the intention of taking over the raising of the children and the running of the household, and that was exactly what she'd done. Adrian just hadn't expected her to do it in less than 24 hours.

"I should go and let you get back to work," she said.

Rome moved as though he'd stop her. "We need to talk, Adrian."

"Yes," she said. "But we can do it later, after things have settled down a bit."

She glanced toward the back porch where Winifred stood, shaking out the bedding. Adrian saw the woman watching them. She couldn't quite like Winifred, but she told herself it was just jealousy on her part. After all, the woman hadn't done anything to earn her ire, except make a few unintentionally unflattering comments. And Rome had asked Winifred to marry him, so a touch of built-in rivalry seemed natural for that reason. Not to mention the fact that Winifred seemed extremely adept at the things Adrian had struggled with since her arrival.

With a whispered good-bye, she left Rome and went to the kitchen. Pouring a cup of coffee, she sat at the table and sipped it slowly as she considered the implications of this new development.

What would Winifred's arrival mean to the

relationship she and Rome shared? Even if she hadn't arrived with the intention of marrying Rome herself, it seemed apparent Winifred wouldn't approve of Adrian and Rome living alone together.

Adrian wished she could tell Winifred she wasn't needed or wanted here. But she couldn't do that.

The woman's talents were very much in demand. And if—*when*, she corrected—when she returned to her own time, Rome would certainly need someone's help. He might even renew his offer of marriage to Winifred if Adrian were no longer in the picture.

That thought hurt, and she began to tremble. Setting aside her cup, she twisted her hands together in her lap. Should she ask Rome to take her to town? Would he understand if she told him she wanted to leave now that he had the help he needed? Would he, deep down, be glad to have Winifred's help instead of hers?

Collecting the shreds of her tattered confidence, she told herself she was being silly. Winifred had been here less than a full day. There was no reason for her to be making difficult decisions on such short notice and so little sleep.

Grasping her cup, she finished the remainder of her coffee. Hunger eluded her, so she decided to wash the dishes Winifred had left in the dry sink.

An hour later, as she finished the last of the

dishes, she heard the children coming out of the barn. She went to the door of the kitchen and waved, offering them a bright smile.

Mimi and Toby spotted her instantly and rushed toward her, their dusty noses and grimy cheeks testifying to the work they'd done.

"Adrian, you're up," Mimi shouted, throwing her arms around Adrian's waist.

"Why didn't you wake me?" she asked, ruffing Toby's hair and scooping a toddling Eli into her arms. He, too, was dirty, but he gave her a grin and she had to admit he didn't seem any worse for the experience.

"Aunt Winifred wouldn't let us. She said she could handle things by herself, and you looked like you needed the rest."

Mimi looked up at Adrian and wrinkled her nose. "You tired, Adrian?"

Adrian clamped down on her ire. The comment seemed innocuous, on the surface. She positioned Eli more comfortably on her hip and pressed her lips to his baby-fine hair. "No, Mimi," she murmured. "I'm fine."

"If she can handle everything, why'd she wake us up so early and make us clean the barn?" Mimi asked, obviously put out over being awakened at daybreak.

"She said my clothes were scraceful," Toby added. "What does that mean?"

"Disgraceful," Adrian corrected, her features tightening in dismay. "And they're not, so don't

267

worry about it. Your aunt comes from the city, that's all. They do things differently there."

"Well, I expect we'll be doing city things, too," Mimi said thoughtfully.

"Why is that?" Adrian set Eli on his feet and took the child by the hand.

" 'Cause Aunt Winifred said now she was here we'd all be dancing to a different tune. Does Aunt Winifred plan to teach us all to dance, you think, Adrian?"

Adrian didn't think that was Winifred's plan at all, but she kept silent. She had to remind herself it wasn't her place to challenge the woman. Winifred was their aunt. Adrian was just . . . well, she didn't know exactly what her position was now.

"Come on, you've worked hard this morning. What do you say we go to the creek and swim a bit?"

"Can we ask Daddy to go along?"

The frown returned to Adrian's face and she bit her lip. As much as she would love to include Rome in their fun, she didn't think Winifred would approve of their swimming together. She slowly shook her head, realizing to her dismay that she was already deferring to the other woman.

"Not this time," she said. "I'm sure he's too busy to take a break right now."

They left the kitchen and started across the yard, but before they had gone more than five feet, Winifred stepped out onto the back porch once more.

"Emily, Tobias," she called. "If you are finished cleaning out the barn, it's time to start your lessons. Come along," she ordered briskly. "And bring your brother; I need to measure him for his new coveralls." Whirling around she reentered the house without giving them a chance to object.

"Adrian, tell her we want to go swimmin'," Toby pleaded, his dirty toes shuffling in a pile of sand.

Adrian glanced at the woeful expression and fought a moment of jealous indecision. She longed to spend a little time alone with the children. But she knew Winifred was doing what she thought was right for them. Children needed instruction, and that was one area Adrian hadn't gotten around to yet.

"We'll go swimming later," she said, her heart aching at their disappointed faces. "You go with your aunt. She knows what's best for you right now."

They mumbled and groaned, but Adrian stood firm. Finally, Mimi took Eli's hand and started for the house. Toby looked back.

"Boy, I can't wait till Aunt Winifred goes back to St. Loose," he whined. "She ain't fun like you."

Adrian smiled at the precious little face, but her heart wrenched painfully. She was glad the children liked her, but she knew there was more to being a real mother than showing children how to have fun. She should have realized they needed lessons, schooling. She should have already started them on a schedule of some sort. With a jolt she realized she hadn't been doing as well at this vocation as she'd thought. She'd neglected important aspects of the children's education.

Going to the house, she was determined she wouldn't think of Winifred as a threat anymore. The woman had the children's best interests at heart, and Adrian could learn a lot from her. She didn't know what the future held for her and Rome, or for any of them. But she could befriend Winifred. After all, despite their differences they had one thing in common. They both wanted the best for Lorraine's children.

Adrian took a deep breath and counted to ten as she watched Winifred tap her palm methodically with a wooden ruler.

The children recited simple words, then slowly repeated the letters as Winifred spelled them aloud. Even Eli mocked her instructions, though he obviously thought it a game of some sort. Adrian could find no real fault with Winifred's program. However, the tapping of the ruler got on her nerves and Mimi and Toby looked miserable shifting on the hard seats.

Finally she couldn't stand the jarring noise

another moment. Setting aside her mending she focused on the long faces of the two oldest children.

"Don't you think they've had enough for their first day?" she asked.

Winifred cut her a startled look and, when the children echoed Adrian's thoughts, rapped the ruler harder against her flesh. "Enough of that," she chided. "Miss Sheppard, I'm afraid you're a distraction to the children. Their lessons are very important if they are to grow up without becoming ignorant, uneducated ruffians. I only have their best interests at heart, you understand," she said, her voice softening once more.

"Yes, I understand that," Adrian told her. "But I wanted to take them for a swim."

"A swim! Dear lord, I'm afraid that's impossible. They could catch their death submerged in water that way." She stared into Adrian's eyes for a long moment, then slowly her smile returned. "Of course, a nice walk down to the creek would be fine, as soon as they've finished their lessons."

Adrian bit her tongue and nodded, ignoring the children's pleading expressions. She reminded herself that Rome would need someone like Winifred to teach the children. And as much as Adrian hated to admit it, the woman had done better in one day than she'd done in a month.

"That sounds fine. I'll just see if Rome needs

271

my help in the meantime."

She touched the children's shoulders reassuringly as she passed them, wishing she could grab them up and take them outside with her into the bright sunshine and cool, early summer breeze of the beautiful day.

As she left the house she heard Winifred's low voice calling the children to attention once more. She went in search of Rome, but he was still inspecting the plants and he told her there was nothing for her to do until he finished.

She went to the creek alone, slipped off her shoes, and let the cold water wash over her feet. Funny how fast she'd gone from indispensable to nonessential. Rome didn't need her help until they could procure new seeds to replant. Winifred had everything in the house well under control.

Self-pity welled in her. She'd come to count on being needed by this family. She'd found fulfillment with them she'd never known before. It warmed her soul to take care of them. Now her presence here seemed superfluous.

She told herself she should be glad. It was time she went to town and got on with her search for a way home. And if her time proved to be beyond her reach, she needed to get on with making a life for herself in this time. Find a job, learn a trade.

If she couldn't marry Rome, she would have to stop living off his hospitality. Especially now that he had a perfect candidate for the position she'd temporarily filled.

"Hello there."

She jumped and whirled around, her heart settling back in place as she saw Rome standing behind her. "Hello."

He looked down at her feet and smiled. "Mind if I join you?"

She shook her head and shifted over on the sandy bank.

Rome removed his boots and socks and sank his feet into the water next to hers. They sat in silence for a long moment and then he nudged her toes with his. She didn't respond and he slid his foot beneath hers and tickled her sole.

"I suppose I can guess what's troubling you."

She glanced sideways at him and raised one chestnut eyebrow. "Winifred."

"Yes, I thought so." He yanked a blade of grass from the ground between his legs and twisted it in his fingers. "I'm sorry, Adrian, I don't know what to say. I wish she hadn't come, that I'd never asked her to. As soon as I sent that letter I realized I'd made a mistake. I was glad when she didn't accept. The funny thing is, I remember Winifred from my days in St. Louis. She wasn't like Lorraine. She was a little spoiled and very accustomed to the niceties of society. I can't imagine why she agreed to come here at all."

"But she did."

He sighed loudly. "Yes, she did. And even if I have no intention of marrying her now, I can't just throw her into the street."

"Of course not," Adrian quickly agreed. "She's Lorraine's sister. She's the children's aunt."

"She isn't the one I want, Adrian. And I plan to tell her that as soon as possible."

His words should have reassured her, but instead her heart sank with dread. "You have to admit she's very adept at running a household and tending children. Did you see the curtains she sewed this morning?"

He shook his head and she looked back out over the water. "She sewed curtains for two windows in the time it took me to wash the breakfast dishes. And she's teaching the children their lessons right now. She seems to care for them a great deal."

"Is that why you're sitting here alone, looking like you've lost your last friend?"

She shrugged and he nudged her shoulder. "You know she'd probably leave on her own in a minute if I told her you'd agreed to be my wife," he said, holding her gaze as his eyes darkened with earnest intent.

"I can't do that," she told him. "I wish I could; it would make things a lot simpler. But I can't agree to marry you just to simplify our situation."

He took her hand. "Is that all it would be?"

She knew what he was asking. He wanted to

know how she felt about him. She met his gaze, her eyes speaking louder than any words could. "You must know I care deeply for you and the children. But I have to resolve some problems in my own life before I can agree to share anyone else's."

"I won't pretend I'm not disappointed," he said. "But I won't push you." He took her chin and lifted her face so they were eye to eye. "Don't be sad. We'll think of some way out of this, I promise you."

His lips came down and brushed tenderly against her mouth. She closed her eyes and let the feel of his body comfort her. His arms closed around her and she pressed closer to his chest. The kiss deepened.

Adrian needed this, his touch, his warmth. She felt displaced, adrift. For the first time since returning to Rome's house the night of her arrival, she'd felt the panic of her situation overwhelm her. What if she couldn't go home? What if she did?

She was no longer even sure which she preferred. If some booming voice from heaven spoke to her at this very moment and asked her to choose, she didn't know if she could. All her life she'd wanted to find someone who moved her the way Rome could. She'd longed to bask in the feelings his children had evoked in her heart. For the first time in her life it was vital to her that she succeed.

And she'd thought she was close to doing just that. Until now. Until Winifred arrived and showed her how inept her performance had been. This time the pain of failure cut like a knife.

Only Rome's kisses, caresses could soothe her. Only in his arms did she feel she'd been right about wanting to stay with them.

She pressed closer and he answered her need by cupping her breast and parting her lips for the deep thrusts of his eager tongue. She arched to welcome the feel of his fingertips, savoring the rough touch of his skin on her thinly covered nipple. She matched his kiss stroke for stroke.

Her hands drifted along the lines of his back, settling in the long, unruly waves of hair lying damply against his neck. She dug her fingers in and pulled, forcing his mouth to press harder against her. She'd never get enough of touching him, kissing him, loving him. And at that moment she thought she'd do anything to stay with him and the children. The thought startled her and she drew back sharply, gasping for breath. Had she lost her senses? Could his kisses have the power to drive rational thought from her mind? She couldn't stay here, in this time, forever. She didn't belong here.

"Adrian?"

"I can't," she whispered, her hands still clutching his neck. Her words were saying one thing, but her touch clearly said another. She didn't want to let him go. Ever.

The sound of a shocked gasp froze them in place. Slowly Adrian turned her head to see Winifred standing a few yards away, her eyes wide with shock.

"Rome," she said breathily. "I believe I need to speak with you in private."

Winifred's spine straightened, throwing her chest out and stretching her neck until she looked like she was trying to peer over a high hedge. Silently she turned, walking briskly back the way she'd come.

Chapter Twenty

Rome pressed Adrian's hand, then released it. He wanted to stay with her and finish what they'd started. But he knew he had to settle things with Winifred immediately. He should have done it the moment she told him who she was and why she'd come to the farm.

But he'd been stunned by her arrival. And before he knew it she was in the house, in Adrian's bedroom.

Now, with one look at the woman's injured expression he knew he could not delay the inevitable any longer.

Her voice had been sharp, not at all like the sweet, honeyed tones she'd used before. He told himself it was the surprise of finding him and Adrian together when Winifred considered herself engaged to him. No wonder she'd been so upset.

"I'll be right there," he told Winifred. Turning to Adrian, he frowned. "I should have done this yesterday. I don't know why I didn't. Wait for me. I'll be back as soon as I've set things right."

She nodded and gave his hand a squeeze before turning back to the creek.

Winifred seemed to glide over the ground, her feet never even raising dust as she marched toward the house. But he could see from her rigid posture her control was feigned. Unless he'd forgotten more about women than he thought, he was in for an unpleasant scene.

He couldn't blame Winifred. He should have told her the instant she arrived that he had no intention of honoring the year-old offer now. He'd tried to think of some way to break it to her without hurting her feelings. But he could see now that was impossible. She *would* be strongly affected; there was no way to avoid that now.

As they reached the house he started onto the porch. She stopped at the bottom and stared up at him. Her demeanor was so starched with disapproval he suspected a 12-pound crimping iron couldn't put a crease in it.

"I'm confused, Rome," she said, clasping her hands together. Her ever-present hanky appeared in her fingers and she pressed it to her face. "Confused and hurt," she added.

Rome stepped down from the porch, keeping one booted foot on the bottom step. He grasped the porch post and cleared his throat. "I need to explain the scene you witnessed at the creek."

She held up her hand like a traffic cop, silencing him. "I don't care to hear the details," she told him, her expression strained. She took a deep breath and seemed to compose herself. "After all," she continued, speaking calmly now. "I'm from the city. I am sophisticated enough to understand men's baser needs."

Frowning, Rome felt his spine grow rigid. He cocked his head as she continued.

"What I do not understand is how you could bring that woman into the house with those children, my own flesh and blood."

"Just a minute, Winifred . . ." he began.

"No, I am not here to judge, despite the fact I can't help but be shocked and dismayed at your behavior. However, you simply must send her on her way immediately."

"Send her on her way? I don't plan to send Adrian away," he said, struggling to speak through clenched teeth. "You obviously have gotten the wrong impression, and that's my fault."

Her eyes widened, her lips thinned, and again he thought how cold her expression looked up close.

"I don't think I misunderstood at all, Rome. Anyone with half an eye could see what is going on between the two of you." She dabbed her eyes daintily. "Why couldn't you take your pleasures in town where such liaisons are usually conducted? I don't know how I will explain this to the children without damaging their delicate young sensibilities. Rome"—she clutched his arm and pressed near to him—"you must listen to reason. She has got to go this instant."

Anger such as he'd never known consumed Rome. His hands rolled into fists. For an instant he found his jaw clasped together too tightly for him to reply. It took several deep breaths before he could speak calmly.

"I will not stand for you talking about Adrian in such an insulting manner. You are a guest in this house, and as such I hesitate to appear rude. But I refuse to allow you to libel a kind, caring woman like Adrian. And as for the children, they love her. So you needn't explain anything to them."

"Well, I am not as naive as those children," she said sharply. "What kind of woman dresses the way she does? And look at how she lets that wild hair of hers fly about unbound. Don't try to tell me she isn't a common strumpet, or that you haven't been intimate with her. I saw that display of carnal exhibitionism at the creek with my own eyes." The hanky fluttered as she fanned her flushed face.

This time he clasped her shoulders before he could stop himself. She gasped, but he thought he saw a blaze of fire light the cool blue eyes. He immediately jerked his hands away, cursing his loss of control.

Bridling his anger, he forced himself to focus on the real problem. He had to tell Winifred his offer of marriage no longer stood. "I sent that letter to you proposing a marriage of convenience nearly a year ago."

"I explained to you," she cut in. "My response must have gone astray."

"Be that as it may, it must be obvious to you that my situation has changed. I am no longer in need of a wife of convenience. I'm perfectly happy with Adrian and her efforts on behalf of me and the children."

Winifred pressed her handkerchief to her lips and made a small, strangled sound. Rome rushed to reassure her.

"You're welcome here as long as it takes you to decide what you're going to do, Winifred. But I must insist you never speak ill of Adrian again. If I hear you do so, I'll forget you're Lorraine's sister. Do I make myself perfectly clear?"

Her face paled sharply, making the cool blue eyes stand out vividly. Without waiting for her reply, he turned around and started back the way he'd come. He still burned for Adrian's soothing touch, hoping it could alleviate the massive storm of emotions roaring through him.

* * *

Adrian stood beside the house, tears streaming down her face, her fingers clasped over her lips to stifle the sobs shaking her body.

Whether her tears were caused by Winifred's accusations or Rome's staunch defense, she wasn't quite sure. Perhaps a combination of the two.

She knew Winifred had every right to her conclusions. In this time, this era, her relationship with Rome would be considered an outrage. And, she told herself, she should have considered that situation in light of the children's presence. A mother, a real mother, would have thought of them first.

Again Adrian had to concede Winifred's superior knowledge of propriety and standards. Despite what Rome said, Adrian had to admit Winifred again had the children's best interests at heart.

And since she couldn't explain her clothing or her liberated ways, the woman would continue to think of her as simply immoral. If Winifred was an example of nineteenth-century attitudes, Adrian would do well to heed the woman's words. Instead of taking offense, she needed to learn from this hurtful encounter.

When she went to town it would not do for her to draw attention to the fact she was different. Too many questions could lead to awkward and complicated explanations.

She waited until Winifred went back into the

house; then she made her way to the barn and climbed into the loft long enough to compose herself and think through her next move. The fragrant hay brought sweet remembrances of her time there with Rome. Had it only been a day since he'd held her and loved her so wonderfully? So much had happened, it seemed like a distant memory.

He would be looking for her at the creek, but she had too many things to sort out right now. And this was one time she would have to deal with her problems on her own.

Her mind continued to drift back to other times, other problems she'd been faced with. Thoughts of her life before the comet came to mind like snapshots being expelled from a Polaroid camera. Hers and Alex's childhoods. Their parents' zest for life. Their tragic deaths, followed by the embittered years of estrangement from Alex and his family. She needed to go back to her time and make things right between her and her brother.

She understood the thinking that must have gone into the writing of her parents' will. They assumed Alex, with his staunch stability and desire to provide a good home for his family, would want the house. And they'd been right in that aspect. But in order to provide him with the means to maintain the monstrous estate, they'd left him in charge of the family business. A company Alex had no interest in running.

The money in their estate would have easily supported the mansion. But, knowing Adrian's somewhat transient ways, they'd chosen to leave the money to her, thinking she wouldn't want to be saddled with anything as solid as tangible property.

Alex had been stupefied by the terms of the will. He'd accused Adrian of coercing their parents into leaving her the money so she could continue her feckless wandering.

With wrenching pain, Adrian remembered the harsh, wounding allegations he'd thrown at her. She tried to tell him she didn't care about the money. She'd offered to give it to him, claiming she didn't want dissension between them over it.

But he'd only grown angrier, saying that her flippant disregard for the staggering amount of assets involved only proved his belief that she was reckless and irresponsible and totally incapable of handling such an enormous sum.

He'd never believed her that the money wasn't important. She would have given it all to him, if only he'd been willing to set aside his hurt and hostility.

She wondered now if he'd been notified of her disappearance. How would he react? Was he regretting their separation, as she was?

Another thought occurred to her then. If she disappeared without a trace, could he have her declared dead? Her will left all the money she'd inherited to him. Finally, after all the years of stubbornly refusing to accept a portion of their parents' money, he would have it all.

He'd accused her of being flighty and irresponsible, never able to hold down a job for long. For the most part he'd been right.

But how would he react when he discovered she hadn't touched a penny of the inheritance since it was turned over to her? Would he realize she'd been waiting for him to come around and accept his share? Would he finally be proud of her for making her own way, even if that way had been a bit rocky and uncertain?

Would he be proud of her now, hiding in a hayloft? No. He'd tell her to stop feeling sorry for herself and do something to better her situation. Don't be dependent on other people, he'd say. Rely on yourself, and the intelligence God gave you.

She sat up, thinking for once Alex's admonitions were warranted. She'd been hiding on this farm ever since fate brought her to the nineteenth century. It was time to do something: make plans for the future, find a way home, or get on with making a life here.

Her contemplation brought her full circle back to Rome. In the deepest part of her soul she knew she wanted her future to include him and his children.

But committing to one thing had never been her strong suit. How could she make a commitment to Rome and the children now when she hadn't even come to terms with what had happened to her? When she'd made a mess of the relationships in her own world?

Besides, she had Winifred to consider now. It wasn't self-pity that told her Winifred was better suited to be Rome's wife and surrogate mother to his children. It was common sense.

If not for those two factors, perhaps she and Rome could have been able to work something out between them. But right now that was impossible. And as long as she continued to hide from her failures, it would remain that way. If she was ever going to take control of her life, she had better do it quickly.

With her resolve firmly in place, she tried to forget Rome's kisses and caresses. The memory of their lovemaking would only muddle her judgment. She knew his touch could make her forget the world she'd left behind and she'd never leave him, even though she knew in her heart she should.

And that would be a terrible mistake. Because she couldn't begin to make a life here until she put to rest, one way or another, the one she'd been forced to leave behind.

When Winifred went to the kitchen to prepare supper, Rome again went to the fields. Eli was napping, Toby busily played in the yard, and Mimi studiously practiced the needlework

Winifred had assigned her as part of her training.

Adrian took advantage of the rare solitude to slip into the bedroom she'd once called her own. She went to Lorraine's trunk and extracted the items she needed. With the help of Winifred's hand mirror and a basin of water, she scraped her unruly curls back close to her head and secured them tightly with pins.

She selected a dark skirt and matching long-sleeved blouse of scratchy serge. As she rolled black cotton stockings up her legs and fastened them with ruffled garters, she felt her mood lighten. The leg coverings might be thick and of an unflattering shade, but they beat panty hose—which she'd always considered a cruel torture device designed by a man who obviously hated women. As she secured the unfamiliar garters, she acknowledged a small twinge of impishness. The lacy additions made her feel sexy, even if no one knew they were there except her.

She reached for her sneakers, then paused. If she was going to do this, she would have to do it right. Kneeling beside the trunk, she withdrew a pair of worn leather bootlike shoes. When she slipped her feet into them, she realized Lorraine's feet were at least a size larger than hers. But she wouldn't turn back now. She found two dainty handkerchiefs and stuffed the pointed toes of the boots. Then she put them on and buttoned them up over her ankles.

As she stood in the middle of the room, trying to adjust to the costume she wore, she wished she had a full-length mirror. She felt . . . different. Transformed, somehow. Until this moment she hadn't allowed herself to fully accept this strange, old world around her. She'd fought the truth by refusing to adjust to her surroundings. She'd been going through the motions of living with what had happened to her. But in truth she'd only been forcing her mind to ignore the facts she found too difficult to deal with.

All that was over now. She would go to town and face whatever awaited her. For the first time in her life she would take charge of her own destiny.

Charged with determination, she lifted her chin and walked into the main room. Mimi's head came up and she glanced briefly at Adrian. She looked back to her sewing, stopped, and raised her head slowly for a better look.

"What do you think?" Adrian asked.

Her task forgotten, Mimi could only stare, dumbfounded. She opened her mouth once but no sound came out. Suddenly her eyes turned hard and the corners of her mouth dropped in a harsh frown.

Adrian felt the girl's disapproval and was about to ask the cause of it when the back door burst open. Rome strode in, sweeping his hat from his head. His eyes lit on Adrian and he stopped midmotion. Comically he stood, his arm extended, his hat in hand as though about to perform an elaborate bow.

"Will someone say something, please?" Adrian coaxed, not liking the stunned silence permeating the room.

The sound of the door slamming shut drew all three startled faces around. Winifred stood holding a huge iron skillet. Adrian recognized it as one of the pans she'd scrubbed clean that morning, but it looked odd.

"I will say something," Winifred whispered, taking another step into the room. "You may don all the finery you want, Miss Sheppard, but you will never be anything but what you are."

Adrian gasped, strangling on the sudden indrawn breath. She staggered back as though Winifred had actually struck her. In fact, she felt the woman's words slam into her like a blow to her middle.

Mimi dropped her needle and cloth as Rome's face hardened into a frightening mask.

"Dammit, Winifred," he snarled. "I warned you."

The hard edge left her features and she turned her gaze to him, her expression softening. "I'm sorry, Rome. I'm simply trying to do what I came here to do, look after Lorraine's children and her household. You cannot let her stay here another moment. This is no environment for children. And she's hopeless at domestic tasks. Just look at this."

She held the heavy skillet in front of Adrian as though it weighed nothing. "They are all like this. You've ruined every one of them. Even a child knows how to season a skillet, and not to leave it wet after scrubbing it. If you truly had a shred of proper upbringing you'd have known it, too."

Rome clutched Winifred's shoulders from behind and she turned to face him. Obviously realizing she'd said too much, she again donned the benevolent mien she'd worn when she first arrived.

"I apologize," she said, lowering her head as though truly repentant. "I'm afraid I get rather overwrought in my zeal to protect these darling children."

Adrian could only stare at the copper flakes dusting the skillet. She remembered Mimi always dried the pans carefully after they'd been washed and then rubbed grease into the metal. Seasoning. She hadn't known that was what you called it, but she should have remembered to do it nevertheless.

Suddenly she felt foolish standing there in the old-fashioned garb. Winifred was right. No amount of clothing could hide the fact that she didn't belong here.

What had she been thinking of to even consider staying with Rome, making a life here on this farm? Winifred was the woman they needed. Rome might consider himself in love with Adrian, but how long would his patience and understanding last in light of her constant blunders? When the bloom wore off of their attraction, would he wish for Winifred's supreme knowledge and appropriate manner? Would he begin to resent Adrian's incompetence and question her further about her past? She couldn't wait around to find out.

The only logical conclusion had been right here for her to see all along. Only she'd stubbornly refused to see it. Until now. She stared at the confused, curious faces watching her.

"I was coming to tell you I'm ready to go into town," she told Rome. "You have the help you need now, with the farm and the children. It's time I got on with my life."

Chapter Twenty-one

"Adrian, won't you change your mind?"

Peering into Rome's beautiful teal eyes, Adrian almost relented. She longed to tell him she'd stay. Instead she tugged the hem of the serge jacket she wore, trying to ease the discomfort of the fitted clothing.

Behind him, the children stood stiffly like little soldiers lined up along the porch, their faces grim, their eyes wet. Having already said goodbye to each of them, she didn't want to prolong the moment.

"I have to do this," she said. "I only agreed to stay because you needed me and I wasn't ready to go back to town. But I am now."

She knew her words hurt him. She'd have to be blind not to see that he cared for her. Even if he'd never said the words, his actions had spoken loudly.

And she loved him more than anything, too. But she couldn't let him send Winifred packing until she knew whether or not she would return to the future. It wouldn't be fair to either them or the children.

If she were to decide she could, and wanted to, go home, he would need Winifred. And although it hurt to admit it, Adrian knew Winifred would make a good helpmate for Rome. The only dissension between the in-laws was caused by Adrian's presence. It would seem, then, that it would vanish with her departure.

After all, the woman had left behind her way of life and traveled a long distance to marry a virtual stranger for the sake of her sister's children. She must be a truly loving person, despite the somewhat erroneous conclusions she'd drawn regarding Adrian.

Who knew, Rome might even grow to love Winifred in time. He obviously loved Lorraine, and Winifred, being her sister, must possess some of the same qualities he'd found appealing in his wife.

Once Adrian was out of the picture he would see that Winifred was the better candidate for the position of farm wife and mother.

That thought, though true, nearly broke Adrian's heart.

Swallowing the rock of misery lodged in her throat, she nodded.

"I'm ready."

She could see the disappointment on his face, but he didn't say anything more. He gathered the small tapestried valise she'd packed with her belongings and a few of Lorraine's things, and tossed it into the back of the hitched wagon.

Taking her elbow, he assisted her onto the hard, wooden seat. She looked back at the porch and wrenching emotions choked her. Eli, his sweet baby face wet with tears, reached out for her with his widespread arms.

Winifred scooped him into her arms and tried to appease him, but he only bucked and cried louder. His tantrum seemed to unleash the emotions the other children had held in check. Toby burst into tears and ran into the house. Mimi glared at Adrian, her pretty face stern with disapproval, her eyes moist.

Only Winifred seemed glad to see the wagon pull out of the yard. She tucked her cheeks close to her molars and nodded slightly in satisfaction.

Adrian felt the warmth of Rome's leg against her thigh, even through the layers of clothing she wore. His shoulder pressed intimately against hers, arousing the desire he'd set free in her. She wanted another moment in his arms before she had to confront what lay ahead. But she knew one touch would be too much, and yet never enough.

A single kiss and she'd forget her plan to go to town. She'd run back to Rome's farm and hide in the shelter of his arms forever. One caress and she'd want a lifetime of loving him.

She twined her fingers and stared straight ahead as the wagon bounced along the rutted road. If she didn't look at him, didn't reach for him, she could leave him. It would break her heart, but she told herself she was stronger than she'd ever given herself credit for.

If she hadn't been, she'd have given in to her own needs and stayed with Rome and the children despite the troubling doubts which plagued her.

Taking her first good look at the scenery, Adrian grew apprehensive. All around her were grassy hills and vine-covered trees that had grown wild in this area for years. There was nothing to hint at what was to come. The roads, subdivisions, and businesses she was used to seeing weren't even glints on the horizon.

This land was untouched, virginal. It waited, poised, for expansion and population growth to drive more and more people into the area. Farms would decrease in size and number. Neighborhoods would go up on empty fields. Pavement, concrete, and telephone poles waited somewhere in the future to be introduced.

Having seen the beauty of a sunrise across a freshly cleared plot of dirt, she felt a sadness to know all this would be gone one day. Oh, a few farms would survive. But a way of life would die. A life she had grown fond of in the past month. More than fond, she admitted, pressing at a tear in the corner of her eye.

She'd found happiness and contentment in this foreign place that she'd never have known existed if not for her bizarre journey. How ironic that she'd found happiness in a place where she didn't belong when that same contentment had eluded her in her world.

Suddenly the wagon turned off the road and cut across a grassy field. Adrian sniffed aside her sadness and cleared her throat.

"Where are you going?" she asked, as Rome directed the wagon toward a huge oak tree.

He didn't answer her. As they approached the tree he pulled back on the reins and shoved the lever of the brake into place.

Still, he didn't so much as glance her way for an interminable moment. He stared straight ahead, his jaw flexing as though clenched.

"I don't want you to go."

A jolt of painful pleasure seized Adrian. Gooseflesh pebbled along her arms and neck. All her life she had hungered for the sound of those words, rife with genuine feeling.

He turned in his seat and she gasped at the look of pain in his teal eyes. She ached to touch his cheek, his jaw, to soothe the lines around his eyes. Clenching her fingers together, she fought the impulse.

299

"I told you when you came to us that I was beyond pride," he said. "If you want me to beg . . ."

She pressed her fingers over his lips as pools of tears flooded her eyes. Her hand spread over his cheek; the other one came up to cup his jaw. Closing her eyes she could feel the roughness his straight razor never quite conquered. She let the stubble abrade her palms, sending frissons of desire and longing zig-zagging through her.

Unable to resist her heart's urgings another minute, she leaned forward and pressed her lips to his. His mouth was warm and firm and he claimed her in a kiss that declared his love more loudly than if he'd shouted it from the peak of a mountaintop.

Adrian quivered at the sweet ravagement he bestowed on her lips. He put every word he ached to tell her into that single, tender consummation of their love. His touch affected her like a drug, easing the pain of withdrawal as it heightened the craving burning inside her.

Her head fell back and his mouth burned a trail along the line of her neck. He buried his face in the fullness of her breasts and held her so tight she couldn't draw breath.

"Oh, Adrian," he murmured. "God, I'll never get enough of you."

She grasped his head and lifted his face. Her throat convulsed with her inability to convey her passion adequately. She wanted him, needed him. Even if it were for the last time, she couldn't deny him.

He read the acquiescence in her eyes, and, holding her gaze, he led her to the back of the wagon.

Rome made short work of the line of buttons she'd tediously fastened an hour before. She tugged the crisp white shirt he wore from the waistband of his trousers and ran her hands over his hot flesh. He pushed her skirt to her waist; she slipped the buttons of his fly out of their slots with a deftness born of raw need.

Her nails raked his skin; his teeth nipped the curve of her shoulder. Desperately they came together, touching, kissing, feeling, memorizing.

His hands cupped her buttocks, padding them against the rough planks of the wagon and holding her in place for his fury of thrusts. She gripped him with her legs and wrapped her arms around his neck as he drove her feverishly toward the zenith of fulfillment.

As they achieved a harmony of perfection together, he buried himself completely in her heat.

Their harsh breaths sounded loud in the silence of their seclusion. The sun shining down on them could not match the fiery glow of their passion. Sweat fused them together, and they lay replete and still for a long time.

Rome moved first, lifting his head and gazing

down into her eyes. She could see the question lingering in the sea-colored depths. She wasn't ready to relinquish their time together, but she could see his questions wouldn't be put off any longer.

With a sigh, she rolled. Rome settled on his back, gathering her close to his chest and snuggling her head in the crook of his shoulder.

"When I came back to your house that first night," she began, "I was running. I think now that I've been running for years. Ever since my parents died I've been searching for something. When I didn't find what I was looking for, I moved on. And until now, I never looked back with any real regret."

"And now?" he asked, hope evident in his voice.

"And now I can't run anymore. There are things I have to face before I can make any kind of life for myself."

"I always thought of you as a gift from heaven, Adrian. Sure, I wondered about your past, where you came from, and who you were before you arrived on my doorstep. Then suddenly it didn't seem to matter anymore. I knew my first image was correct. You were a gift, a precious present sent to save me from the grief and despair I'd allowed myself to become tangled in."

"No, Rome. I can't be anyone's salvation. Up until a month ago I could barely take care of myself. I wandered aimlessly, never striving very hard for success. Moving on when failure inevitably found me."

She shook her head and he stroked the damp strands of hair away from her face, pressing his lips to her ear. Adrian knew her old ways would never be good enough for this man and his children. But she was afraid she didn't know how to change after all this time.

She had to prove to herself she could stand on her own before she agreed to the kind of commitment Rome needed. She had to try to find some answers in town, even if the thought seemed farfetched. Even if the only answers she found were inside herself.

Her relationship with Rome involved more than the normal obligations inherent in pledging one's life to another. Adrian's life would never truly be hers to give until she settled her past and the question of her bizarre arrival here. It was time to face her fears. Those she harbored inside herself and those which had been thrust upon her by her fateful journey.

"I don't know what I'll find in town. But there are some realities about myself and about my situation that I have to face."

"Let me help you, the way you helped me."

But she was already shaking her head. "No, this is something I have to do by myself. Something I should have done years ago. Something I'm only confronting now because I have no choice."

If she had faced up to her fears years ago and stopped running would she and Alex still be close? Had her feckless, irresponsible nature only added fuel to the fire of his bitterness? He struggled to succeed at a business he despised in order to hold on to the only home he'd ever known. Despite the fact she hadn't supported herself by drawing from the funds she'd been left, Alex didn't know that. Her shiftless behavior acted as salt to the wounds of his resentment.

"The children will miss you; I'll miss you. We need you; don't you care about that now?"

Pressing a kiss to his chest, she told herself he didn't mean to hurt her. He was trying to understand. Only she knew this was something no one could understand unless it had happened to them.

"Don't," she pleaded. "If I have to go, it's better to go now, before the children get more attached to me." She didn't add that she'd already become hopelessly, endlessly bound to them. And their father.

"Winifred will be there to help you. She's more skilled than I could ever learn to be. They'll get used to her."

"They don't love her the way they love you."

"They didn't exactly love me when I first arrived, either. But they got used to me and they'll do the same with her."

"I'll never feel about her the way I feel for you."

Again tears stung her eyes and she had to blink them back before she could respond. "That may be; I don't know," she said, fighting the exultation his confession set off in her. "All I know is that I have private demons to face before I can be any good for anyone, including myself. I don't know if I'll find the answers I'm looking for, but I won't ask you to wait while I decide whether or not I can be a wife and mother at this place—and time—in my life. I've never stuck with anything for more than a few months. What if I let you send Winifred away and then I decided to run away again? I can't do that. I can't take on that much responsibility on a permanent basis until I know I can honor a lifelong pledge like that."

Rome rolled to his side and leaned up on his elbow so they were facing each other. "I don't know what you're talking about, Adrian. You're devoted to the kids; I've seen that with my own eyes. You're wonderful with them. And what we have together, well, I don't know how you can still be unsure."

She tried to touch his forehead, to brush the waves of hair back, but he pulled away. A hardness came into his eyes. He thought she was rejecting him, his love. He couldn't be more wrong.

But even if she knew beyond a doubt that she wanted to stay here in this world with him, she didn't know if she could. She hadn't even tried to get back to the future. What if she tossed aside her doubts and returned to the farm with him? Would she ever feel secure? Or would she always wonder if fate waited for her around the next corner to snatch her back through this crazy time warp? For once she would have to stand and face her fears.

There had to be answers somewhere out there to the questions plaguing her. All she knew was she'd never find them hiding away on Rome's farm.

She didn't want to hurt him, but she had to make him understand. And she couldn't tell him the truth about her presence here, so she chose the next-best thing. A partial truth. A statement which she was sure would show him the kind of person she really had been.

"I told you I was married," she said, bolstering her resolve.

His features turned stony and he nodded sharply. "You said he was gone."

Drawing her shirt together, she pushed to a sitting position. Her clothes were hopelessly wrinkled and she stalled for time by smoothing them down around her.

"I knew you must have thought I was widowed. I purposely let you think that because I didn't want to tell you the truth."

"I see," he said, rising and leaning his back against the seat of the wagon. He adjusted his trousers into place but didn't fasten them. She couldn't stop her eyes from going to the wedge of chest revealed by his unbuttoned shirt and low-riding waistband.

"He didn't die. Our marriage ended the same way all my other ventures ended. When things got tough, I left. I've never stood and fought for anything before. My standard operating procedure was always to run away when a situation got difficult."

"Taking care of my children didn't come easy to you, but you didn't run away."

She laughed dryly and picked at the knots in the weave of her skirt. "That's because I was running from something a lot bigger than three small children."

"Your husband?"

Her head snapped up and she saw a glint of anger turn his eyes deep turquoise. His full lips which could bring her such pleasure thinned with irritation. He was wondering if she'd added adultery to her list of faults.

"No. Tate is out of my life for good. I never would have made love to you if that wasn't the case."

"Then I don't understand. If he's not dead, where is he? And why aren't you with him?"

"I can't begin to tell you where Tate is now," she said, purposely hedging to avoid that line of questions. "But I can tell you why I'm not with him."

He arched an eyebrow and she took a deep breath.

Marti Jones

"Tate wanted to start a family. I'd never stayed with anything long enough to even wear the new off it. I couldn't imagine being saddled with children, the ultimate commitment."

"So, you weren't ready to have children. That isn't a sin, Adrian."

"No, I suppose not. But what about divorce, Rome. Do you consider divorce a sin?"

"Your husband divorced you because you weren't ready to have children?" His incredulous tone cut through her. She wished she deserved his championing.

"No," she said, shaking her head as she carefully watched his expression. "I divorced him."

Chapter Twenty-two

Rome didn't utter another word following her bald statement. He remained silent, his hurt and confusion radiating out in waves until the wagon reached the outskirts of town. She could see his shock. Though he tried to hide it, Adrian knew she'd finally convinced him she had to go. He hadn't argued further. Now, she almost wished he would.

"Are you going to be all right?" he finally asked.

Adrian stepped down beside him into the middle of the dirt street, her blurry gaze traveling up one side of the small town and down the other. *Wooden buildings, planked walkways, hitching posts!*

She swallowed and fought the panic rising

within her. All her survival instincts screamed at her to get back in the wagon and return to the farm with Rome. This was not the time to decide to be strong after years of running away.

The problems she had encountered being a nurse in a modern hospital were nothing compared to this. Facing death by near-drowning couldn't hold a candle to facing the fear this town created in her.

Her home was a burg! It was a—a wide spot in the road! This wasn't possible. A place could not go from being this small hamlet to a thriving, bustling, populated town with condominiums and automatic teller machines in a hundred years.

There must be some mistake.

"This is Newhope?" she whispered.

Rome followed her shocked stare and shifted uncomfortably. "Yeah."

"Are you sure?" she asked, her eyes widening as a horse passed and stopped beside them to lift his tail and make a revolting deposit in the middle of the street.

Rome saw her shiver of disgust and cocked one eyebrow at her. "Yep, this is Newhope. What were you expecting?"

Adrian whirled to face him, angry that he could be flippant at a time like this. "What was I expecting?" She shook her head. Somehow she thought she'd find a younger version of the Newhope she'd known. But there was no sign of the town she knew. Nothing even vaguely familiar. "I guess I expected—more."

She saw the confusion fade from his eyes, replaced by the concern he couldn't hide, and she sighed, tucking her hair behind her ears and risking another long, close look at the town.

Her actions were as much to avoid his direct gaze as anything else. "I don't know what I thought I'd find," she admitted. "But it sure wasn't this."

Could she do this? she wondered. It would be the toughest obstacle she'd ever encountered. And the fact that her love for Rome and the children pulled at her to abandon this mission and closet herself in the relative security of the farm only added to her doubts.

She met his eyes and her heart thrilled at the love she saw there. This man deserved more than a woman looking for refuge. He needed a wife who would never question her commitments. A lover who lay beside him each night out of love, not fear.

Adrian found herself momentarily startled by the depth of maturity it took to make that vow. A warm, fuzzy pillow of pride spread out from her chest and she raised her chin a notch. Maybe, just maybe, she was finally growing up.

"I'm going to be fine," she told him, certain now that whatever happened she would do all right. She battled one last surge of panic, then nodded sharply. "Let's go."

They left the wagon at the livery and made their way to the planked walkway. As they strolled toward the center of town Adrian took the time to stop and look in each of the windows they passed.

Wes Logan's Harness Shop. Adrian gazed at the leather goods displayed on a table at the front of the room. In the back, a wizened old man bent double over a piece of stretched hide.

Anderson's Clothing and Dry Goods. Behind the glass were an array of fabric bolts, miscellaneous barrels, and farm implements of every size and description.

Rome walked along beside her, not questioning her peculiar fascination with each shop.

They passed a bakery, and the round little woman rolling dough at a table in the back lifted a flour-covered hand in greeting. Adrian smiled and waved back. Some of her dread seemed to leave her.

It reappeared as they approached the next window. *Sal's Barber Shop and Dentist Establishment.*

"Ugh," Adrian cried, turning away as a burly man with his sleeves rolled to the elbow grasped a pair of pliers and pried open the jaws of his terrified victim.

"Good reason to take care of your teeth," Rome offered, seeing her horror. "Sal ain't the best doc we ever had around these parts."

Adrian took another step and Rome's hand

came up and gripped the small of her back, turning her toward a pair of wide double doors with opaque glass windows. She raised an eyebrow.

"Hungry?"

Her eyes went to the shingle hanging above their heads from the porch roof. *Quinn's Eats*.

"This is the restaurant you mentioned?" A look of indecision crossed her face and suddenly her composure seemed to crumble like a fragile shell around her.

"It's not bad, really," he said, pushing open one of the doors.

Immediately the smell of beef and bread reached her nose. The yeasty aroma caused moisture to rush to her mouth and her stomach growled and rumbled.

Rome heard the sound and smiled. "I told you."

From out of the kitchen a huge barrel of a man emerged carrying a heaping tray of food. His red hair was shaggy and his orange freckles stood out like a rash on his ruddy cheeks. He saw Rome and gave a shout, nearly rattling the dishes on the tray.

"Haven't seen ya in a spell, Walker," he called. "Sit, I'll be with you in a shake."

Rome motioned toward a small table at the far side of the room and Adrian sank into the seat, grateful to put her adventure on hold for a brief time. The sights she'd seen had taken a toll. Her legs felt watery; her stomach quivered. She wondered if she'd be able to eat at all.

The proprietor deposited the plates on a table occupied by a couple of farmers and shuffled back to the kitchen. Adrian took a moment to study the restaurant. It was rustic, with plain wooden walls and floors. The tables were unpretentious, serviceable pieces, the chairs straight-backed with seats carved out to fit one's backside.

"What are you thinking?" Rome asked, seeing her concentrated frown.

"Well, it's not the Waldorf."

His brow arched and he glanced around. "Nope, I suppose not. But the food's better."

Blinking, she stared at him in awe. "You've been to the Waldorf? In New York?"

He grinned and, with the tip of his finger, reached over and touched her chin, closing her gaping mouth.

"Yes. I wasn't born and raised in Newhope, you know."

"No," she whispered. "I don't know. In fact, I really don't know very much about you. Well, except that you have three children, you're widowed, and you own a farm."

"That's all the important stuff," he said. "The rest is history."

Funny, she thought. She'd never questioned Rome's life before she came into it. Another example of her selfishness, she supposed. Now she found she wanted to know everything about him.

"But how did you come to live here if you're not from around here?"

"I was a deck hand on a riverboat that ran the Mississippi from St. Louis to New Orleans. I'm originally from Memphis."

"Memphis? So, that's how you met Lorraine?"

"Right. We made port in St. Louis one fall and the Captain asked some of us to a party at his house the next night. Lorraine was there. I took one look at her and fell in love. She was the prettiest thing I'd ever seen. Real elegant, too. But not a snob, you know."

Adrian could only nod. After a month of living with this man she was just beginning to realize he had a rich, vibrant past she knew nothing about.

"Her folks were well-to-do, but they liked me fine. When the boat put up for the winter, I got a job and stayed in town. We courted over the weeks that followed and I asked her to marry me. I told her I wanted to take the money I'd saved and buy a farm down South where I could raise crops and work the land. That suited Lorraine fine. All she'd ever wanted was a place where she could raise children that was quiet, away from the city.

"Her folks sent us to New York for our honeymoon trip; then we moved down here. I worried that she wouldn't be happy on the farm after living so good in the city, but we were content."

Adrian heard the truth in his words and she was glad he and Lorraine had found happiness for a while. Rome was a good man, just as she'd thought from the first moment she met him. He deserved to be happy. But, of course, his happiness hadn't lasted long. She'd known of Lorraine's death; now she knew a little about her life.

Being from a wealthy family would explain the fine things she'd found in Lorraine's trunk and the beautiful dishes that had seemed so incongruous in the tacky little farm house.

The kitchen doors swung open again and a woman emerged. She could have been the owner's sister, they looked so much alike, with their red hair and florid complexions. She was as big around as the man, but short where he'd been tall.

"Ah, Rome," she drawled, waddling to the table. She cupped his face with her hands and planted a smacking kiss on his cheek. "Where have you been? And where are those darlin' younguns of yours?"

Rome laughed and returned the woman's kiss, then motioned toward Adrian. "Mary, this is Adrian Sheppard. She's been helping out at the farm. Lorraine's sister arrived a few days ago, and she's tending the children while I bring Adrian to town."

"Yep, your sister-in-law stopped here for a night. Seemed in a hurry to get out to your place, though. She left a'fore daylight, without so much as a good-bye." She turned to Adrian. "You come in answer to the newspaper advertisement, did you?"

"No, actually, I kind of got lost and wandered onto Rome's farm. He was gracious enough to let me stay and help out until I decided what to do."

"Did he now?" Mary said, her reddish-brown eyebrows climbing toward her hairline.

Adrian could see her comment had only raised Mary's curiosity, but she didn't offer further information and Mary didn't ask.

"Well, you're a right pretty thing. In fact, you look like you could be kin to me and Bob with that hair and all. Yep, I can see why Rome would like having you around."

"Thank you," Adrian said, flushing. She could see the speculation in Mary's eyes, but the compliment had been genuine.

"What can I get you?"

"What's the special today?" Rome asked.

"Roast with gravy, new potatoes, peas and butter beans, and yeast rolls."

. "That sounds good," he said, looking at Adrian. She nodded. "We'll both have that."

Mary puttered back to the kitchen, and a comfortable silence descended on the table.

Adrian told herself this wasn't as bad as she'd thought it would be. She'd put off facing the reality of her situation for a month out of fear, but so far she hadn't seen anything too frightening.

Rome cleared his throat and she met his eyes. "I was thinking," he said. "Mary is always complaining about needing help in the kitchen. Quinn's having a hotel built next door. He wants it to be open by the time the railway reaches us at the end of summer. If you want to stay here a while I could speak to them about letting you work for room and board."

Adrian glanced around the dining room. At least it was a plan, she thought. "That sounds like a good idea. But, if you don't mind, I'd like to be the one who talks to them about it. I need to do this on my own."

"Sure."

She could see he was disappointed that she didn't want his help. She wished she could tell him what his safekeeping had meant to her over the last four weeks. Without him, she would have been totally adrift in this bizarre world, with no hope of making her way.

Now she'd had time to adjust to what had happened, if such a thing were possible. She'd come to terms with the impossible. And, again with his help, she'd faced the actuality of it and survived with her sanity intact. She reached out and touched his hand.

"You've done enough. Now it's time for me to see if I can make it here on my own."

He clutched her hand. "If this is about what Winifred said—"

"No, it isn't. Not really," she added, when he narrowed his eyes in doubt. "Winifred's arrival made me reevaluate my predicament, and by taking over the chores and the care of the children she enabled me to do this without feeling like I was abandoning all of you."

"Can't you at least tell me what it is you're looking for? Let me help."

Smiling, she savored the warmth of his hand and the feel of his fingers entwined with hers. "Maybe one day I can tell you all about it. Right now, it's better this way."

Straightening, he released his hold. Their food arrived and they ate as they exchanged small talk. He retained his affability, but a coolness permeated his manner. After the fiery passion they'd shared, the heat he'd bathed her in when they made love, his aloofness chilled her and she felt the loss more keenly.

Despite her anxiety and apprehension, Adrian polished off every bite of the meal. The waistband of Lorraine's skirt pinched where before she'd had plenty of room.

She looked at Rome's plate and saw that he'd barely touched his food.

"What's the matter? After eating my cooking for a month I'd think you'd inhale this ambrosia."

319

"Your cooking wasn't bad," he said, but she caught the hint of a grin.

Chuckling, she pushed aside her empty plate. "If you cooked as well as you lied, I'd have turned the kitchen over to you the first day."

He seemed to relax, and Adrian felt relieved to have put their relationship back on easy terms. Soon, he would leave to return to the farm and she didn't want to part company with harsh feelings between them.

While they ate, the other customers had finished and gone. Mary and the big red-headed man came out of the kitchen together and pulled two chairs over to sit with them as they sipped coffee. "I'm Bob Quinn," the giant of a man said as he offered his hand. "I hope everything is satisfactory.

"This coffee is delicious," Adrian said. "I haven't had a decent cup in a month."

"Oh, well, there's plenty more where that came from. Let me get you some."

"No, thank you. I'd like to talk to you and Mr. Quinn for a minute, if that's all right."

The couple exchanged curious glances and Mary nodded. "Sure thing, honey."

Adrian looked at Rome but he stared down into his mug. She'd asked him to let her handle this. It was what she wanted, she told herself again. Besides, when it came to seeking employment she was pretty much an expert.

"Rome said you might be looking for

someone to help out around here. I was wondering if you'd consider giving me a job for a while."

"You want to work here?" Mary's eyes darted to Rome, then quickly back to Adrian. But Adrian knew what she was thinking. Why would she want a job as a waitress and cook when she'd been living with Rome and his children for a month? Unfortunately, Adrian had no answer for that question. She just knew this was something she had to do.

"Yes. I don't need much money, but I'll need a place to stay while I'm here. Also, I can't promise you how long I'll be here."

Rome's head came up and for a brief instant their eyes met. Then he covered his expression by bringing his mug to his lips once more.

Mary watched Rome for a long moment, then shrugged and looked at her husband. Adrian didn't see Bob make a move of any kind, but apparently Mary had gotten his consent. She nodded.

"All righty," she said. "You're hired. I sure won't mind the help, I can tell you that for the truth. But as far as a room goes, we can only offer you a small one. We've got a man staying in the one we usually let to visitors."

"A man?" For the first time Rome joined the conversation. "Who is it?"

Mary shrugged. "A feller named Evan Garvey. Been here about a month. Some kind of writer,

I reckon. Spends most of his time out riding about the countryside or up in his room pounding on the keys of a gizmo he calls a type-a-writer."

Cutting a look toward Adrian he asked slowly, "You say he's been here about a month?"

"That's right. Hey, you don't know this feller, do you, Adrian. He musta got here about the time you did."

She could see Rome was waiting for her answer. What did he think, that this man was some kind of friend of hers? Or did he wonder if she'd told him the whole truth about her husband? She told herself there was no way she could know Rome's thoughts. And besides, they made no difference.

"I'm sure he's not anyone I know," she said, knowing without a doubt she could be confident on that score at least.

Mary bobbed her head again. "No matter. You'll meet him soon enough, I reckon. If you want to come with me I'll show you your room and we can discuss our arrangement a bit more."

Adrian set aside her napkin and pushed her chair back. The sound of the wooden legs scraping the floor seemed loud in the sudden silence. Rome rose slowly. They stared across the table, their gazes locked.

They could have been alone for all they were aware of Mary and Bob. Teal eyes met brown, and words weren't necessary. God, how she loved him.

More than anything she wanted to go into his arms and ask him to take her home, back to the farm to live with him and the children. But she couldn't do it. She cared too much for him to make him settle for half a person. Until she proved to herself she wouldn't run again when things got tough, she had nothing to offer him and less than nothing to contribute to the lives of three impressionable children.

So she offered him what she could. She smiled. He returned it. Then she faced Mary.

"I'm ready when you are," she said.

Chapter Twenty-three

Rome hefted the cotton sack filled with flour into the back of the wagon and paused to look across the street to the restaurant. He'd never get his supplies loaded if he didn't quit thinking of Adrian and trying to catch a glimpse of her at Quinn's.

And, after all, why should he give a damn? She hadn't even looked back as she'd followed Mary from the dining room. She made her decision and it didn't matter to her that he and the children had come to love her. Winifred had arrived and Adrian saw her chance to get away. Dammit, why had he agreed to take her to town? He could have lied and made up excuses why they couldn't go.

But Rome knew that wouldn't have done either of them any good. He couldn't force her to stay with them if she didn't want to. And deep down, he knew he couldn't have kept her if being with him wasn't what she wanted.

If only he could figure out what it was she wanted. She talked about living with him as though it had been the wrong thing for her to do. He understood pain, and hiding from reality. After all, he'd gotten to be pretty good friends with a whiskey bottle for the same reasons. But he couldn't understand what Adrian was running from, and she sure as hell didn't show any signs of confiding in him any time soon.

She'd shared with him a passion that threatened to burn them both alive, but she never opened herself to him completely. He'd always felt she was holding back. Of course, he'd suspected from the moment she arrived she was trying to escape from someone or something. Her odd clothes, the panic in her eyes that didn't fade for days. And, the desperation with which she'd clung to him and the children, despite the fact she'd obviously known nothing of being a farmer's wife or even a mother, for that matter.

He held his questions with great restraint so as not to scare her off; he was that desperate for the help she could give him. But they'd never gone away, always just below the surface. Especially when she did things like wearing the corset cover as though she didn't know it was underclothing. And, the unrestrained passion she'd shown when they made love. No other woman he'd ever been with had been that unrestricted in bed except a few practiced whores. And Adrian Sheppard was damned sure no whore; he'd bet his soul on that.

Still, that didn't explain what, or who, she was. All he knew was that she was the woman he wanted for his wife. No other would do now. Not since he'd held her and loved her. Not since he'd seen her caring for his children as though they were more precious than gold.

Winifred was family and she'd be good to the children, he supposed. Still, something about her attitude since her arrival hadn't rung true to him. And as far as taking her for his wife, there would be no question of that now. After Adrian, kissing Winifred would be like kissing his own mother. Making love to her would never compare to the moments he'd spent with Adrian.

No, since Adrian came into his life he'd realized one thing. He couldn't marry just anyone, not even for the sake of his farm and his children. He had to have Adrian and no other. He had to convince her to come back with him.

He tossed another sack into the wagon and leaned his elbow along the rough, railed side of the bed. Cutting another glance toward the restaurant, he saw the door open. His spine straightened and he felt a fist of longing reach up and grab his gut.

Then a man emerged and he released his breath. He started to turn and collect the next item to be loaded, then stopped. This must be the man staying with the Quinns. The one who'd be living under the same roof as Adrian while she was here.

Rome felt his gut tighten again, this time with jealousy. The man was young, late twenties maybe, and tall. He had broad shoulders and black hair, cut short in the fashionable style.

His suit of clothes appeared to be new and he filled them out as though they'd been tailor-made. He closed the door of the restaurant and placed a stylish bowler hat on his head.

Rome disliked him on sight.

"Dandy looking fellow, ain't he?"

Will Anderson sidled up next to Rome and handed him a carton filled with odds and ends Rome had purchased. "A queer bird, though," he added, squinting against the afternoon sun.

"Strange how?" Rome asked, trying to appear unconcerned as he set the carton in the wagon bed beside the rest of his purchases.

"Showed up about a month ago. Wouldn't say much about his background."

"That isn't so strange," Rome said, thinking of Adrian and her curious arrival and questionable silence.

"No, I reckon not. A body's got a right to privacy, that's for sure and certain. But he had this coin, looked like a silver dollar."

The stranger they discussed sauntered down the walkway toward the other end of town and Rome focused his attention on what Will was saying.

"A silver dollar?"

"Yeah. Looked like a silver dollar anyway. And it was the real thing, I made sure of that. But the odd part was it was dated nineteen hundred and twenty-one."

Rome looked down the street, saw the man disappear into the livery. He blinked and stared at Will.

"What did you say?"

"One-nine-two-one. That was the date on this silver dollar he had. Said he'd trade it for a suit of clothes and that typewriter I took off a newsman a couple years ago when he got hard up and needed money for train fare back to Mobile."

"You gave that man a suit of clothes for a worthless coin?"

Will flushed and shuffled his long, boat-like feet on the uneven planks. "I didn't figure it was worthless," he said defensively.

"Well, what else could it be? It was obviously a fake."

"No, I don't think so. This fellow, he said he'd had it a long time. It belonged to his grandpappy or something. Said he figured the date

329

was a mistake and that'd make it worth a bundle to folks who collect things like that." Again he shuffled, poking his hands into his pockets. "I reckon he's right about that," he said smartly. Then added in a worried tone, "Don't you?"

Rome narrowed his eyes in thought. Something about the man's story didn't ring true. Could he be a swindler in town to dupe Will and the Quinns into giving him a free ride? If so, would Adrian be safe living under the same roof with him?

"Hey, Will, your boy still saving for that horse Houchin has for sale?"

"Yep, got near five dollars put back already," Will said, his chest poking out proudly as he spoke of his oldest son.

"I've got a job for him. I'll pay him good if he'll take these supplies out to my place and give a message to Lorraine's sister for me."

"Sure thing, Rome. He'd be glad to do it. You plan to stay in town a spell?"

Rome watched the door of the livery until the stranger came out, leading a horse. He pulled himself clumsily into the saddle and rode at a slow pace out of town.

"What? Oh, yeah. I think I'll stay over a couple of days."

"What's the matter? You think that fellow ain't what he appears to be?"

Turning toward Will, Rome narrowed his eyes. "What exactly is it he appears to be?" he said, studying the shopowner.

"Well, some kind of writer, I reckon." At Rome's raised eyebrow he stammered, "Well, what else would he want with a typewriter?"

Shaking his head, Rome went back to loading the wagon. What indeed? he wondered.

"You mean to tell me you gave this man a room, and he hasn't paid you a penny?"

Rome leaned against the frame of the partially constructed hotel and eyed Bob Quinn with disbelief.

"He said he'd lost all his money when his wallet was stole at the train station. But he'd got this type-a-writer from Will over at the general store and he said I could use it for co-latrill, or something like that, if he couldn't get the money by the end of the month. Besides, he's been helping me out with the hotel whenever he can."

"And has he? Got the money he expected, I mean?"

"Not so far as I know. Least he ain't paid me none if he has. Why are you so interested, anyway?"

Rome shrugged casually. "Just curious. It isn't like we get a lot of visitors through here."

Quinn scratched his hairy chest with the claw side of his hammer. "That's true. 'Course, I hope that's gonna change with the railroad coming through." He waved toward the skeleton of the planned hotel. "In fact, I'm banking on it."

Anxious to get back to the subject of Evan Garvey, Rome nodded, then looked thoughtful. "Where does Garvey plan to get the money?"

Quinn's face lit up. "I told you, he's a writer. He's got a bunch of stories he's been crankin' out on the gizmo and sending to Mobile. Says they'll make good fiction pieces for the newspapers and magazines."

"But he hasn't actually sold any that you know of, has he?"

"Nope, but I know he's sent 'em to them places."

Rome felt a cloud of apprehension engulf him. "Let me guess," he said, his mouth twisting in an annoyed grimace. "You paid to post them for him?"

Quinn nodded his shaggy red head and grinned.

"Don't fret now, it's only a couple of plates. You'll get the hang of it soon enough."

Adrian knelt on the floor of the kitchen and scooped the shards of crockery into a dustpan. Mary had been patient with her so far, but she could tell the woman was growing concerned about the number of dishes she'd broken.

"I promise I'll be more careful next time," she vowed, gathering up another tray and heading for the dining area. She made it all the way across the kitchen and turned to share a timid smile with Mary. The woman smiled back and nodded succinctly.

Just then Bob Quinn came barreling through the doors and the tray flew out of Adrian's hands, landing with a resounding crash as another two place settings were instantly reduced to rubble.

"Dad burn it, Bob," Mary scolded loudly. "How many times have I told you not to burst through that door like that? It's bad enough when you knock into me, but Adrian ain't figured out how to dodge that door without losing her grip on the tray."

"Sorry," the big man muttered, bending to help Adrian clean up the mess.

"Me too, Mary," Adrian said, apologizing profusely to the red-haired, red-faced woman.

"Don't fret," Mary said. "It weren't your fault. This time."

Mary fixed another tray and Adrian carried it out to the customers she'd waited on. As jobs went this one was pretty cut and dry. However, she'd learned quickly that balancing a half-dozen dishes as she weaved through a room full of tables wasn't a talent she possessed.

Had she been in her world, with more options, she'd have reverted to her old ways and thrown in the towel the first hour. But she didn't have any choices here, in this place and time. And she needed to see if she could make it on her own in this world.

More than anything she wanted to go after Rome and beg him to take her back with him to the farm. But she stiffened her resolve and went back to work. If she did decide to go back to Rome and the children it wouldn't be because she'd failed again.

From the corner of her eye she saw Evan Garvey enter the room and take a seat.

She knew his name because Mary had introduced them earlier when he'd come down on his way out. He was handsome in a way that transcended time, she thought now. In other words, he looked as though he'd be perfectly at home in either this world or hers. But there was something about him that interested Adrian. His manner of speech didn't have the slightly stilted, old-fashioned edge she'd come to expect from people she'd met since her arrival.

He even used slang terms she'd thought were modern. Shrugging, she dismissed the thoughts. Obviously she was mistaken. A case of wishful thinking, no doubt.

Being careful not to drop anything, she unloaded the plates of food and glasses of iced tea onto the occupied table. The men thanked her, and, tucking the tray under her arm, she moved on to Evan Garvey's table.

"Hello, Adrian," he said. "How's the first day of work?"

"Fine, I suppose." She withdrew a pad and a stub of a pencil from her pocket. Mary could listen to a half dozen orders and get every one right without ever writing them down. But Adrian had discovered after the first few minutes that she tended to confuse things if she didn't list them carefully.

"What can I get you?"

"The special sounds good. Has Will brought the mail yet?"

"Will?" She stopped writing and glanced down at him.

"Will Anderson, the man who runs the general store. He usually brings the mail around lunch—I mean dinnertime. It's his way of getting a piece of Mary's pie without his wife knowing."

Adrian grinned, but she couldn't help the twinge of unease she felt around this man. "I don't know if he's been here. But I'll ask Mary and let you know when I bring your order out."

"Thanks," he said, clearing his throat. He looked discomfited and Adrian offered him a slight smile as she went back to the kitchen.

Rome watched the scene from the doorway of the dining room, a scowl marring his features. If that man wasn't a scoundrel he'd eat his hat, he thought, noticing the way the man shifted in his seat and dabbed at nervous perspiration on his brow.

And what was Adrian thinking smiling at him that way? Couldn't she see he was a no-good cad, who'd probably cheated Will with his phony money and bamboozled the Quinns out of room and board? No telling what he'd try next.

Rome was glad he'd decided to stay in town for a few days. That fellow was up to something. And Rome would just bet it was nothing good.

Chapter Twenty-four

Adrian finished the last of the dishes and hung her sodden dish towel on the rack over the sink. She'd never been so bone-tired in her life. Always one to tip generously, at least 20 percent of the bill, she decided then and there she hadn't given those poor, overworked waitresses nearly enough.

Her feet ached, especially in the ill-fitting, low-heeled shoes. Needles of pain drove into her spine between her throbbing shoulder blades. Even her face felt tight and sore from smiling at the customers all day.

All she wanted was to go upstairs and sink into a hot tub and stay there until her skin shriveled up and resembled a prune. However even that was not to be. Mary had told her there was no bathroom in the house. Once more, she'd be forced to use an outhouse and haul buckets of water up to a hip tub if she wanted a bath. As much as she wanted that soak, nothing could persuade her to haul any*thing* any*where* after the day she had had.

She stared down at her poor hands, red and swollen from the work she'd done. Why had she thought taking care of one small family on a farm was difficult? It was a piece of cake next to this. Which only made her want to go home all the more.

Home. She wanted to go home. But she didn't mean back to her time or even her little apartment. She'd been thinking of the farm. Rome and the children.

She lifted her head and stared through the kitchen window at the dark night outside. She wished she were in her rocker in front of the fireplace, receiving good-night hugs and kisses from Mimi, Toby, and Eli. She wanted to look across the small room and see Rome reading the *Farmer's Almanac*.

Would she always think of their place as home? she wondered. Why had she thought she could leave them so easily? Where was her resolve to settle her past? She'd made the toughest decision of her life for the sake of Rome and the children and she had to see it through or admit to failure once again.

Besides, there was still the problem of Winifred, and her seemingly endless skills.

Was it fatigue and self-pity that had her long-ing for the feel of Rome's strong arms and the sound of his warm, rugged voice? She longed to brush back his hair, picturing it in her mind as it always was, a little too long, a little too unruly. Just the way she liked it.

Was it self-pity? It felt suspiciously like love. But until she had something definite to offer him, she couldn't go back. It would be unfair to give him false hopes just because she was in need of comfort.

She dragged herself upstairs to her room and dropped down face-first on the mattress. She didn't bother to undress or wash off at the ba-sin. Exhaustion overtook her and she fell asleep thinking of Rome, and wishing he were beside her.

She didn't see Rome the next day, but Quinn told her he'd decided to stay in town a few days. Each time the door to the restaurant opened she would glance up, hoping to see him stand-ing there. If he were trying to make her regret her decision, he was doing a good job of it. She'd been doing just that.

The day passed slowly. Adrian accustomed herself to the work expected of her, but, to Ma-ry's dismay, she broke another tray of dishes. This time she knew the blame lay in her pre-occupation with Rome's absence. Had he changed his mind and returned to the farm?

She went to her room that night more miserable than ever before. She missed Rome and the children terribly. She resented knowing Winifred was seeing them every minute of the day. She tried to tell herself Winifred was the best woman for the job, but she couldn't help feeling she had something to offer Mimi, Toby, and Eli that their aunt couldn't.

"You're being ridiculous," she chastised her reflection in the mirror over her washbasin that night. "She is their aunt. She loves them. She'll make the best replacement for their mother. You can't even wait tables without breaking things."

Again she crawled into bed exhausted. Again she wished for Rome's comforting presence beside her.

"Hello, Adrian," Evan Garvey said the next morning as he came into the dining room and took a seat for breakfast.

"Good morning, Evan," she answered absently, her gaze going to the door again before she turned to go back to the kitchen.

She delivered a tray of eggs, ham, sausage, biscuits and coffee to the man from the livery and then went to take Evan's order. His mind seemed preoccupied this morning as well, and she stole another look at the door while she waited for him to tell her what he wanted. Finally she copied his order and went into the kitchen.

Mary busily kept pots and pans going on all eight burners of the massive stove at one time. The woman seemed to have an uncanny knack for knowing just when to stir, flip or remove something from the oven.

She could pull a perfectly browned batch of biscuits from the oven without ever having checked them once to see if they were done. There could be no doubt Mary had found her calling.

As she set the tray down on the crowded work table in the center of the kitchen, Adrian bumped a glass tumbler and just managed to catch it before it slid over the edge onto the floor. She shot a glance in Mary's direction, and saw the woman exhale a relieved sigh.

She would not quit this job, Adrian told herself. No matter how difficult it became, it was too important that she succeed this time. She had to prove to herself she could stand by a commitment, even a small one. She felt as though she'd changed since her arrival here, but she'd thought that before. Rome and the children were too important for her to risk hurting them.

Besides, until she found the answers she sought, she'd need this job to support herself. It wasn't as if she could get another one at the snap of her fingers as she'd always been able to before.

For an hour she hustled to and fro, taking orders, removing dishes, and refilling coffee cups without a single mishap.

Evan drank nearly a pot himself as he perused something written on a sheet of paper. He didn't even notice her the last time she refilled his cup. His head was bent over the page as he scribbled frantically.

Suddenly he jumped to his feet. He bumped into Adrian and she barely managed to keep her grip on the metal pot.

"Sorry," he mumbled, shoving his chair back as he fished some coins from his pocket and dropped them on the table.

"It's all right," she called as he hastened from the room. At least it wasn't anything breakable. Mary had told her that morning that she would have to let her go if she continued to break things. The woman was kind, and truly sorry but she couldn't afford to replace any more dishes.

Adrian scooped the coins into her pocket and carefully loaded the dishes on the tray. She successfully delivered them to the kitchen and collected the next order.

So far so good, she thought. She hadn't broken a single thing all day.

As she came out of the kitchen, she stopped, her feet frozen in place. Rome sat at the table near the door, a newspaper open in front of him. Swallowing, she picked up a clean mug and carried it over. Setting the cup on the table, she poured coffee into it, black the way he liked it.

"Good morning, Rome," she said.

He glanced up from the paper and smiled and her heart slammed against her ribs. It was suddenly warm in the room and she tugged at the high neck of the blouse she wore.

"Good morning, Adrian. How is the job working out?"

He sipped his coffee and Adrian watched the full lips touch the smooth rim. He blew lightly on the black liquid, pursing his lips in imitation of a kiss, and her pulse raced.

Fanning herself with her notepad, she answered simply, "Fine. What can I get you?"

"What's the special?" he asked, just the way he had the first time she'd come in here with him.

For a long minute she watched the way he squinted against the steam coming from his cup, just the way he used to squint against the morning sun as it came over the fields at dawn.

He looked up and their gazes met. Adrian smiled warmly, wondering if he'd known what she was thinking.

"Adrian?"

"Yes, Rome?" she whispered.

"The special?"

Adrian blinked away her musings and cleared her throat. "Oh, right. Um, let me see. Biscuits and cream gravy with bacon," she murmured absently.

"That sounds good," he said, raising his paper and disappearing behind it once more.

Adrian stood rooted to the floor for a full minute, watching him swallow more coffee. He hadn't said a word to her about returning to the farm with him or even sitting in the swing out front. Had he finally given up on her? And why did that thought fill her with such distress?

She collected herself and turned to go to the kitchen.

"Adrian."

She whirled at the sound of Rome's voice, certain her eagerness must show on her face like a neon sign. "Yes, Rome?"

"More coffee," he said, lifting his cup.

"More coffee?" she stammered, thinking she must have heard him wrong.

"Yes." He lifted the cup higher. "More coffee. Please," he added, as though that lack of courtesy was what had her flustered.

She looked down at the empty pot she carried in her hand. "Right," she said, nodding. "Coffee."

She refilled his cup twice before delivering his meal.

He ate, pushed himself away from the table, and cordially waved good-bye as he counted enough money out for his breakfast and a good-sized tip.

Adrian appreciated the gratuity, but a few words and a little of his time would have been better. Her lips pursed in a frown and the customer behind her had to call twice before she heard him and went to take his order.

Rome stepped into a wedge of early morning sunlight streaming through a gap in the roof over the walkway. He rolled the newspaper in his hand and tapped it slowly against his thigh. He had to return to the farm soon. He struggled with his disappointment. Adrian had looked miserable, but she hadn't mentioned changing her mind after two days of waiting tables. He'd thought that she'd be ready to go back with him. Had he made a mistake leaving her alone yesterday so she could think things through without his interference? Was he wrong to assume she would come to the conclusion he desired if he stopped pushing her so hard to marry him?

He hoped not. He still loved her and wanted her to come back with him to the farm more than anything. He wanted to marry her, share their lives, raise the children, and maybe even have a few of their own. But none of that was possible until Adrian overcame whatever problems were keeping her from making the commitment.

He might have been able to give up except that he knew beyond a doubt she loved him. And that made worthwhile every effort on his part to give her unfettered opportunities to work her problems out herself. No matter how hard it was for him to pretend he wasn't anxious to have her back at the farm and away from the handsome boarder, Evan Garvey.

He'd passed Garvey as he came into the restaurant earlier. The man had nearly run him down in his hurry to leave the place. Although Rome hadn't found out anything definite about the guy, something about Evan Garvey continued to bother Rome. Something he couldn't put his finger on.

Was he just getting paranoid? He'd thought the same thing about Winifred when she arrived so unexpectedly. He'd even gone so far as to wire an old friend in St. Louis and inquire about her life the past few years since her parents' deaths. He suspected there was more to her belated appearance here than she'd said.

With that thought in mind, he decided to check the telegraph office for a reply this morning. He'd give Adrian another couple of days before pressing her to come home with him. His instincts urged him to storm the restaurant and take her, if he had to carry her over his shoulder kicking and screaming. But he knew that kind of behavior would never work with a woman like Adrian. She wouldn't return to him unless, and until, she resolved whatever was bothering her.

Chapter Twenty-five

Quickly tiring of the never-ending supply of dirty plates, cups, pots, pans and utensils, Adrian sank her hands into the hot, soapy water.

At least the evening rush was over. Once the last of the dishes were done she could go to her room and collapse.

"Hey, pretty lady."

A smile quickly spread across Adrian's lips and she whirled around. The smile died and she felt something in her heart die with it.

"Oh, hello, Evan."

"Uh, oh," he said, pushing away from the door frame. "You were expecting someone else."

She hated she'd been so transparent. And she

despised being so sappy about Rome's cool aloofness. But she couldn't help the tears of disappointment welling in her eyes. Blinking, she shook her head, refusing to let Evan see how she felt.

"No, actually I wasn't expecting anyone at all. You startled me."

"Sorry. I thought I'd come down and sneak a piece of Mary's pie. I was so busy earlier I missed dinner."

"Let me fix you a plate. I put some leftovers in the larder."

"Don't go to any trouble."

Adrian gathered a plate and one of the funny, three-tined forks. "No bother."

Actually it was, but she wasn't about to let Evan mess up the kitchen she'd cleaned. If she fixed his plate she could tidy up while he ate.

She dished up a slab of chicken-fried liver and some purple hull peas. Setting it in front of him she reached for a glass to pour him some milk.

"Not my favorite," he said. "But I guess we've got to get those vitamins."

Adrian chuckled and poured his milk. "That's just what I thought when Mary told me what the special was tonight."

She turned to put the empty pitcher in the sink and a dizzying thought seized her. The pitcher slipped from her hand, hit the corner of the zinc enclosure, and shattered.

Evan jumped to his feet, took one look at Adrian's face, and misread her concern.

"Don't worry. Mary's upstairs already. We'll clean this up and she'll never know it happened."

Adrian nodded woodenly, but she couldn't force a reply past her stiff lips. Had Evan said vitamins? Had she misunderstood him?

Her hands trembled so badly he took them in his own and pushed her into a chair while he swept up the broken crockery. After cleaning the floor, he unplugged the sink and let the water run out the pipe that led outside. Then he carefully gathered the slivers that had fallen into the sink and put the whole mess at the bottom of the trash barrel by the back door.

"There now, no harm done. If Mary says anything I'll tell her I broke the pitcher when I came down to get a snack."

Still stunned and confused, Adrian glanced at his plate. "You didn't eat your liver," she said dumbly.

He looked as if he wanted to choke and she shook herself. Something had happened here. But what she was thinking was impossible. Wasn't it? It was at least very improbable. Maybe she was just mistaken, she told herself again.

"I'm not hungry anymore," he said. "I think I'll go on up to bed. Good night," he mumbled, skirting her where she sat on the chair.

Gradually, Adrian began to clear away his dishes. She scraped the food into the hog's slop jar, poured the milk in the sink and rinsed the plate and glass. But her mind continued to whirl with possibilities.

Finally, she decided she had to be confused. As a nurse she'd learned about vitamins and such. And she could have sworn no one had even known of their existence until the nineteen hundreds. But it had been a long time since her classes. It was possible, in her present state, that she was mistaken.

She wiped off the table and went to the stairs. Climbing them seemed a chore after the long day. The last few tense moments had taken their toll as well. She felt drained. What kind of life was this? she thought in frustration. What good was she doing proving she could face up to the reality of her situation here if all she did was move like an automaton through each day?

Was she torturing herself by leaving Rome for nothing? If all she had to look forward to here in this time was a lifetime of servitude she'd rather hide on the farm, where at least she was loved and could love in return.

But would she wonder later whether she'd gone to Rome out of love or need? Would he always have doubts about her reasons as well? She didn't think she could live with that. And he deserved so much more.

At the top of the stairs she grasped the newel post and paused. God, she missed him. She missed Mimi and Toby and Eli. When she thought of Rome her heart ached. Thinking of the children made it feel as if it had been ripped out of her chest.

She wanted to be with them. Her arms ached to hold the baby; her fingers itched to run through Mimi's soft, fine hair. She longed for one of Toby's mischievous smiles.

But her soul yearned for Rome. The sight of him, his touch, his scent, his warmth. To be held in those strong, capable arms would be heaven right now.

Slowly, she put one foot in front of the other. At the door to her room she paused, wondering where Rome was and what he was doing. Was he thinking of her? Wishing, as she was, that they were still together?

She pushed open the door and, without even lighting the lamp, dropped onto the bed. As she lay there she became aware of a stillness in the room. She told herself the eerie feeling was a result of her exhaustion, but then she heard a rasp in the dark and a small flame jumped to life.

Adrian screamed and scrambled to the far side of the bed. In the glow of the flame she saw the distortion of a man's face. Someone was in her room, and Mary and Bob Quinn were at the other end of the hall. They probably hadn't even heard her scream.

Before she could cry out again, the match was held to the wick of the lamp and the room filled with blessed light.

"Evan! What the hell are you doing in here? You nearly scared me to death."

Evan uncrossed his legs and rose from the chair beside her bedside table. "I thought you'd light the lamp when you came in and you'd see me. When I realized you'd gone immediately to bed, I figured I'd better let you know I was here."

"You couldn't have found another way to do it?" she hissed, absently rubbing her chest in an effort to ease her racing heart. Every time she tried to swallow she felt a lump in her throat.

"Sorry, I wanted to talk to you alone."

"Geez," she snapped, uncurling her legs from under her and finding a more comfortable position on the bed. "We were alone in the kitchen. If you had something to say why didn't you say it then?"

"I had to see you in private, where I knew we wouldn't be disturbed. The kitchen's too open and sometimes Quinn sneaks down for a snack."

"How did you know my door was unlocked?"

"This room doesn't have a key." At her look of startled confusion, he laughed and waved his hand. "Never mind, that's another story," he told her.

"Just what do you have in mind?" she asked, glaring at him with reproachful eyes.

He followed her gaze to the door and chuckled. "Not what you're thinking, I'm afraid. Not that I'm not interested," he quickly assured her. "But, maybe you should read this first."

He held up a small stack of papers she hadn't noticed he was holding.

"What is that?"

"It's the story I sent to Mobile. I'm trying to earn some money by publishing fiction pieces."

"You sneaked in here to ask me to read your work?" She hoped her tone conveyed the fury rising within her. She couldn't believe this man's audacity.

He continued to sit there, calm and serene in the chair. His short black hair was rumpled slightly as though he'd run his fingers through it. She noticed for the first time that his eyes were dark, almost black. And he squinted as though he needed glasses but didn't wear them.

His bulk filled the chair, but a healthy, muscular build. Almost like the men she'd known in her time who worked out in gyms to stay fit after sitting behind a desk all day.

She saw him shift in the chair and her attention went to the pages in his hand. Making no attempt to hide her growing anger, she went to the door and pulled it open.

"I'm very tired, Evan. All I want to do is go to

bed and sleep. I'm sorry, I don't have the energy to read your story right now. And the next time you want a free critique I'd appreciate it if you'd have the courtesy to knock first and wait to be invited in."

His lips twisted in a condescending grin and Adrian's ire blazed. Instead of leaving as she'd asked, he merely crossed one long leg over the other and settled into the chair.

"I think you'll find this interesting reading," he said.

"Look, I don't care how fascinating you think your work is, I'm not interested. Now, please leave."

Finally, he stood. Adrian expelled a relieved sigh, but continued to hold her staunch position. As he approached, she felt a shiver of apprehension. After all, she didn't know anything about this man.

"Just promise me you'll read the first line," he said, surprising her.

Adrian turned her head to the side, refusing to meet his questioning gaze. He took her hand and pressed the pages into it. "The first line," he repeated. "That's all I ask. If you don't want to read any more after that, I won't bother you again."

She clutched the pages rather than have them fall to the floor, and he stepped out of the room. Closing the door, she threw the bolt into place and leaned back against the sturdy wood. She would ask Mary to find the key to the door and from now on keep it locked at all times.

She went to the chest in the corner and dropped Evan's story on top of it. How dare that man come into her room and ambush her, all to get her to read his stupid story. God, she couldn't believe how brazenly he'd sat there, as though it were nothing for him to be in her room. What if Mary had come to her room for something and seen him there? Rome might even hear of it. And then what? Would he think her unfit to take care of his children?

"You gave up that position," she reminded herself. What difference could Rome's opinion possibly make now? But as she unbuttoned her blouse and tugged the bottom out of the waist-band of her skirt she knew it still mattered to her. Deep down, Rome would always matter a great deal to her. Regardless of what happened in her life from this point on.

Discarding the blouse, she reached for the buttons of her skirt. Unfastening them, she dropped the skirt and stepped out of it. Then she reached down, scooping it off the floor. As she turned to hang it on the wall peg, she heard a jangling sound and looked down in time to see a shiny coin roll across the floor and disappear under the bed.

"Oh, great," she mumbled. "It isn't as though I make a bundle in tips to begin with."

She still had not gotten used to the small amount of money it took to live in this time. Rome had paid her when he brought her to town for the month she'd filled the position as housekeeper and nanny for him. She'd wanted to refuse the salary, but knew it would be foolish when she was about to venture out on her own in a strange world.

However, she hadn't used so much as a single, curious-looking nickel of it. And she'd already filled a small jar with what she'd gotten from the customers.

Releasing the tapes on the side of her single petticoat, she hung it beside her skirt. She splashed water on her face and used a small cotton cloth to clean each tooth. She hadn't forgotten her first glimpse of the town's "dentist," and she wanted to make sure she would not be needing his services anytime soon.

Finally, she was able to crawl into bed. She rolled onto her stomach and fluffed her pillow several times, trying to ease her aching bones into a comfortable position. Slowly her eyes drifted shut.

Once more, her thoughts returned to Rome. What was she going to do about her feelings for him and the children? She told herself a hundred times a day she was doing what was best for them. But that didn't stop the despair that had become her constant companion.

If it weren't for the fact that Winifred was taking better care of them, and was more fitted to the job, she thought she might break down and go back to them. It would be so much easier than living this day-to-day existence, missing them unbearably. And after all, hadn't she always taken the easy way out?

Not this time, she told herself. This time her actions would affect more than just herself. If she really cared about Rome and the children she would have to do what was best for them no matter what she wanted.

And as much as it hurt her to admit it, she knew that right now that meant leaving them with Winifred.

How could she ask them to let her stay and be wife and mother to them when she wasn't even sure she could stay? That would be the ultimate cruelty, and she refused to subject them to her unstable existence no matter how she wished she could.

Shifting on the bed again, she let her hand drop over the side. Her fingers brushed the wood floor and she remembered the money that had rolled under there earlier. Without much effort, she felt around and located the coin. Picking it up, she tossed it to the bedside table and reached over to extinguish the lamp.

Her eyes lit on the coin. Her body went rigid. Frozen in place, she stared at the silver disk. Suddenly she was wide awake. Her heavy lashes flew open and she bolted to an upright position.

Trembling, she reached for the coin. As her fingers approached it she drew back, feeling a moment's hesitation. What would happen? Would anything happen? She'd had it in her pocket all day and nothing strange had occurred.

But where had she gotten it? She thought back to the customers and the tips she'd received. Who had given her this particular coin?

There was no way to be certain, but Adrian had a sneaking suspicion she knew where it had come from.

Snatching up the money, she darted to the chest and grabbed the sheaf of papers Evan Garvey had asked her to read.

Just the first line, he'd said. All he asked was that she read the first line.

She read it, and her legs gave out beneath her. She crumpled to a heap on the floor and reread the words he'd typed.

Who could have conceived of something so horrendous as being hurled back through time?

A hysterical giggle escaped Adrian's cold lips. Her eyes refused to leave the page, fastened on those words like they were her lifeline.

Who could conceive it? she thought crazily. She, for one. She could certainly imagine it happening. After all, it had happened to her.

And if Evan Garvey was trying to tell her something, as she suspected, it would seem it had happened to him as well. She looked down at the quarter clutched in her shaking hand. Squeezing it, she felt the small ridges along the edge cut into her palm.

A real, Washington quarter. Part silver, part nickel. She read the date and cried out in sheer pleasure. Nineteen seventy-eight!

Chapter Twenty-six

Propriety never entered Adrian's mind as she sped down the hall toward Evan's room. She barely took the time to grab her robe from the bottom of the bed and throw it over her chemise.

She burst through the door without knocking despite her earlier admonitions to him.

Evan sat in the chair by his bedside table, his legs crossed just the way he'd been in her room. Adrian slid to a halt, waving the story in front of her.

"What took you so long?" he asked, his foot bobbing casually in the air.

"I'm not crazy." She gasped. "You're from the future."

He laughed and motioned for her to shut the

door. Dazed, Adrian did as he directed, waiting eagerly for his reply.

"Did you read the entire story? Or just the first line."

She sucked in great gulps of air, wondering how he could be so calm. She wanted to run and hug him, touch him, feel him and know he was from the same world as she. She needed a link to her time and this man was a miracle connective.

"Oh, my God. Omigod," she cried, pressing her fingers to her lips. "It's true, isn't it?"

He chuckled again. "Read the story, Adrian. We've got a lot to talk about, but I think you'll find some of the answers you're looking for in there."

"I'm too excited to read. Just tell me, I'm right, aren't I?"

He stood and strolled casually to the door. Opening it, he took her by the shoulders and led her out into the hallway. "Read the whole story, Adrian. I'll see you in the morning."

"But—but, Evan."

He walked her out of the room and closed the door behind her. For a full minute Adrian stood rooted to the floor outside his room. How could he simply dismiss her like that? She needed answers and he had them. She realized she still held his story in her hands and she looked down at it. Or was he trying to tell her she had all the answers she needed right here?

Scurrying to her room, she closed the door and sank into the chair by her bedside table. Her fatigue had disappeared with the first few words she'd read. She could never sleep now. Evan had known that when he brought the pages to her.

Again she read those incredible words, that extraordinary first line. Quickly her eyes moved on to the next line, and then the next. Hungrily she devoured the story and then, turning back to the first page read it all again.

Bursting into the dining room the next morning, Adrian saw Mary and hurried to her.

"Where's Evan?" she asked, breathless from dashing to get dressed and downstairs as soon as possible.

Mary drew a sharp breath and stared wordlessly. Then her gaze cut to the side and Adrian whirled around. Coming face-to-face with Rome would have been enough to steal her own breath. The black scowl he wore added to her apprehension.

"Rome."

"I was waiting to talk to you," he said, his lips tight and thin over his teeth. She could see the anger he didn't even try to hide.

"I'm sorry. I needed to see Evan Garvey. . . . "

She cut her explanation off as his eyes darkened dangerously. Just the mention of Evan's name was apparently enough to fuel his fury.

363

"How are you?" she asked instead.

"Fine. Can we talk privately for a minute?"

She glanced at Mary and the woman nodded. Adrian motioned Rome to a table in the far corner.

She was inordinately glad to see him, ashamed to admit she was thankful for the smallest crumb where he was concerned. She told herself she was pitiful, waiting breathlessly like a love-struck adolescent for just a glimpse of her beloved. But, Adrian knew a glimpse might be all she could hope for now.

"I'm leaving, Adrian," he announced without preamble as soon as they were seated.

She gasped, pressing her hand to her pounding heart. "Leaving?"

He nodded. "I have to get back to the farm. Will's boy'll return with the wagon today."

"I see." She steadied her racing pulse and blinked several times to clear her whirling thoughts. "Will I see you again?"

He studied her face a long moment, then looked away and shrugged. "That's up to you. I wanted to let you know, whether you decide to come back or not, I won't be marrying Winifred."

Adrian had to stifle a joyful cry at his words. She could see there was more to that decision than he was telling her, but even that nagging thought couldn't mar the happiness she felt welling in her.

"So if you change your mind about . . . anything, you know where to find us."

A lump wedged in her throat and she found she couldn't force a reply out. She nodded, feeling the tears come to her eyes. He was going to walk away and she couldn't speak the words that would stop him.

And with Evan's revelation she had another set of worries gnawing away at her insides now. If she let Rome walk away, would it be the last time she ever saw him?

Two local farmers came into the dining room and took a seat. They greeted Rome and he lifted a hand in return but didn't speak.

"Wait," Adrian said. "I have to get their orders, but I'll be right back."

He nodded.

She hurried to the table, quickly took two orders for the special, and called them back to Mary. Then she returned to the table.

"Rome, I have to talk to Evan Garvey this morning." She saw his features tighten once more and she held up her hand. "But I want to see you again after that. Can you wait for just a little while, before you leave town?"

She could read the doubt and indecision in his teal eyes. Pride warred with the real affection he obviously still felt for her. Adrian's heart hung suspended for a split second.

"All right," he said. "I can wait a few hours. But no later than that if I want to reach the farm before nightfall."

"Thank you," she whispered. Mary poked her head out the kitchen door and called for Adrian to collect her orders. She stood to go, then turned back to Rome. Grasping his hand, she took a minute to memorize every detail of his face. She wondered how she'd feel if this were the last time she ever saw him.

Pain seized her, and for the first time she realized what she'd be giving up if she let him go back to the farm without her. Could she do it? Even if it were the best thing for him and the children? It would just about kill her to let him go.

Some of what she felt must have shown on her face, for a dim light of hope flashed in the sea-green eyes watching her. Briefly, the lines around his eyes smoothed out and a ghost of the lighter side he'd recently shown her could be seen. But then it was gone, and the doubt returned.

Her leaving had hurt him deeply. He couldn't understand. She couldn't explain without telling him the whole truth about her past, and all the failed plans she'd made in her life up to this point.

He left, and she watched him go, beyond the point of tears now.

The morning rush took her mind off her grief for a time, and then she looked up and saw Evan rush in, a frown lining his brow. Quickly she deposited two plates of eggs, hominy grits, and biscuits and refilled coffee cups at another table on her way toward him.

"What is it? Is something wrong?" She noticed the high color in his cheeks, the almost frantic gleam in his eyes.

"You read the story?"

Adrian followed him to the same table she'd shared with Rome earlier, and they sat across from each other. "Of course I read it. You knew I would. But how did you know I was from the future, too?"

"Your speech, your actions. I listened to you talk and I began to wonder if it was possible. The scene in the kitchen was a test of sorts."

"And you're from the Newhope of 1995, just like I am?"

"It was all in the story," he told her with a decisive nod.

"And the rest of it, that was all true, too?"

"Yes, yes. Now, can we talk about this? We don't have much time."

"You mentioned that in the story. How can you be sure?" she whispered desperately. "You theorized that the particles of the comet somehow broke through the time barrier. That this time actually runs parallel to our time and if we find the opening we can go home. But, I don't understand the part about the debris and this time limit."

"I've spent the last month trying to figure out how I came to be here. I went back to the spot where I came through."

"The airfield? Were you there to watch the comet, too?"

"No," he said, grinning roguishly. "I was leaving a friend's house when my car broke down."

"A friend?" she asked incredulously, remembering it was the middle of the night.

"A lady friend," he confessed. "Anyway, I was going to have to walk to get help. Then I saw a car at the edge of the field."

"My car," Adrian said.

He nodded. "I suppose so. Anyway, I was heading for the car hoping to find someone I could hitch a ride with back into town when the comet appeared."

"And whatever force drew me through time took you along, too."

"That's my guess. Of course, I didn't know until you showed up in town that anyone else had been drawn through."

"Neither did I." She breathed. "It never even occurred to me. I thought I was finally losing it for sure."

"Well, I don't know what you've been doing for the last four weeks but I've been busy trying to find a way back. And I've discovered some of the chunks of matter that fell from the comet. They glow a phosphorescent green at night under the light of the moon. But the glow is fading. Each day the rocks get dimmer. It only makes sense that the opening between the two times is closing, resealing itself where the comet somehow damaged it. We have to go back through before it disappears altogether."

"How can you talk about sense? None of this makes sense," she hissed, noticing the curious looks they were getting from the customers.

"Not if your idea of normal is thinking of time as being a linear thing with a beginning, a middle, and an end."

"What other way is there to think of it?"

"Didn't you ever watch 'Star Trek'?"

Adrian sat back, still unaccustomed to being able to discuss modern, twentieth century things as commonplace again.

"Of course. I mean, I was no Trekkie, but I've seen a few episodes."

"They explained time as a continuous, circular phenomenon. Sort of like a cinnamon roll."

"A what?" she cried, her eyes widening. She stared at him as though he'd gone mad.

"Shh," he warned, seeing the sidelong looks they were earning. "All right, maybe that wasn't a good simile. But if time does pass around itself like the layers of a roll, it would make sense that you could go from one time to another if you somehow broke through the barrier separating the layers."

Pressing her fingers to her temples, she shook her head. "I'm more confused than ever. Are you sure that's what happened?"

"Pretty sure. Last night, after you left my room, I went back to the field where I first appeared. The fog was blanketing the ground, just the way it was that night. And the moon is almost full again. I found the spot where I guessed the opening to be and I threw a rock through it." He leaned in, and Adrian found herself holding her breath anxiously. "The rock disappeared."

Somewhat deflated, she sat back. "How do you know you didn't just lose it in the dark?"

"Dammit, Adrian, I'm serious," he snapped.

"So am I. That's a pretty flimsy theory for us to base our lives on, isn't it?"

"So we fling ourselves through the fog. If I'm wrong, we end up with a couple of bruises. We're no worse off than we are now."

She chewed her lip, her mind racing with a hundred thoughts. It all seemed so bizarre. Could Evan be right? If he was, that meant she could go home. But it also meant she would never see Rome or the children again.

She shook her head. "I just don't know, Evan. It's all so strange."

"Not to me, it isn't. What's strange is sticking around here in this backward time without computers or cars or anything civilized."

Adrian thought of the beautiful mornings she'd spent on Rome's farm. There was something to be said for a simpler time. "I don't know," she whispered. "It's not all that bad."

Evan scoffed, looking across at her now like she was the crazy one. "Adrian, wake up. You can't stay here. We've got to make plans if we're going to do this before it's too late."

Plans. The one thing she was never very good at making. Flying by the seat of her pants for the last decade had not prepared her for the tough decisions she was being forced to make now.

She wanted to see Rome, talk to him. But what would she say? *By the way, did I mention I'm from the future? And now I have to decide whether to go back where I came from or stay here.*

"I need more time."

Evan shook his head. "We don't have any more time. I'm going out again tonight to try another experiment. But we have to be ready to go tomorrow night. It's too dangerous to wait any longer than that. And I for one am not taking any chances of being stuck here forever."

If only she could talk to Rome.

"Adrian?"

"I'm not very good at making decisions like this," she told Evan. "I have to think."

Evan's dark eyes widened with astonishment. "What is there to think about? You don't want to stay here, do you?"

Her head came up and she bit her lip. Did she? Was that why she was hesitating?

"I just don't know," she said, shaking her head. So many thoughts were careening through her mind she felt dizzy. If she stayed she'd never see Alex again, never mend the rift between them. Of course, if she left Rome and the children would be lost to her forever. She had to make the most important choice of her life and this time there was no one to make it for her. And there would be no going back and changing it once it was done.

Evan took her hand across the table and squeezed it. "I know this is frightening. You think I'm not a little scared when I think of hurling myself into what might be a black hole? But it's our only hope, Adrian. We've got to get back to our time, and this is the only way."

Desperation and indecision threatened to overwhelm her. She clutched his hand, needing to know she wasn't alone in this situation.

That was how Rome found them when he walked into the dining room a moment later. His gaze fell to their clasped hands and he stopped short. Adrian met his eyes. For a moment they just stared at each other. Then he turned on his heel and started for the door.

Adrian jumped to her feet. She didn't know what she'd say to him; she only knew she had to stop him. She had to make him understand.

Evan hadn't seen Rome's approach or departure, and when Adrian rose so fast she toppled her chair he leapt to his feet.

Adrian rushed out into the small foyer of the restaurant just as Rome was reaching for the knob on the beveled door.

"Rome," she called out.

He stopped, his hand on the brass knob. Evan slid to a halt behind her.

"Rome, please wait."

Slowly he turned, and she saw his features harden at the sight of Evan. She rushed forward and clutched his arm before he could turn away once more and leave.

"I need to talk to you," she told him, knowing her eyes were beseeching.

"I just came to tell you my wagon's coming up the street. I'll be leaving in a few minutes."

Adrian's heart skipped a beat, then thundered against her ribs. Instantaneously she ran her choices through her mind, trying to sort them out.

She could let Rome go and attempt to return to the future with Evan. She could stay in this time, in this town, and try to figure out what she wanted. Or she could go home with Rome.

Her heart raced and she felt the flutter of a thousand butterflies in her stomach. This was the most important decision in her life and she had very little time in which to make it.

As she stood frozen by fear and doubt, she looked through the opaque glass and saw the silhouette of the wagon come to a stop outside the restaurant.

Chapter Twenty-seven

Suddenly Rome grasped her shoulders. He drew her to him in a fierce embrace. "What'll it be, Adrian?"

Evan moved forward and Rome shot him a scathing look over Adrian's shoulder.

"I can't go on like this forever," he said. "I love you. I know you love me. I don't understand what you came to town to prove, but I was willing to give you time to do it. Only now I need some kind of an answer. Am I wasting my time waiting for you to come to your senses, Adrian? Is there some other reason you can't marry me?"

He cut his eyes toward Evan and she heard Evan's startled gasp.

"So," Evan said, stepping forward. "That's

what you've been doing for the last month."

She couldn't see his face but she heard the disbelief in his voice. Rome's grip tightened and he cut Evan a black look as he waited for her answer.

Vaguely she heard a ruckus outside the doors of the restaurant but she couldn't force her gaze away from Rome's tense face.

"What is it, Adrian? Weren't you happy with me and the children?"

"Yes, oh, yes. Rome, I don't think I've ever been so happy in my life," she said, as surprised by her declaration as the two men listening.

"Then what is it?" Rome asked, his hold gentling until it was almost a caress.

"I wasn't good at running a farm. I couldn't cook or sew. I didn't even *think* about the children's schooling until Winifred came. I don't know anything about this—your life," she stammered, realizing she'd almost blurted out the truth. That she didn't know anything about this world, this time. "Winifred will make a much better wife for you than I ever could."

"Is that was this was all about? You thought if you were gone I'd want Winifred?"

Adrian didn't answer but she heard Evan swear behind her.

"That's crazy. There's more to being a mother than sewing a few dresses," he said. "If the children need new clothes, we can buy them from the mercantile or pay someone to make them.

And there's more to being a wife than cooking, Adrian," he told her, drawing her closer against his chest. "Much more."

"Adrian?"

She stiffened at the sound of Evan's voice. Without loosening Rome's hold, she gazed over her shoulder at the other man.

"Adrian, you can't even consider this," Evan said, stepping toward her. "You know you don't belong here. Come with me."

She felt Rome's hands tense, cutting into her flesh. She stared at Evan for a long minute, and he nodded. Then her eyes went to Rome and his turquoise gaze held hers.

The door of the restaurant burst open and Rome barely managed to turn her in time to keep her from being hit by the swinging portal.

Winifred marched in, her face a blaze of fury. "Rome Walker, what are you up to?" she demanded.

"Winifred, what are you doing here? What's the matter? Where are the children?" he asked, releasing Adrian.

"I'll tell you what's wrong," she said through clenched teeth. "Your children are uncouth, undisciplined hellions. You wouldn't believe the horrors I have endured since you left. Snakes in the milk bucket, frogs in my bed. There was no way I was staying there alone with those brats another minute."

At that moment Will's son barreled through

the door, out of breath and struggling for wind. "Pa told her you was here, Mr. Walker. I tried to beat her over, but she got past me. She's been hollering like a pig with its tail stuck in the gate ever since I let her outta the springhouse."

"The springhouse?" Rome asked, seeing Winifred's scathing glare at the youngster. "What were you doing in the springhouse? And where are the children?"

Winifred was pushed aside as the three little imps in question shoved through the growing melee. She glared at them with loathing.

"Pa, Adrian," Mimi cried, rushing forward. She had Toby and Eli each by a hand.

Adrian's face lit up as they entered. Oh, how she'd missed them! She immediately moved forward and scooped the baby into her arms, smiling at Rome's daughter. Mimi grinned back.

"Will someone tell me what's going on?" Rome said.

Mimi looked at Winifred and wrinkled her nose. "She was horrible after you and Adrian left. She doesn't care anything about us."

"Did you scare Winifred and then lock her in the springhouse?"

Mimi and Toby shared a look of chagrin. Eli only giggled and jumped in Adrian's arms.

"We don't want Winifred for our ma," Mimi said, by way of an explanation. "We want Adrian, don't we, Toby?" The little boy hastily agreed with a bouncy nod.

Mimi continued. "We thought if Winifred left, Adrian would come back. Adrian ain't the best cook, and she don't know much about some things. But she was real nice to us and she looked after us real good. Like Ma used to."

The words stole Adrian's breath. Her heart swelled ten times its normal size. Joyful tears coursed down her cheeks as she hugged baby Eli to her breast.

"Adrian, don't even think about it," Evan warned.

"You stay out of this," Rome snapped.

Winifred noticed Evan for the first time. Her blue eyes widened and her pale face seemed to take on a grayish tinge.

"Oh, Evan, you don't understand. This *is* where I belong," Adrian said, smiling at Rome through her tears. "I've finally found something worth sticking with, something I never want to give up on, no matter how hard I have to struggle."

Rome's gaze riveted on her face and the lines of fatigue and hardship smoothed out once more. A sparkle shone in the teal depths of his eyes. A smile played at the corners of his full lips.

"Do you mean it?" he whispered.

Adrian nodded happily and an endless peace and satisfaction settled over her for the first time in her life. She knew, without a doubt, she'd made the right decision this time.

Mimi, who'd been paying close attention to the adult drama being played out, shrieked in delight. "Adrian's gonna be our ma," she sing-songed to Toby as she took his hands and danced him in circles around the foyer floor.

Eli giggled and bounced harder until Rome had to take him. He held out his free arm and Adrian went into his embrace. Lowering his head, he kissed her long and hard, not caring who saw them.

When they parted they faced three happy children and two disturbed adults.

Evan continued to shake his head, occasionally sneaking a glance at Winifred. Winifred tried to ignore him but she finally gave up and met his gaze. Evan approached her leisurely.

"So I take it your scheme didn't work quite the way you planned. My offer is still open."

"Don't be ridiculous," she hissed. "And stop talking to me, someone might notice and wonder how we became acquainted."

"Um," he said, putting his finger to his lip as he watched Rome, Adrian, and the children. "And then you'd have to explain how after drinking myself silly, I wandered into your room by mistake the night you stayed here. And, about how you invited me to stay, and what followed."

"Oh, stop it," she said through clenched teeth. "I told you at the time it meant nothing. A moment of weakness. Besides, you said you were leaving for good soon."

He chuckled and raised an eyebrow at her. "Funny, I don't remember thinking you seemed particularly delicate at the time. In fact, you were insatiable if I remember correctly. Why'd you sneak off in the middle of the night?"

"I didn't. It was morning. Why are you still here?" She glanced quickly at Rome.

"That's another long story," he said vaguely, looking at Adrian.

Adrian couldn't ignore Winifred's presence any longer. They still didn't know what to do about Lorraine's sister. As happy as Adrian was, if Winifred stayed it would be a cloud over her happiness.

"Rome," she whispered. "What about Winifred?"

His features tightened and he turned toward his sister-in-law. Rubbing his hand over the stubble on his jaw, he shook his head.

Winifred looked up and caught them staring in her direction. She frowned and lifted her chin.

"Don't you think for a minute I'm going back to the farm with that woman, Rome Walker. Nothing could be worse than that."

Adrian gasped at the waspish words, and Mimi and Toby gathered close to her as though closing ranks in protection.

Rome's lips tightened and his eyes narrowed. "Really, Winifred?" he said sarcastically. "Not even prison?"

The delicate features went slack with shock; her pale skin turned ashen and she sucked her breath in sharply. "How did you find out?" she demanded through clenched teeth.

Adrian and Evan exchanged curious glances. Adrian shrugged her shoulders as if to say she knew nothing of this new development. She saw Mimi perk up her ears and decided this confrontation was no place for the children.

"Come on, you guys," she said, taking Eli from Rome. She grasped Toby's hand and motioned Mimi into the dining room.

"We'll wait for you in the other room."

"Adrian, ask Mary to keep an eye on the children," Rome told her. "I think you should be here for this."

Hiding her surprise, Adrian herded the children to a table and went to ask Mary to sit with them. The older woman agreed, bringing cookies and milk to the table for them all.

In the foyer, a variety of expressions met her return. Rome appeared angry, but tried to hide it from Adrian. Winifred had recovered slightly and had adopted an unconcerned mien. Evan seemed amused by the whole episode.

"Did you think I wouldn't find out the truth, Winifred?" Rome cut to the heart of the matter.

Adrian came to his side, and his arm went around her waist.

"You had Adrian thinking you were the perfect choice for my wife and the mother of my children. Why don't you tell her the truth, Winifred?"

She shook her head. "You're bluffing," she charged.

"No," he said, pulling a folded piece of paper from his shirt pocket. He unfolded it and held it out to the woman.

"I knew something wasn't right when you showed up the way you did. I remembered you as a selfish, spoiled woman from my time in St. Louis. That was why I wasn't surprised when you didn't answer my letter after Lorraine's death. For you to show up a year later, ready to give up your life in the city for country living didn't ring true, despite your efforts to appear sincere. So I wired my friend Capt. Poole. You remember Poole, Winifred."

Her cheeks blanched. The thin lips turned white with rage.

"He was very interested to hear you were at my farm."

Scarlet spots flashed on her cheeks, and her ice-blue eyes shot daggers at him. "You told that bastard where I was? Do you realize what you've done?"

Adrian stared with growing horror as the layers of Winifred's persona peeled away like the skin of an onion, revealing the real person within.

"What I've done is to help locate a wanted thief."

It was Adrian's turn to stare in disbelief. Even Evan lost his amused smirk as Rome and Winifred stood toe to toe in the standoff.

Chapter Twenty-eight

"You didn't think he'd go to the authorities, did you, Winifred? You thought because of your affair with the captain, he'd keep his mouth shut when he realized you'd embezzled money from his business."

"I don't know what you're talking about," she said.

"Capt. Poole hired you two years ago when you went to him and told him you'd already spent all of the money your parents left you. No doubt you used your wiles," he said, eyeing her insultingly. "Although why that would convince him to make you his secretary I can't imagine."

She huffed in outrage and Adrian squeezed his arm. She knew he was angry at the woman for using him and his children to cover her crimes, but she couldn't see any reason to grind the woman's last shred of pride into the ground.

Rome patted her hand and she felt some of the tension ease from his muscles.

"You needed more than the small salary he paid you in order to maintain the life-style you'd grown accustomed to. So, you started skimming funds from the business. Only you weren't very good at it and he discovered the discrepancies. When he threatened to go to the authorities if you didn't return the money, you threatened to tell his wife about the affair you'd been having."

"I didn't have the damned money any longer," she hissed. "I told him it was gone. What was I supposed to do?"

"You didn't count on one thing, though. The company, and therefore the money, belonged to his wife. He had to tell her what you'd done. He confessed the whole thing as soon as he realized you'd run. She forced him to press charges against you."

Taking a deep breath, Winifred seemed to gain control of her emotions once more. She sniffed and met Rome's accusing stare with a haughty smirk. "He never was much of a man," she said indelicately.

Rome turned a deep red. Adrian, more accustomed to frank language, merely pursed her lips in a frown. Evan surprised them all by laughing out loud.

" 'Atta girl," he coaxed, cheering Winifred on.

Once more her gaze went to Evan and this time she didn't hide her interest as she smiled back at him.

"His telegram was very detailed, Winifred. As was his next course of action. He intends to see you prosecuted for your crimes. Apparently it's the only way to appease his wife."

Her bravado fell away and she actually shuddered. Clasping a trembling hand over her lips, she glanced around frantically. "What am I going to do?" she whispered. "I can't go to jail."

Adrian almost felt sorry for the woman. Then she remembered the way Winifred had tried to trick Rome. And, she'd nearly succeeded. Adrian had been ready to leave forever and let this woman—this criminal—raise the children.

"I don't know what you're going to do, Winifred. But you won't be doing it at my farm. I'll pack your things and have them delivered to you immediately. After that, you're on your own."

Winifred rushed forward and grasped Rome's arm, forcing Adrian aside in her desperation. "You can't just throw me into the streets, Rome. I'm family. Think of Lorraine. Think of the children."

He brushed off her hold and clasped Adrian's hand. "I am thinking of them. Adrian and the children are everything to me. I won't let you befoul this family with your misdeeds."

Taking Adrian by the elbow, he turned her toward the dining room.

"Rome," Winifred cried. "Wait, please. You have to help me."

Turning back to look at her he chuckled dryly. "Help you? Like you helped me? Pretending to be sweet and efficient and so concerned for the children. You knew exactly what you were doing all along, didn't you? You planned to make Adrian look bad so she'd leave, all because you needed a place to hide out."

Placing his arm around Adrian's shoulders reassuringly, he pulled her to him.

Winifred took a step in their direction. "It wasn't very hard to do," she gloated. "The woman is incompetent. I'd still make the best wife for you," she purred, placing her hand lightly on his chest.

Rome removed Winifred's hand and looked down at Adrian, concerned about what effect Winifred's insults would have on her. But she only grinned and shrugged her shoulders.

"Cooking isn't everything," she said, speaking to Winifred, but never taking her eyes off Rome's handsome face.

They walked away, leaving Winifred standing in the foyer. As Adrian reached the door of the dining room, a thought occurred to her and she stopped.

"Wait here a minute," she told Rome. Pulling the pad and pencil from her skirt pocket, she hastily scribbled a note. Tearing the page from the booklet, she went to Evan.

"You're still going to go, aren't you?"

"You bet. In fact, I might just leave tonight. No sense waiting, right?"

Adrian smiled and grasped his hands. "Take care," she said.

"You bet." He pressed a quick kiss to her cheek. "I hope you'll be happy, Adrian."

"I will," she said, no trace of doubt in her voice. She handed him the note. "Will you do me a favor?"

"Anything."

"Deliver this for me when you get back. The address is at the top."

Evan regarded her with open curiosity. He glanced down at the folded paper in his hand. "Can I ask who it's to?"

"My brother," Adrian said, a catch in her voice. "I just made him a very wealthy man. I hope he finally understands how much I love him."

"I'll make sure he does," Evan said. He winked and tucked the paper into his pocket.

As Adrian left the foyer she heard Evan speak

to Winifred. Interested, she paused at the door and listened.

"I knew the first moment I saw you that you were a lady who liked adventure," he was saying in a very familiar, flirtatious tone. "Poole, whoever he is, must be a fool. You're too bright and ambitious to bury yourself in a nothing little burg like this. If you'd like, I think I can help you out of the predicament you're in."

Adrian heard Winifred huff. "Well, I don't see how that's possible. There's nowhere in the world I can hide from Poole's spiteful wife."

Evan took her arm and smiled into the cool blue eyes. "Not in this world maybe, but I have a plan I think you might be interested in."

Staring in shock, Adrian watched them go to the entrance of the restaurant. As he pulled open the beveled door, Evan looked back and winked.

"What was that all about?" Rome asked, coming to stand beside Adrian.

She shook her head. "You'd never believe it," she told him.

"Are you ever going to tell me about that guy?"

She studied his dark expression. She loved the fact that he was jealous. She couldn't resist teasing him a bit more.

"One day, Rome Walker, I'm going to tell you everything there is to know about me. But I'm going to wait until we're old and gray and sitting in our rocking chairs in front of the fireplace with a dozen grandchildren around us. That way you can't get away from me."

He encircled her waist with his arms and pulled her to him for a kiss. "What makes you think I'd ever want to get away from you?" he asked. "Or that I'd let you get away from me? Uh-uh, you said you'd stay and I'm holding you to that promise for life. No backing out now."

Adrian looked at the door of the restaurant where Evan had gone. She flung her head back and laughed. "Boy, that's the truth," she said. "There is no going back now."

He kissed her, his lips full and ardent on hers. Pulling back, he frowned.

"No regrets, Adrian? No doubts?"

Biting her lip, she thought about the choice she'd made. A lightness filled her and she smiled. "No regrets and no doubts," she said.

They walked arm in arm into the dining room and Mary and the children greeted them with happy, knowing smiles.

"She agree to marry you?" Mary asked eagerly, her hands folded together in front of her ample middle.

"She did," Rome said proudly.

Mary looked to the heavens and breathed a sigh of relief. "Thank goodness," she said. "I'm about out of dishes."

Everyone laughed. **Adrian** flushed, but she took the teasing with good humor. It no longer mattered if she performed every task perfectly. Love made up for a lot. And she had enough of that to cover a lifetime's worth of little mishaps.

A LOVE THROUGH TIME

TIMESWEPT

MARTI JONES

Although tree surgeon Libby Pfifer can explain root rot and Japanese beetles, she can't understand how a fall from the oldest oak in Fort Pickens, Florida, lands her in another century. Yet there she is, face-to-face with the great medicine man Geronimo, and an army captain whose devastating good looks tempt her even while his brusque manner makes her want to wring his neck.

_51991-7 $4.99 US/$5.99 CAN

Time's Healing Heart

Marti Jones

No man has ever swept Madeline St. Thomas off her feet, and after she buries herself in her career, she loses hope of finding one. But when a freak accident propels her to the Old South, Maddie is rescued by a stranger with the face of an angel and the body of an Adonis—a stranger whose burning touch and smoldering kisses awaken forgotten longings in her heart.

Devon Crowe has had enough of women. His dead wife betrayed him, his fiancee despises him, and Maddie drives him to distraction with her claims of coming from another era. But the more Devon tries to convince himself that Maddie is aptly named, the more he believes her preposterous story. And when she makes him a proposal no lady would make, he doesn't know whether he should wrap her in a straitjacket—or lose himself in desires that promise to last forever.

_51954-2 $4.99 US/$5.99 CAN

DREAM WEAVER

MARTI JONES

Bestselling Author Of *Time's Healing Heart*

Brandy Ashton peddles homemade remedies to treat every disease from ague to gout. Yet no tonic can save her reputation as far as Sheriff Adam McCullough is concerned. Despite his threats to lock her up if she doesn't move on, Brandy is torn between offering him a fatal dose of poison— or an even more lethal helping of love.

When Brandy arrives in Charming, Oklahoma, McCullough is convinced she is a smooth-talking drifter out to cheat his good neighbors. And he isn't about to let her sell snake oil in his town. But one stolen kiss makes him forget the larceny he thinks is on Brandy's mind—and yearn to sample the innocence he knows is in her heart.

_3641-X $4.50 US/$5.50 CAN

Now And Then

TIMESWEPT

BOBBY HUTCHINSON

Indian legend says that the spirit can overcome all obstacles, even time itself. Yet Dr. Paige Randolph doubts that anything can help her recover from the loss of her child and the breakup of her marriage. But when a mysterious crop circle casts her back one hundred years, her only hope of surviving on the savage Canadian frontier is to open her heart to the love of the one man meant for her and the powerful truth of the spirit world.

_51990-9 $4.99 US/$5.99 CAN

An Angel's Touch *Where angels go, love is sure to follow.*

Don't miss these unforgettable romances that combine the magic of angels and the joy of love.

Daemon's Angel by Sherrilyn Kenyon. Cast to the mortal realm by an evil sorceress, Arina has more than her share of problems. She is trapped in a temptress's body and doomed to lose any man she desires. Yet even as Arina yearns for the safety of the pearly gates, she finds paradise in the arms of a Norman mercenary. But to savor the joys of life with Daemon, she will have to battle demons and risk her very soul for love.

_52026-5 $4.99 US/$5.99 CAN

Forever Angels by Trana Mae Simmons. Thoroughly modern Tess Foster has everything, but when her boyfriend demands she sign a prenuptial agreement Tess thinks she's lost her happiness forever. Then her guardian angel sneezes and sends the woman of the nineties back to the 1890s—and into the arms of an unbelievably handsome cowboy. But before she will surrender to a marriage made in heaven, Tess has to make sure that her guardian angel won't sneeze again—and ruin her second chance at love.

_52021-4 $4.99 US/$5.99 CAN

Dorchester Publishing Co., Inc.
65 Commerce Road
Stamford, CT 06902

Please add $1.75 for shipping and handling for the first book and $.50 for each book thereafter. NY, NYC, PA and CT residents, please add appropriate sales tax. No cash, stamps, or C.O.D.s. All orders shipped within 6 weeks via postal service book rate. Canadian orders require $2.00 extra postage and must be paid in U.S. dollars through a U.S. banking facility.

Name _____
Address _____
City _____ State _____ Zip _____
I have enclosed $_____ in payment for the checked book(s).
Payment <u>must</u> accompany all orders. ☐ Please send a free catalog.

Timeswept passion...timeless love.

Forever by Amy Elizabeth Saunders. Laurel Behrman is used to putting up with daily hard knocks. But her accidental death is too much, especially when her bumbling guardian angels send her back to Earth—two hundred years before she was born. Trapped in the body of a Colonial woman, Laurel arrives just in time to save a drowning American patriot with the kiss of life—and to rouse a passion she thought long dead.
__51936-4 $4.99 US/$5.99 CAN

Interlude in Time by Rita Clay Estrada. When Parris Harrison goes for a swim in the wild and turbulent surf off Cape May, she washes ashore in the arms of the most gorgeous hunk she has ever seen. But Thomas Elder is not only devastatingly sexy, he is also certifiably insane—dressed in outlandish clothes straight out of a ganster movie, he insists the date is 1929! Horrified to discover that Thomas is absolutely correct, Parris sets about surviving in a dangerous era—and creating her own intimate interlude in time.
__51940-2 $4.99 US/$5.99 CAN

Dorchester Publishing Co., Inc.
65 Commerce Road
Stamford, CT 06902

Please add $1.75 for shipping and handling for the first book and $.50 for each book thereafter. NY, NYC, PA and CT residents, please add appropriate sales tax. No cash, stamps, or C.O.D.s. All orders shipped within 6 weeks via postal service book rate. Canadian orders require $2.00 extra postage and must be paid in U.S. dollars through a U.S. banking facility.

Name_____
Address_____
City _____ State_____ Zip_____
I have enclosed $_____in payment for the checked book(s).
Payment <u>must</u> accompany all orders.☐ Please send a free catalog.

DANCE of the FLAME

ELAINE BARBIERI

**Elaine Barbieri's romances are
"powerful...fascinating...storytelling at its best!"**
—*Romantic Times*

Exiled to a barren wasteland, Sera will do anything to regain the kingdom that is her birthright. But the hard-eyed warrior she saves from death is the last companion she wants for the long journey to her homeland.

To the world he is known as Death's Shadow—as much a beast of battle as the mighty warhorse he rides. But to the flame-haired healer, his forceful arms offer a warm haven, and he swears his throbbing strength will bring her nothing but pleasure.

Sera and Tolin hold in their hands the fate of two feuding houses with an ancient history of bloodshed and betrayal. But no matter what the age-old prophecy foretells, the sparks between them will not be denied, even if their fiery union consumes them both.

_3793-9 $5.99 US/$6.99 CAN